BRAVE
HEARTS

ADDITIONAL CAROLYN HART CLASSICS

Skulduggery

The Devereaux Legacy

Escape from Paris

Death by Surprise

Castle Rock

CAROLYN HART

BRAVE
HEARTS

CAROLYN HART CLASSICS

*With a
New
Introduction
by the
Author*

SEVENTH
STREET
BOOKS™

59 John Glenn Drive
Amherst, New York 14228–2119

Published 2013 by Seventh Street Books™, an imprint of Prometheus Books

Cover image © Everett Collection/Shutterstock.com
Cover design by Jacqueline Nasso Cooke

Inquiries should be addressed to
Seventh Street Books
59 John Glenn Drive
Amherst, New York 14228–2119
VOICE: 716–691–0133 • FAX: 716–691–0137
WWW.PROMETHEUSBOOKS.COM

17 16 15 14 13 • 5 4 3 2 1

Library of Congress Cataloging-in-Publication Data

Hart, Carolyn G.
    Brave hearts / by Carolyn Hart.
        pages ; cm.
    ISBN 978-1-61614-797-6 (pbk.)
    ISBN 978-1-61614-798-3 (ebook)
    1. World War, 1939-1945—Campaigns—Philippines—Corregidor Island—
Fiction. I. Title.

PS3558.A676B7 2013
813'.54—dc23

                                                                2013012108

Printed in the United States of America

AUTHOR'S NEW INTRODUCTION

*B*rave Hearts is a true picture of the fate of American forces and civilians in the Philippines after the Japanese invasion. The fighting was brutal, the treatment of civilians capricious and often deadly. Though the characters in the book are fictional, *Brave Hearts* offers a realistic and often heartbreaking picture of what happened in the Philippines. My hope is that readers who know little of that past will be touched by the heroism of the "battling bastards of Bataan," the gallant nurses on Corregidor, and the American civilians who plunged into jungles and scaled mountains to seek freedom.

AUTHOR'S NOTE

These historical figures appear in this book: General Douglas MacArthur, his wife, Jean, and their son, Arthur IV; President of the Philippines Manuel Quezon, his wife, Aurora, and their children, Maria Aurora, Manuel Jr., and Zeneida; U.S. High Commissioner to the Philippines Francis B. Sayre and his wife, Elizabeth; Financial Adviser to the High Commissioner Woodbury Willoughby Jr. and his wife, Amea; Major General Jonathan M. Wainwright; and U.S. Ambassador to the Court of St. James John G. Winant. All other characters without exception are creatures of fiction and purely inventions of the author's imagination.

The gold in the Philippines existed and was rescued by submarine from Corregidor. But, if part of the gold had been left behind and Spencer Cavanaugh had been a special envoy . . .

1

atharine Cavanaugh paused at the top of the steps leading down into the River Room at the Savoy Hotel. She looked at the dancers, in the middle of an energetic rhumba, and saw beneath the gaiety a ferocious determination to have a good time. The laughter, the sensuous beat of the music, and the swirl of cigarette smoke combined into a familiar montage of wartime London, dancers and lovers waiting for the bombing to start, as everyone knew it would.

For an instant, the dancing couples became a huge gray pile of rubble and bones in her mind's eye. She willed away the image and started down the steps.

Her escort followed. He was a man with whom to spend an evening, another evening of laughter and bombs. The current escort, Captain Smithies, took her elbow and bent down to speak. She responded lightly, cleverly, not listening to his words or hers. Her smile touched her face but didn't touch her heart.

She knew that some she saw in the River Room that night felt emotion. A young couple sat at a side table, their hands interlocked over the snowy white linen as they stared into each other's eyes. Tears streamed down the girl's face. Were they a honeymoon couple and this his last night of leave?

Catharine slipped into her seat at a table beside the dance floor. Her heart ached for that couple, for all the frantic, intent merrymakers, for herself.

She shook her head impatiently and lifted a glass of champagne. This wasn't a moment to grieve; it was a moment to laugh and smile. Perhaps she was luckiest of all in that she didn't feel.

She sat at the luxuriously appointed table in a pool of quiet as her companions talked, a breathtaking, lovely woman with fine chiseled features, glossy soft black hair that hung around her face, and enormous violet-colored eyes. She wore a soft blue silk dress that clung to her with grace, revealing a slim, supple body.

Catharine drank champagne and had no sense of fate on this early evening in May 1941.

Jack Maguire ignored the others at his table. He stared at the reflection in the pillar opposite the table. It was made of some kind of reflective material, perhaps mica, masking the structural steel supports installed by the Savoy management to make the dining room safer in the event of a bombing. Jack didn't care about that; he cared only about the reflection so dimly but so strikingly seen. He watched the pillar without moving, almost without breathing. He could just glimpse her face, half the room away. Sometimes dancers moved between them, but, each time, he waited, and then he would see her again.

God, she was lovely: high cheekbones, deep-set eyes, and a soft mouth that looked both prim and vulnerable. She was American, too; he felt certain of it. American women had a certain flair even now with no new dresses in the shops. She had that casual elegance that set her apart from the other women at the table, who looked utterly British.

He turned, moving his chair back until he had a clear view across the dance floor. Yes, there she was. He felt a surge of excitement. She was even lovelier than she'd appeared in the shiny facade of the pillar. Her eyes were a deep violet like the color of spring wildflowers in the Albanian mountains.

Why had she caught his gaze? It wasn't just her beauty. There were more striking women around the room, women who looked quite approachable. But there was something about this woman, something about her face, something about her eyes . . .

She was with a vivacious crowd, women in evening gowns, the

men, of course, in uniform. There were few men in the Savoy or, for
that matter, in all of London who weren't in some kind of uniform.
Jack moved his shoulders restively. Odd to think he was in a uniform
of sorts, too, though it was the plain uniform accorded all correspondents, with red shoulder tabs instead of insignia. Jack's uniform was
crumpled and sloppy and didn't quite fit. That was fine with him. He
wasn't a soldier; he was a writer and a damn good one—if that mattered, in a world gone mad. Even as his mind wandered, he kept on
watching her, wondering about her.

She wasn't smiling. She sat in a grave repose despite the high, insistent wail of the saxophones and the dull shuffling of feet as servicemen
danced with women they'd just met. Carroll Gibbons's band blared
into "In the Mood." It wasn't Miller, but it wasn't bad.

The waiter stepped between Jack and the dance floor, and Jack
couldn't see her any longer.

"Would you care for dessert, sir?"

"No, thanks." Jack waved him on and found her again.

She wore a pale blue silk dress. He knew from years of looking at
people, and dealing with all kinds, that the dress was very expensive. Of
course, only the rich could afford the River Room at the Savoy—the
rich, the politicians, and the hard-drinking newspaper and radio correspondents who preferred to cover the Blitz in convivial surroundings.
The Jerries hit the West End every night, and the Savoy, with its belowground dining and temporary sleeping areas, was right in the heart
of the action. Jack's table companions, a correspondent for *Time* and
another for AP, were ordering their third drinks and well into a heated
exchange on tactics.

The woman in blue didn't look as though she belonged in the
loud and jazzy crowd. Unbelievably not one of the men with her was
paying the slightest attention to her. Jack's eyes skimmed the three
other women at her table, all expensively dressed, without interest.
Three of the men were in RAF blue. The fourth wasn't in uniform,
but Jack recognized him. Lord Laswell held an important post in
the Ministry of Information. Lord Laswell was doing all the talking.

Everyone at the table listened intently to his every word, everyone but the woman in blue.

Jack felt the beginnings of a grin. She wasn't listening to the bombastic old fool. Her head was tilted a little to one side, and Jack knew she was listening to the music, "Begin the Beguine." Her hair fell softly on either side of her face in sleek dark waves like a calm sea on a moonless night. There was a timelessness and poignancy about her that touched Jack as nothing ever had.

The dance ended and the music paused. In the sudden quiet, he heard, ever so faintly, the up-and-down wail of the air-raid sirens, the strident warning rising and falling. The band immediately swung into "Itty-Bitty Fishies," and dancers flocked to the floor; no one even looked up. There might have been an instant, just an instant, when faces smoothed out and emptied, but it was gone before it could be noted. Dancers jitterbugged gaily, diners talked brightly, and laughter rose higher and higher.

The woman in blue looked toward the ceiling for an instant; Jack knew she was afraid. They were all afraid, of course, but the whisky, the music, and the bright, hard chatter masked the communal fear. All Londoners lived with fear now. It haunted their nights and corroded their days. No one ever spoke of it.

Jack saw fear every day, the lines of strain etched on the faces of the portly bartender, the girl in the tobacconist's shop, the housewife standing in a queue, clutching her ration card. He'd written about that fear and the terrible, bright courage of a great city withstanding the bloodiest siege of all time. He'd written about the burned-out blocks, the smoke and fire that roared like summer thunder as grimy-faced, exhausted men fought blaze after blaze in nights that never seemed to end. He'd written about the shattered homes and the shattered lives and a child's dead hand sticking up through the rubble, bone white in a misty autumn rain. He'd written his stories, drunk great quantities of Scotch, and tried not to feel the pain and the sorrow, but, tonight, something within him burned with a searing ache as he watched a woman's lovely face and saw that brief upward glance. He wanted to hold her, to say it would be all right, to still the almost imperceptible flutter in her throat.

He picked up his glass and drank down the rest of the Scotch. What did he really see? A beautiful woman. A woman turning to her dining companion and smiling, hiding fear beneath that smile. A woman who was alone despite her companions. He knew that, sensed it. She was terribly alone.

Jack's mouth twisted in a self-deprecating grimace. What did he see and what did he invent? What was she really like, that dark and lovely woman? He wanted to know so much that he hurt inside . . . the feel of that soft and vulnerable mouth with its faint touch of scarlet. How would she make love? Would her hair, that thick and brilliantly black hair, sweep softly against her lover? Would her mouth open and seek and her hands reach out to caress? Or was she a lovely shell without fire or warmth, aloof, her soul a mystery even to herself?

Jack leaned forward a little, his gaze intent; then, suddenly, with no warning, she looked at him. Their eyes met and locked; he felt breathless, delighted. She was looking at him. Her eyes widened, and he thought of a startled doe in the Minnesota woods turning and slipping soft-footed between huge green firs. He held her gaze, willed her to look at him, and he felt her tense. It was there in the sudden lift of her chin, in the deliberate blankness of her face. Abruptly, she turned and spoke to the officer beside her, but Jack felt a rush of triumph. She had looked at him.

He had to know her.

He turned back to his own table and, reaching into his pocket for some pound notes, handed them to his friend. "Take care of the check for me, Sydney."

Sydney, still arguing about the role of De Gaulle, waved his hand absently.

Jack was already crossing the dance floor. He didn't know what he would do or say when he reached her table, but he had made up his mind. He had to know her.

Jack Maguire never counted on tomorrow and rarely thought

about yesterday, but he always played his hunches. He felt it now, certain as the beat of his heart; he had to know her.

He was midway across the dance floor when the lights flickered and went out. The crump of bombs was louder, closer. Jack knew a transformer had been hit.

The band kept on playing. The maître d' called out reassurances, his voice calm and resonant. "We'll have torches in a moment, ladies and gentlemen." Before he finished speaking, waiters were moving through the room and handing flashlights out to each table.

Jack peered into the shadowy mass of people forming orderly lines to move out. He hesitated. Would her party go to the bomb shelter and the rows of cots for those who would choose to spend the night? Or would they go upstairs and out into the raid? He waited a moment longer, then moved toward the stairs. She would pass there. He would find her.

He waited beside the stairs and strained to see the faces of the dark figures moving up the steps, following bouncing spots of light. Finally among the few remaining, he felt a sweep of disappointment akin to despair, knowing he'd missed her.

Catharine Cavanaugh pulled her raincoat tighter around her. The rain swept up the street in a thin gray sheet. It was miserably wet and cold for May, cruelly wet and cold. But that wasn't true, of course. April was always the cruelest month. Then she felt the old, familiar dull ache in her chest. Sickness welled deep inside her. Charles died in April. The memory came to her, and she tried to will it away, tried not to remember the thin, straggling line of crocuses that marched in an uneven row just past the new grave, the new and pitifully small grave. Catharine licked her lips. It was four years ago now. Would the pain ever stop?

Suddenly the sirens shrilled. She looked up, but she didn't see any planes, only the wet and bumpy barrage balloons that moved like sluggish whales against the leaden sky. She ducked her head and kept on walking. It wasn't far to the house now. She ignored the tattered placard with the yellow arrow pointing toward the underground steps. She was terrified of being caught belowground, caught and crushed.

This was the first raid since that night at the Savoy. Unbidden, a face came into her mind, the dark, intent face of the man sitting on the other side of the dance floor. They had looked at each other for a moment. She felt a faint stain of color in her cheeks despite the fine, cold spatter of the rain. He'd looked at her so boldly.

It was odd how clearly she remembered him, how sharp the picture was in her mind. He had a beaked Roman nose, full lips, and a blunt, square chin. It was a tough face, a weary face, but his bright sapphire-blue eyes were brilliantly alive and unforgettable. Twice this past week, she thought she'd glimpsed him on the street. Once she followed a broad set of shoulders down Regent Street, which was extraordinarily silly of her. After she caught up with the man and looked up into his face, she wondered what in the world she would have said had it been the man from the Savoy. When she turned and started back the way she'd come, she felt a flutter of panic. What was wrong with her? What possessed her to follow strangers?

And here she was, thinking of him again.

Catharine picked up her pace—not that she was especially eager to go home. She pushed that thought away, too, and hurried up the steps to the house. The brass knocker shone from fresh polish, and she smiled. Trust Fontaine to ignore the rain. She slipped her key in the lock, but Fontaine was opening the door. He took her parcels. "There's a fresh fire in the drawing room, Mrs. Cavanaugh."

Catharine slipped off her gloves and let Fontaine take her raincoat and hat. She smiled. "Thank you, Fontaine. Are there any messages?"

"Yes, madam. Mr. Cavanaugh called to say that he has made plans for you to dine out this evening, if that is agreeable."

Catharine nodded and turned toward the drawing room. She felt suddenly weary. What did Spencer have planned tonight? It wasn't like him to do anything on the spur of the moment, and it had been quite a while since they'd gone out together. Their usual schedule of entertaining was curtailed by the war. He spent most evenings at the embassy, and she often went out to dinner or the early theater with friends she'd made through the War Relief work.

Catharine walked slowly into the drawing room. The fire crackled and hissed; she crossed to it, held out her hands, and realized she was chilled from the long walk in the rain. Again, desperately, she willed away memories and forced her mind to stay in this room, this room as it was today. It was a lovely room. Only the shiny black sateen of the blackout curtains reminded her of the war. This room had existed for more than two hundred years; she took great comfort in that and in the substantial Hepplewhite sofa and Empire chairs.

Abruptly, above the rain and the hiss of the fire, she heard the uneven rumble of the powerful German bombers and the thud of crashing bombs. Catharine jerked around, walked to the Steinway, and sat down. She began to play a polonaise, loudly, forcefully. As the music swelled and rose in a glittering cascade of sound, she lost herself in it, and the tension began to seep out of her shoulders. She felt at peace when she finished.

"That's very lovely, Catharine."

She paused just an instant before she turned and looked up at her husband.

"I didn't hear you, Spencer."

"I'm sorry. I hope I didn't startle you."

"Not at all." She closed the piano lid and stood. "Did your day go well?"

He frowned, a quick, nervous frown that she recognized. Spencer frowned so often now.

"It's touch and go. Touch and go," he said somberly.

Catharine wished she could say something to ease the strain in him, but she knew him well enough, for all their distance now, to know she couldn't help. He'd always been very ambitious, determined to succeed in the Foreign Service. Perhaps it was his very absorption in his future that first attracted her in Paris. He was so different from Reggie. She knew that no matter what happened, Spencer would plunge ahead, determined, intent on his goal.

It was much later, several years after they were married, that she'd realized clearly and dispassionately that Spencer would always move to his own advantage—and she'd realized also that her wealth was a marked advantage to his progress in the State Department. The MacLeish fortune made possible very lovely homes no matter where they were posted and exquisite dinner parties that put Spencer on an equal social footing with the scions of great families who often served as ambassadors.

Spencer had always put the first priority on his work, but, since Charles's death, he'd redoubled his efforts and worked harder than ever. Catharine didn't begrudge the long hours. Each of them had to grieve in his own way. He worked nights and weekends, coordinating American shipments of foodstuffs and arms across the Atlantic to England; now standing alone against Hitler. She knew that not even Spencer could separate in his mind how much pressure came from the war and how much from himself.

"Are the figures very bad?"

"Worse and worse." Spencer shook his head. "If the wolf packs keep it up, there isn't any hope. The tonnage loss is staggering—and Britain can't fight on if the supplies don't arrive." He pushed his hand through his thinning blond hair and managed a tight smile. "But we can't live with it every minute. We have a very special invitation tonight, thanks to you, Catharine. Lord Laswell wants us to join him at the Savoy."

Catharine's eyes dropped away from Spencer's. She looked down at the muted pattern in the dusty rose rug. It was at the Savoy . . .

"Lord Laswell said his wife found you very charming."

Slowly, Catharine looked up at Spencer. She wondered what he would say if she replied, "Oh, yes, that dreadful, empty-headed woman." Instead, she said quietly, "That's nice."

Spencer was smiling at her warmly. "You know, Catharine, I really do appreciate your efforts, the way you go out with our British friends. I know this night club business isn't your kind of thing, but you've been very good to cement relations."

No, nightclubbing didn't thrill her. She went, as part of a rather desperately jolly young set, because it was harder to hear the sirens and the bombs when the music played.

She wondered what Spencer would say if she told him that. Would he understand?

He was still beaming at her. "In any event, it's turning out very well indeed. It could be important to know Lord Laswell."

Oh, yes, she understood Spencer. It never hurt an ambitious American diplomat to be on good terms with a powerful British peer.

"The Savoy," she repeated slowly.

2

J ack Maguire paused at the top of the steps leading down to the Savoy dining room, just as he had every evening for the past six nights.

Tonight his perseverance was rewarded.

He saw her at once, at the same table where he'd first glimpsed her. And there was Lord Laswell again.

He started down the steps, smiling. He'd wondered how he would feel when he saw her again. Would the magic be gone? Tonight she wore a silver dress that revealed bare shoulders and the soft fullness of her breasts; the magic was still there. She was lovely, remote, desirable.

He moved quickly down the steps into the dining room. When he reached her table, his eyes still intent on her, the rather supercilious-looking blond man beside her looked up inquiringly.

Jack looked directly at her. "I don't know if you remember me. I'm Jack Maguire."

He would never forget the instant before she answered. Time stretched out; sound and movement faded away. There was nothing in the world but her; nothing mattered but her answer.

She looked up, her violet eyes dark with uncertainty. "I . . ." She paused. "Of course, I remember you, Mr. Maguire."

He heard the tiny tremor in her voice.

"It was at the War Relief meeting, wasn't it? Mr. Maguire, I don't believe you've met my husband, Spencer Cavanaugh."

Spencer rose. As they shook hands, Jack appraised his adversary.

Cavanaugh was tall, slender, and elegant; his tuxedo fit perfectly. His face was smooth and expressionless, like a banker's. He was too polite to show irritation at Jack's arrival, but his disinterest was clear. He did introduce Jack around the table, and he asked perfunctorily, "Won't you join us, Mr. Maguire?"

Jack smiled. "For a moment. I'm meeting friends for dinner, but they haven't arrived yet."

When the waiter brought a chair, Jack gestured for it to be placed next to hers. As he sat down, Spencer asked, "Are you involved in the War Relief effort, Mr. Maguire?"

"No. I'm a correspondent with INS."

For an instant, Spencer's face froze; then he said carefully, "Oh, of course." He turned to the rest of the table. "Maguire here is a newspaper chap." He said it pleasantly, but he'd given warning.

"And you, Mr. Cavanaugh?" Jack asked, his own voice smooth and pleasant.

Spencer looked a little affronted. "I thought since you'd met Catharine . . ." He paused and cleared his throat. "I'm State Department. Financial adviser at the embassy."

"Yes, of course," Jack said agreeably. "I'd forgotten for a moment. Challenging work, I know."

"Not the sort of thing to discuss in public," Spencer said stiffly.

"Certainly not."

Lord Laswell broke in. "Too much talk altogether these days. Can't help but aid Fritz. We must . . ."

Spencer turned toward his host, and Jack looked at Catharine.

She looked back, unsmiling.

The band slid into "Harbor Lights."

"Would you like to dance?"

She didn't answer, but she slowly stood, paused for an instant, then turned toward the dance floor. Following, he once again sensed in her an impulse to flight, though she walked gracefully and unhurriedly ahead. When they reached the dance floor and she turned to face him, Jack felt a rush of triumph. In only an instant, she would be in his arms.

He held her lightly and smiled down at her grave and serious face. "You are very lovely."

She stiffened a little. "I don't know you." She stared up at him, her violet eyes huge and dark and questioning. "Why did you come up to the table?"

"You know why."

Slowly, she shook her head.

"Yes, you do. I saw you—and I had to know you."

She tried to smile. "That's very kind of you."

"No. It isn't kind. Or sensible. I saw you—and you looked so alone."

"That first night?"

He nodded.

"I was with friends."

"You were all alone."

"Yes." The word was faint, just a breath of sound. The hand resting on his arm tightened for a moment. "You see a very great deal, Mr. Maguire."

"Jack."

"Jack." She said his name tentatively, but it marked a beginning, and they both knew it.

The plaintive song was almost over, and Catharine glanced back toward her table. He felt the beginning of a withdrawal.

"Catharine, meet me tomorrow."

The music ended.

They still stood in a dancers' embrace. Her eyes were enormous now, filled with uncertainty. She pulled away and started across the floor.

Spencer didn't see them coming. He was deep in conversation with Lord Laswell.

"At four o'clock," Jack said urgently. "At the little bridge in St. James's Park."

The muffled roar of faraway explosions woke Catharine. She lay rigid in her bed, listening; then, slowly, she began to relax. The bombs weren't coming nearer, at least not yet. Her hands were clenched in tight fists.

She fought the fear, contained it. All across London, millions lay in their beds, frightened, too, or moved in restless sleep in the underground stations, or stumbled wearily down steps to cellars.

Was Spencer awake now, too?

Surely he must be. No one could sleep through the dull rumble of destruction, louder now, louder and nearer. Did he, too, lie and stare sightless through the dark, made doubly dark and airless by the blackout curtains?

But they didn't comfort each other.

Spencer. How long had it been since she and Spencer had held each other, talked, loved? So long. Such a long and lonely time.

Catharine moved uncomfortably. She remembered the feel of strong arms, the warmth of a hand at her waist, and the melancholy strains of "Harbor Lights."

What madness impelled her to pretend that she knew him?

Not madness. Hunger.

She wanted to know him. The thought rang as clear, sharp, and distinct as a single bell at dawn. She wanted terribly, passionately, desperately to know him, to know who he was, where he came from, and where he was going, to know whether her instinctive response could become a miracle of closeness or was just a product of her own loneliness.

He saw that she was alone despite her laughing companions. It was profoundly true, profoundly and painfully true, and she wanted to know the man who saw that.

She loosened her tightly clenched hands. The explosions were farther away now. Others would die tonight, but not she.

She remembered the sound of his voice. It was a little hoarse, but deep and confident. "Meet me tomorrow. At four at the little bridge in St. James's Park."

She could do it very easily, of course. There was a meeting at three not far from there. She could walk to the park and, despite the piled-up sandbags and barrage balloons, there would be signs of spring. Anyone might want to walk in the park in the spring.

She was a married woman. She had never been unfaithful to

Spencer, never considered it. It was unthinkable. Once again, Jack's face filled her mind, touched her heart.

Jack lit another cigarette as he paced impatiently up and down. It was only five minutes after four, so there was no need to panic, but he felt a welling sense of fear. She must come. She must.

Then he saw her. Happiness flooded through him, and he knew it had been years and years since he had felt this alive.

She walked with her arms swinging loosely. Her sleek black hair was rolled at the nape of her neck beneath her yellow hat. The drawn-back hair emphasized the striking beauty of her face, the clean line of bone from jaw to chin, and the vividness of her violet eyes. Her stride checked for just an instant when she saw him; then she came ahead.

Jack dropped his cigarette, ground it out, and hurried to meet her. He reached out to take her hands. "You came."

"I don't know why. I don't know anything about you," she said breathlessly.

"Where shall I start?"

"Anywhere."

"Jack Maguire. Third of four Maguire boys. Grew up in Chicago. Good Catholic family. My brother Ralph's a priest. Everybody's respectable but me."

She laughed, more at ease now. "Why aren't you respectable?"

He grinned. "There's something a little disreputable about dodging around the world covering prize fights and executions and wars."

"You've done all that?"

"Sure."

"Why?"

He stopped and looked down; his face grew serious. "I guess I've been looking for something all my life."

She stared up into intensely alive blue eyes. His hand reached out and gently touched her cheek, a feather-light stroke. "I think I've been looking for you."

She felt the sudden burn of tears in her eyes; then she turned and walked away, jamming her hands into the pockets of her raincoat.

He followed and had to bend near to hear her.

"I'll disappoint you. I'm just Catharine Cavanaugh." She drew her breath in sharply. "Mrs. Spencer Cavanaugh—and I shouldn't be here."

He reached out and gripped her shoulder and turned her to face him. "But you came."

"Yes."

"Why?"

She shook her head at that.

"Why, Catharine?" he repeated insistently.

"Oh, God," she replied bitterly. "For so many reasons—and I guess all of them are wrong."

"Do you love your husband?"

That was the question, the direct challenge, the demand. She stared up at him, her face strained and taut.

"Answer me, Catharine."

Finally, and the pain in her eyes hurt him, she whispered, "No."

"Why did you marry him?"

"You don't ask much, do you?"

Abruptly, he pulled her into his arms, curved his arms around her, pressed his face against her hair. She stood rigid in his embrace, and then he said gently, "Please, Catharine. Tell me."

Her hands came free from her pockets, and she reached out and clung to him. She clung to him for a long moment, then pulled free and looked away, looked across the water toward Duck Island. "I'd have to go back a good many years."

"Go back."

She stared at the glittering water and, for the first time in ages, permitted herself to remember. "It was the summer I was seventeen . . ."

It was a sunny, clear afternoon, and the air had that particular soft, silky feel that she would always, the rest of her life, associate with Pasadena. She'd just finished playing tennis with her father, and they looked up at Ted shouting.

"Hey, Dad, Cath, I've got a friend for you to meet."

Catharine shaded her eyes, looked past her brother, and saw a tall, slim man with dark blond hair, sleepy blue eyes, and a curving blond mustache.

"This is Reggie, Sis. He's the best polo player in England. Besides that, he shot down thirteen planes in the war."

Reggie shrugged away Ted's grand claims, but it was too late. Catharine was enchanted, and she fell headlong in love, a dreamy, wonderful first love.

The woman looked back at the girl, then said quietly to Jack, "I suppose I rather overwhelmed Reggie. I thought he was marvelous—and I told everyone so—and he was too much of a gentleman to make me look a fool."

"He must have been the fool," Jack interposed.

Catharine shook her head, her eyes dark. "We spent every minute together that summer, and I thought it was all settled. Then, without a word to me, he went back to England."

She looked up at Jack and wondered what he thought. Could he picture the girl she had been? An eager, confident, happy girl, so different from the woman of today. At seventeen, she was so sure—and willing to plunge ahead no matter what convention might dictate.

Catharine looked back across the water. "I went to England." A simple sentence, but what boldness it had required. She marveled now at that act. She had been so decisive, so certain. Oh, God, so very certain.

Catharine slowly shook her head. "He was too gentle to fend me off, though I began to realize there were times when he drank too much. He drank when he remembered the planes he'd shot down. Once he told me, 'I could see his face. Catharine, he was just a kid. Just a kid.' And his voice broke. Reggie tried to send me home. He said he could go for a while and then it was too hard and he had to drink and that wasn't right for a girl like me." Catharine watched the pelicans gather for their feeding. "But I was so sure. I wouldn't let him go."

Jack offered her a cigarette. He lit it and one for himself. "What happened, Catharine?"

"The day before the wedding, he took his biplane up—and flew it straight down into the ground."

Jack blew out a thin stream of blue smoke, and, once again, he wanted to take her in his arms.

"You poor damn kid."

"I went to Paris, art school. I learned how to paint still lifes, and that's what my life was, a still life. A few years later, I went to a party at the American embassy. I met Spencer."

He looked at her sharply. Her voice was even and uninflected, neither happy nor sad.

"Spencer was very nice to me." She grimaced a little. "That sounds terribly prim, doesn't it? But he was gentle and caring, and he wanted so much to marry me. Finally, I thought, why not? I married him, but you're right, I didn't love him. I didn't want to love him. I didn't want ever again to love anyone."

She hadn't been fair to Spencer. Had she ever been fair to him? But there had been happy days, many of them, and if she saw his faults, she saw his strengths, too: devotion to duty, good heartedness. If Charles had lived, they might have found in him an anchor for their lives.

But Charles had not lived.

She stared hopelessly at Jack.

"The first time I saw you," Jack said gently, "I could see the pulse fluttering in your throat. I wanted to hold you in my arms and tell you it was all right."

He reached out, but she stepped back, her composure broken.

"I'm sorry," she said, choking back tears, "I shouldn't have come today. I shouldn't have come." And she turned and ran blindly down the path.

3

"I have to see you."

His voice was so strong over the telephone, it was almost like having him stand beside her. Catharine remembered with incredible precision the way his thick black hair curled behind his ears and the piercing brightness of his blue eyes.

She clutched the phone, tried to answer, couldn't. Her throat felt tight and choked.

"I'll come over there."

"No," she managed. She took a deep breath. "Jack, we've nothing to say to each other." Oh, she knew that wasn't true, but this was dangerous and foolish and would lead only to heartbreak. She would break this off before it could grow.

"You're wrong, Catharine. We've worlds of things to say to each other."

Yes, her heart agreed, but her mind knew this was madness.

"Jack," and she made her voice reasonable and patient, "I know I've given you a wrong impression. I can't blame you for misjudging me, but you must understand, I'm married. I'm not free; I can't see you again."

"Why can't you see me?" he pressed.

When she didn't answer, he continued, "Don't you have friends, Catharine?"

"Of course, I have friends."

"You were at the Savoy that first night with men other than your husband."

The difference was that she wanted him, and she hadn't cared at all for those nice young RAF officers, but she couldn't tell him that, could she?

There was a chuckle at the other end, and Catharine's face flamed. She didn't need to tell him.

"Aren't you presuming about my intentions?" he asked delightedly.

She had presumed about both his intentions and her response—and he knew it very well indeed. She had revealed herself terribly. She laughed, too. The two of them stood by telephones and laughed, and Catharine felt young and happy for the first time in years.

"You're very obnoxious, you know," she said finally.

"Obnoxious and persistent. Now, when am I going to see you again?"

She heard herself saying, "I don't know. My schedule is very busy this week."

"What about right now?"

"No, I have a guest coming for late tea, and I'm going to a concert tonight."

"Tomorrow then."

"All right," she said abruptly. "Tomorrow."

They agreed to meet at the Park Square entrance to Regent's Park at three. Catharine replaced the receiver. She felt as if she'd cut a link to something strong and vital, but she could feel the softness in her face. Tomorrow. Thursday. She would see him then.

But slowly, happiness faded, replaced by a gnawing realism. If she met him, wouldn't it make it that much harder, ultimately, to say goodbye? What would happen to them? He had laughed and she had shared his laughter, but didn't she know in her heart exactly what he wanted—and she, too?

Jack wouldn't settle for friendship. She didn't need to be told that. If she met him, didn't she know in her heart, especially in her heart, where that road would lead?

Of course, she did.

Catharine walked slowly across the drawing room to stand by the back windows and look out at the neat garden, given over now that it was wartime to tomato plants, rows of lettuces and radishes, and a few stalks of corn.

If she met Jack tomorrow, there would be other tomorrows.

The front door chimes rang softly.

Catharine closed her eyes briefly and when they opened, her face was set in a pleasant smile. She turned to greet the young woman brought by Fontaine to the drawing room.

"Miss Redmond, Mrs. Cavanaugh."

Catharine walked across the room, her hand extended. "Priscilla, I'm so glad you could come."

She'd met Priscilla in War Relief work. Priscilla was unmarried, a devoted daughter to an invalid and widowed mother. She took what free time she had and devoted it to raising funds for those widowed and orphaned by the war. Her rather dowdy gray skirt and high-necked silk blouse reflected both modest circumstances and gentility.

Priscilla smiled shyly. Juggling a notebook and a sheaf of papers, she reached out to take Catharine's hand. Her pale cheeks carried an unaccustomed flush of excitement.

"I'm going to be able to go to America for the Society, Catharine. Mother's going to stay with my oldest brother and his wife in Surrey. Oh, I am so looking forward to going." She walked with Catharine toward the fire. "And I certainly appreciate your willingness to help me with introductions. This will be my first time in the New World."

"I'm delighted to be of help," Catharine said warmly. She led the way to two Empire chairs near the fireplace. "Would you like a cup of tea?"

"Very much."

Catharine nodded to Fontaine. She and Priscilla chatted stiffly until the tea came. Catharine poured the tea into delicate Spode cups and offered sugar and cream.

"Where in the world did you come up with Darjeeling tea now?" Priscilla asked.

"Somehow Fontaine has a store of it. I hesitate to ask how it was acquired."

They both laughed.

They bent over Priscilla's papers and she eagerly described the tour she was planning in America to raise money for the War Relief Fund.

"The first stop will be in New York City, of course. I'm very excited."

Catharine nodded. "I'll send a letter to my brother, Ted. He's a lawyer there. I know he and Betty will help set up some meetings."

Priscilla listed the other stops, ending in Washington, D.C. She looked up shyly at Catharine. "Some of the board members think I might raise as much as ten thousand pounds."

"Oh, yes, I should think so," Catharine agreed. "Perhaps even more. Americans are absolutely shocked at the bombings, and they are so eager to help the people who have been bombed out, especially the children. I understand people hang onto Ed Murrow's every word."

"That's so generous," Priscilla said softly. "Do you know, if we—if England—make it through the war, we are going to owe so much to Americans, and to people like you, who have given so much of their time and money, too." She paused and looked at Catharine inquiringly. "It's so wonderful of you to care so much for children when you have no children of your own. You don't have children, do you?"

Catharine sat very still, her face absolutely empty. She could see Charles's face so clearly. He was standing in his crib, his small hands tight on the bar, his head thrown back, and he was laughing. He was the master of his kingdom. And then he would lift his arms to her. She would pick him up and feel his warmth and solidity and the soft, sweet tickle of his breath against her cheek. He had wispy blond hair and the darkest, deepest blue eyes, laughing eyes. Charles had laughed so often.

The pain, the familiar, aching, hideous pain, swept through her.

Catharine bent forward to pour Priscilla another cup of tea. Catharine's black hair fell forward, hiding her face. "No," she said numbly, "I don't have any children." Was it a lie? But she didn't have Charles. Not anymore. "Won't you have another cup of tea?"

"Oh, yes, please," Priscilla said cheerfully. "But, really, I do think it's marvelous of Americans such as you who have no children to be so con-

cerned about the survival of other people's children. I don't know what
the War Relief Society would do . . . I say, watch that—"

Catharine stared at Priscilla's cup, full to the brim, overflowing.
"Oh, yes. Sorry. I was thinking of something else. Tell me, when do you
leave for the States?"

"Soon, I hope, but they don't tell you very far in advance. It depends
upon when a convoy is scheduled and, of course, if I'm lucky enough
to get a spot, but the government does realize how important the Society's work is."

"I know your trip will be a success," Catharine said. She didn't, of
course, mention the danger of an Atlantic crossing and the marauding
German wolf packs. Some things, so many things, one didn't mention
now. "I have a friend in Philadelphia who . . ."

The sirens began to shrill, the familiar, sickening up-and-down
wail.

". . . will be sure to help you." Catharine told Priscilla about Sophie
Connors; Catharine was pleased that her voice didn't change or waver.

Priscilla answered just as evenly.

As they talked, Catharine looked curiously at her guest. What did
Priscilla really think and feel behind those mild, myopic eyes? She was
so perfectly of her class and time; earnest, sincere, well-bred. Where was
the human being behind that even, controlled voice? Was she afraid?

The heavy, broken drone of the bombers was so loud now that Priscilla raised her voice to be heard; yet neither of them mentioned the
attacking planes.

Catharine pictured a bomb striking, the swirl of dust and the rattle
of falling masonry. Somewhere in London people were dying, people
who had expected to live this day.

Catharine's throat felt dry as dust. Where was Jack now? Was he
safe? Oh, God, she hated the terror that ached inside her, and she realized that for the first time since Charles's death, she'd permitted herself
to care for someone, to be vulnerable to the pain, once again, of loss.

Catharine felt the familiar weakening wash of fear. As always she
wondered if she were the only one so terribly, horribly afraid? Priscilla

sat there so primly, balancing her full cup of tea on her lap, talking, on and on.

Then both Catharine and Priscilla looked up. The sound of the bombs was changing. Instead of the faraway crumps, they heard a high, shrill whistle. The whistle deepened.

Priscilla's voice trailed away.

Noise throbbed around them, a rumbling, violent roaring like a runaway express train.

Catharine stared at Priscilla and saw her own fear reflected in Priscilla's pale blue eyes.

"Do you hear?" Priscilla cried. "The bombs are coming nearer and nearer. We're in a bombing run. My brother's told me about them."

Catharine knew she was right. She and Priscilla waited helplessly hundreds of feet below as the bombers hurtled along their predetermined path, raining down death.

Priscilla bolted to her feet; her teacup crashed to the carpet, and tea splattered out. Catharine watched the small patch of spreading wetness with absorbed eyes as the clamor of the exploding bombs obliterated all thought.

"We have to take cover," Priscilla shouted.

Catharine never went to the cellar during raids. She hated the idea of the narrow stairs that twisted down into the dark, damp, musty cellar. It was a double cellar. The staff always took shelter in the back cellar during raids. Fontaine had arranged several chairs and a lamp in the front cellar for Catharine and Spencer, but she had never gone down. Now she was a hostess and Priscilla was her guest. Automatically, she stood. "We can go down to the cellar." She didn't know if Priscilla could hear or understand her words, but she was following Catharine across the drawing room.

Priscilla pressed close behind her as Catharine opened the cellar door, flipped the light switch, and started down the steep steps, bending a little to avoid the low pitched ceiling. They were almost to the bottom of the stairs when an enormous explosion rocked the house. The walls shook; the cellar light went out.

Catharine reached behind her and clasped Priscilla's hand.

"There are some chairs just past the steps," she shouted.

They felt their way. Priscilla sat in the first chair. Catharine let go of her hand and took another step or two.

"There's a flashlight. I'll see if I can find it," but she was listening to the numbing roar of the bombers.

"They're just above us," Priscilla cried. With a catch in her voice, she said tightly . . . "Oh, God, I'm going to die—and I've never loved a man."

The words hung in the dusty, dark air. Catharine felt an instant of intimacy that would forever wipe away her picture of Priscilla as a prim, reserved stranger. The words echoed and reechoed in Catharine's mind. Catharine felt a surge of pity. She was reaching out to catch Priscilla's hand again when the cellar burst with noise. Pressure moved against Catharine. She felt herself lifted and flung. Dust, smoke, and an acrid smell of gunpowder choked her. The walls toppled in, and she heard a faint, choked-off scream from Priscilla.

4

"They're giving us bloody hell tonight," the ARP warden said wearily. "God, I think it's the worst yet." The phone rang, and he looked at it helplessly. "I don't have any more men to send out." The phone rang again, and he picked it up. He listened and began to make notes. "I'll send a rescue unit as soon as possible, but it may be a while. Give me the address again." He scribbled the numbers. "Seamore Place?"

Jack's heart began to thud. Catharine's house was on Seamore Place.

"Warden, what's that address?"

The warden looked at him absently. He'd forgotten Jack was there. "Seamore Place. A direct hit midblock. They think some people are trapped . . ." His words trailed away; Jack had turned and was already at the door.

Jack ran down the darkened street. Catharine's house was four blocks from the warden's post. He'd chosen to come to this post tonight because it was close to Catharine, and it didn't make any difference which post he covered when the raids began. He always got a story, at one post or another. Tonight, he'd come to be close to Catharine, that was all, but now . . .

The heavy thud of his footsteps echoed in the empty street. Everyone had taken shelter. Between bangs of AA guns, Jack heard the tinkle of shell casings striking the pavement, the clatter of incendiaries on the rooftops and the streets, and the heavy, uneven drone of the bombers. But he kept on running, skirting an enormous crater in one street, seeking another path when rubble, the spilled-out walls of a church, blocked his way.

A gas fire burned and hissed as he approached the corner of Seamore Place. Heat pushed against Jack as he forced himself on, sweat streaming down his back and legs despite the chill of early spring. He rounded the corner and stumbled to a halt. An agony of horror knotted the breath in his chest.

Fire danced high into the sky from the blazing house at the corner. As Jack watched, the house slowly dissolved, the walls sliding inward and thousands of sparks crisping up into the air. Smoke spiraled lazily up. Firemen struggled with heavy hoses to save the house next door.

Jack blinked his eyes against the stinging soot and smoke, straining to see down the block. Where Catharine's house had stood was a gaping emptiness against the darkening sky, a crumpled, tumbled heap.

Jack stumbled over the fire hoses.

"Hey, mate, get back. It's dangerous here."

Jack ignored the shout and dodged around the fire truck, his eyes clinging to that open space where no open space should be. He ran desperately toward the emptiness. "Catharine!" He shouted it against the roar of the hoses, the rumble of the fire, the clatter of incendiaries, and the drone of the bombers.

"Catharine!"

The stench of cordite burned her nose and throat. Catharine struggled to breathe. It was utterly dark. She realized with surprise that she wasn't injured, although her head ached from the concussion, and she would be bruised and sore. When she tried to move, she discovered she was lying in a pocket of rubble. She had some inches of leeway, but her shoulder touched an immovable beam. She lifted her hands, felt the rough wood. Panic flared. She turned, twisted, shoved, then sank back, her heart thudding. She was buried beneath the ruins of the house, and the oak beam which trapped her also protected her from the crushing weight of the debris.

Faintly, she heard faraway thumps in the dark, cold, and quiet space. She knew the raid went on, but that was all she heard.

"Priscilla?" She heard her voice, thin and high. "Priscilla?"

No answer.

Nothing.

Only a tiny crackle as pieces of mortar sifted down through the wreckage.

She and Priscilla had just reached the floor of the cellar when the bomb hit. What had happened to Fontaine and his wife and the two maids?

"Fontaine?" She tried to shout. Her call sounded loud in her own ears, terribly loud against the awful silence.

No one answered.

No one moved.

"Priscilla?" she cried again, but without hope.

Catharine lay in the terrible silence and thought of her life—and of love.

Reggie. She had wanted so badly to love Reggie. He'd taken his two-seater up one sunny Friday morning, turned the nose down, and kept his hands steady on the controls until the plane crashed into a Surrey hillside.

"Reggie . . ."

She could picture him clearly, his smiling light blue eyes and sandy hair and that dark blond mustache that made him look so carefree; but he wasn't carefree at all. The love she'd offered hadn't been enough to help him fight the demons in his mind, the guilt and horror that he tried to wash away with whisky. He'd chosen death because he felt he wasn't worthy of love. She understood that now. It didn't ease the pain. She struggled with her own guilt. If she hadn't followed him to England, if she hadn't been seventeen and so certain of herself and the future, a sunny, happy future . . . But she had been seventeen and certain. Now she was thirty-two, and she would never be certain of anything again.

She and Spencer had almost been happy. But she didn't love him, and he didn't love her. In the utter loneliness of this quiet, dark pocket, she couldn't escape the truth. They had come close to happiness with Charles. Those were the bright days, the laughter-filled days. Spencer had been so very proud of his son. He'd taken so many pictures of Charles's first birthday party.

Catharine had teased him. "I believe you're going to use up all the film in Paris. For heaven's sake, Spencer, there will be other birthdays."

But there hadn't been any more birthdays for Charles.

The pictures were upstairs in her sitting room in the roll-top desk . . . oh, the war mustn't destroy their pictures of Charles . . .

The happy days. They'd walked in the Bois de Boulogne and taken picnic lunches and, for the only time in her marriage, she and Spencer had come together with pleasure and almost with passion. But in the icy, numb days after Charles's death, she and Spencer had moved apart; they'd never come together again. The tie between Catharine and Spencer died when Charles died.

She knew that Spencer didn't blame her for Charles's death. It was more that their grief snuffed out any spark of love, and it had never rekindled.

Catharine lay in the darkness and thought of Jack. It was odd how words could turn your mind. Priscilla's high, cultivated voice crying out, "Oh, God, I'm going to die—and I've never loved a man." And neither, thought Catharine, have I.

"Catharine."

It was a faint call, filtered through the mound of rubble that covered her.

"Catharine!"

Tears burned her eyes. From somewhere above her, Jack called her name.

"Careful there, careful! The whole bloody mess'll go down if you pull on that," the rescue worker shouted.

His mate yelled, "There's somebody down there. I heard a cry."

The ARP workers wore rubber boots and thick padded gloves. One of them held a blue-shaded lamp.

The stocky man with the rough voice repeated, "I heard her. Right about here." He began to shift the debris. "Come on, lads."

Jack crouched at the edge of the sidewalk. He strained to see through the dark in the dim pool of light from the lamp.

Then a cry went up. "Here's one, but she's gone. Give me a hand, will you?"

Jack crouched, and his chest ached. One of the workers gave a heave. A mound of debris moved, and the worker began to tug. He and a second man clambered awkwardly over the heaped rubble, carrying a sagging, still form. When they got to the sidewalk and gently laid her down, Jack was there. He bent down and saw a dark sweep of hair before he realized the hair was dark with soot and grime, but a loose tendril was blond. It wasn't Catharine.

The rescue workers were turning away. Jack called after them. "There's another woman down there."

"We're still looking, mate."

Jack followed and waited at the edge of the broken-up masonry.

Twenty minutes. Thirty. An hour. Jack waited, unmoving. He'd watched before as rescue parties scrambled among shattered houses, trying to find someone alive, anyone alive. Sometimes, everyone survived. Sometimes, no one. Death might strike at the head of the table, bypass the foot. There was no rhyme or reason in a bombing. So he knew there was hope. And one of the rescuers said a woman had called out. He didn't look again at the still form on the sidewalk. Please, God, let Catharine live. He wished he could help dig, but he knew he must wait as thousands of Londoners waited this night to learn whether the answer was life or death. Let her be alive, he prayed. At last he understood the heartbreak of war.

Tomorrow men and women like him would file stories—stories of the night that fire and death rampaged across the West End. Correspondents would describe the bomb destruction.

He knotted his hands in tight, hard fists and waited.

Dust cascaded down into her face, clogged her nose and throat. Catharine twisted her head. "Don't." She coughed. "Please, I'm choking."

"Miss." The voice was deep and rough. "You just hold quiet now. We'll have you out as quick as we can. You hold quiet." Then he shouted to the others, "I've found one alive. Get me a rope."

The rubble shook and settled. More dust swirled around her, but she held her breath. Then the beam that trapped her began to move. There were grunts of exertion and calls of encouragement. The beam lifted, and she was free. Gloved hands gripped her arms; a dim blue light shone in her face.

"Are you hurt, miss?"

Cautiously, she moved. Her head ached from the force of the concussion, her back was stiff, but she was lucky this night.

"Careful, miss. We can get a stretcher."

"No." Her voice was hoarsened by the dust. "No, I'm all right. The beam protected me."

The man picked her up as easily as he might have lifted a child and mounted the rubble. "She's all right," he called out.

"Catharine?" Jack's voice carried across the mound of debris.

"Yes."

Jack took her in his arms when the man gently swung her to her feet on the sidewalk. They didn't speak, but Jack held her. Catharine felt strength flowing back into her.

Then the ambulance attendant brought a cup of hot tea. Catharine took it and turned to face the warden, who wanted information about the others in the house. He also needed her to identify Priscilla's body.

Jack held her arm, and they walked to the covered stretcher at the curbside. The warden pulled down the cover and flashed on the pale blue light.

Priscilla's face was pale and lifeless. Only a few hours ago, they'd talked and laughed . . .

"Priscilla Redmond," Catharine said quietly. "She's . . . she was with the War Relief Society."

Jack waited with Catharine while they dug out Fontaine and his wife and the two maids.

"All gone?" Catharine asked.

The warden nodded.

"I must call Spencer," Catharine said wearily.

A neighbor's son spoke up. "The phones are all down."

"Where is he?" Jack asked.

"At the embassy." She spoke in a monotone.

"We've got to get you to shelter," Jack said quickly.

The neighbor's son stepped forward. "My mother sent me to offer our house. We're taking in several people tonight from the houses that were hit."

"That's very kind." Catharine wavered unsteadily on her feet. Suddenly, she wanted so much to lie down, to close her eyes and try not to remember. She felt leaden and sick.

Jack slipped an arm around her shoulders and supported her as they walked slowly down the street, away from the wreckage. They didn't talk, and she was grateful. He was glad she lived. She knew that. Jack didn't know Priscilla, the Fontaines, or the two middle-aged maids, but he understood that words couldn't help.

It was enough that he was there and she felt his warmth.

When they reached the neighbor's, he gave her shoulders a hard squeeze. "I'll call the embassy from my office. Don't worry, I'll get word to Spencer."

"Thank you, Jack. He often stays the night. He called this afternoon and said he wouldn't be home. Tell him where I am. Tell him not to try and come. There's nothing he can do tonight."

"I'll take care of it."

She was starting up the steps when Jack said, "Catharine, remember. I'll see you tomorrow in Regent's Park."

"Tomorrow." She said it slowly as if it were a word in an unfamiliar language. It was in another lifetime that they had laughed on the telephone and promised to meet. It was a lifetime ago for Priscilla and the Fontaines and Millie and Agnes.

"Tomorrow," Jack repeated.

5

Spencer wrinkled his nose at the smell of cooking fish. These flats really weren't very nice, but Peggy never complained. At the thought of Peggy, his steps quickened, and the flowers he carried rattled a little against the florist's green paper.

The hall light provided barely enough illumination for Spencer to find his key. As the door opened, he called out her name.

He smelled cooking here, too, but it had a savory scent, and he knew Peggy'd done it again, hoarded her rationing coupons to buy a piece of beef for him. It would be a simple meal, and he'd never cared much for simple meals. He liked fine, rich French cuisine, but nothing ever tasted quite so wonderful as the simple meals Peggy cooked for him. Ever since he'd escaped the comfortable mediocrity of his childhood, he'd tried to avoid any contact with the commonplace, the usual. Then the irrelevant skein of thought broke because Peggy stood in the doorway to the cramped kitchen, and all he felt was complete pleasure. Her golden red hair glistened even in the dim light of the dingy apartment. Her eyes, so softly blue they reminded him of a midsummer sky, glowed with warmth that was only for him. He felt younger, very strong, and immeasurably happy.

"I came as soon as I could."

She smiled. "I know you did." It was half past nine, but she smiled. Peggy never complained about the hole-in-wall circumstances of their meetings even though he knew that it mattered to her. She was conventional and proper. Sometimes, in the darkness of his house on Seamore Place, in the middle of the night when the bombs crashed down and the antiaircraft guns banged and made sleep impossible, he wondered where he was going and what would happen to them. Divorce was unacceptable. It could spell the end of his career—it would be a stain on his record, and his postings wouldn't be to the fine embassies, to the places that really counted. Divorce meant a fellow wasn't quite steady, and steadiness was important in the Foreign Service. Divorce would also spell the end of comfortable living, of being able to afford all the niceties that marked him as a member of the right set, because the money belonged to Catharine.

But Peggy was as warming to his spirit as a crackling fire in the chill of December. She adored him. Even to think in those terms made Spencer uncomfortable. It wasn't sophisticated, and he'd built a life where form mattered equally with substance, perhaps mattered more than substance. Yet, here he was.

Her soft, round face glowed with pleasure. "I'm so glad you could come," she said simply.

He held out the bouquet of spring flowers, sweet-scented violets, bright primroses, and sharply yellow daffodils.

Peggy took the flowers, then stood on tiptoe to kiss his cheek. "You always do the nicest things," she said happily. As she bustled around the kitchen, hunting for a vase and finally settling for a water jar, he absorbed her pleasure and felt the tension from the long, discouraging day at the embassy drain away.

After finishing two bowls of stew, he dried the dishes as she washed, and he listened with a smile as she chattered on in her soft Southern accent, "I got a letter from Mama today, and she says Father Coughlin's still got people shouting for him in the streets. Spencer, I don't know how anyone can still listen to him!"

He murmured something in reply, but his eyes were watching the soft ripple of her white sweater over her full breasts and the curve of her hips. She was so small and soft and when she turned to him he forgot the war, forgot his hunger to succeed.

Peggy squeezed out the dishcloth and hung it to dry, then looked up and saw the tenderness and heat in his eyes. She smiled so sweetly and lovingly that his heart ached.

He was reaching for her when the telephone rang.

They both stiffened and looked toward the phone. No one had this number except the duty officer at the embassy, who thought Spencer kept the flat for nights when the bombing was too heavy for him to try to reach his home.

The phone rang again.

Spencer reached out. He was to be called only in the event of an emergency. "Hello."

"Spencer, this is Frank. First thing, Catharine's all right, absolutely okay and staying with neighbors."

"All right? What do you mean?"

"Your house got it tonight. Apparently, from the message we received, it's gone, and there were some casualties."

"You're sure Catharine's all right?"

Peggy looked at him sharply, and her hand went up to her throat.

Spencer was nodding. "Right, right. I appreciate your calling. Now, what's the address where Catharine's staying?" He listened. "Oh, did she say that? She sent word for me not to come?"

When he hung up the phone, he turned to Peggy. "It's bad. Everyone killed but Catharine. The whole staff and a woman who was visiting."

"Your house was hit?"

"Destroyed."

"Oh, my God." Peggy's face blanched, looked suddenly old. "If you hadn't come here tonight, you could have been killed. Oh, Spencer." Tears flooded her eyes.

He reached out, pulled her into his arms. For an instant, he thought of Catharine. He should go to her. But she'd sent word not to come. His arms tightened around Peggy. He felt twistings of guilt and a surge of thanksgiving that he and Peggy were alive.

The swans, their feathers a glistening white, glided in a stately procession across the shining water. It could be any spring day in any park, Catharine thought, until she glanced up at the bobbing barrage balloons, then looked across what had been a smooth, open expanse of lawn at the gun emplacements piled round with sandbags.

"But it is spring," she said suddenly, emphasizing the verb.

"Yes, it is." Jack nodded seriously. "It's a lovely day and not even the war can ruin that." He reached out for her hand. They walked in companionable silence to a bench. His hand's warmth and strength helped push away the awful remembrances of the night before: the dust and the fear and the nearness of death.

"Tell me about Chicago."

"Have you ever been there?"

"Never."

"I'll take you someday." He said it matter-of-factly.

She clung to his hand and watched him, loving the way the sunlight gilded his strong face, loving the look in his eyes. He would take her to Chicago someday—if only he could, but that could never happen. She almost told him so; then she willed away the cold truth. She could pretend, couldn't she? She could sit by his side in the soft spring air, feel the warmth and strength of his handclasp, and not think beyond this moment.

He was smiling. "We'll walk along Lake Michigan, and the wind will blow your hair, blow and whip it into tangles."

"So it really is a windy city?"

"Very, very windy. Very dirty. Covered with coal dust, and there are always wrappers and newspapers rustling in the streets, and the people walk very fast and work hard. The beer is wonderful. You'll like it."

"If I went with you, I would like it."

As she watched him, she wanted suddenly to sketch him. She hadn't drawn or painted in years, but she wished she had a sketch pad and soft charcoal. He wasn't conventionally handsome; his face was too bold for that—the vivid, challenging blue eyes deep set beneath craggy brows, the strong mouth that looked both tough and sensuous. His mouth . . . she would like to touch his mouth with her fingertips.

They looked at each other. Silence fell between them, but they needed no words as their awareness grew.

Catharine swallowed. "Tell me more about Chicago."

"I haven't been there in fifteen years."

She was terribly conscious of his nearness.

"Where have you been these past fifteen years?"

"Everywhere," he said matter-of-factly.

"Tell me."

"The Yangtze River in a gunboat. The Yucatan jungles with desperadoes. I've seen the Taj Mahal at moonrise and the rose-red city of Petra on a baking summer day. These last few years, I've moved around because of the house painter. I listened to him at Nuremberg; then I covered the fall of Czechoslovakia and Belgium and Holland. And France."

"You don't feel nearly so detached as you sound, do you?" she asked gently.

"No."

"Now you're watching a city being battered to pieces." She bit her lip. "Jack, why do you stay? You don't have to. You could go home."

"Go home where it's safe? Being safe has never been one of my priorities." His bright blue eyes watched her. "Why don't you go home, Catharine? You don't have to stay either."

"Oh, but I do."

"Why?"

"It would look very defeatist if the diplomats' wives went home."

"So we're both damn fools," he said drily.

He was so near; Catharine felt her pulse race. Abruptly, she stood and walked toward the water and the railing.

Jack came up beside her and slipped his arm around her shoulders. For an instant, she stood stiffly; then, slowly, she relaxed. She loved the touch of his arm, the warmth of his body next to hers.

Their eyes met and held as they had on that first night at the Savoy. His head bent toward her. Slowly, she lifted her face. Their lips touched.

It was, at first, such a gentle kiss, almost a ghost of a kiss, it was so light, tender, and soft. Then, abruptly, excitingly, their mouths opened, their tongues touched, and Catharine felt a rush of desire. She wanted nothing more than to be in his arms and to explore his taste and being.

It was wild, glorious, and magnificent, but Catharine knew that if she continued, she would lose herself. She tried to pull away, but he held her tightly. His mouth warm against her cheek, he asked, "Do you really want me to stop?"

"No."

They kissed again; then she said breathlessly, "Jack, we must stop. This can't come to anything, and that's not fair to you."

"Let me worry about what's fair to me. I want you, Catharine."

She tried to quench the desire that raged within her at his words.

"I'm married," and the words were so weary. "Oh, God, I shouldn't have come." She pulled back, her hands against his chest, tears in her eyes. "I keep saying that, don't I?"

He still held her hard against him. "I know why you came."

She looked up, her eyes dark with pain.

His hand gently brushed an angry scratch that flamed on her cheek. "You almost died last night, and you feel the same way I do. There's so little time, and you and I could have something wonderful."

She took a jerky breath and nodded. "But can that be enough for you?"

"A bomb may get me tomorrow. Or the next day. We can't count on any future." His eyes softened. "But we can have today."

Then, piercing the sky, rising and falling, rising and falling, the sirens sounded.

Catharine's head jerked up. She stared up at the empty blue sky, her eyes wide and strained.

He pulled her close. "Don't be frightened. There's a shelter . . ."

"No," she cried. "Oh, God, no. I can't stand to be buried. Not again. Not ever again."

He stroked her hair, tangled his hand in the soft, sleek waves of her hair. "My apartment's just a block from here—and it's on the top floor."

"The top floor?" She looked at him in astonishment.

"It lets quite cheap—and I get a spectacular view of the barrages."

"The top floor," she repeated.

"Tiptop."

Suddenly, they both began to laugh.

6

The scruffy brown rug on the floor of the boxlike living room was so faded it could scarcely be differentiated from the linoleum floor. A saggy leather sofa sat against one wall, but sunlight streamed in through the open west windows and a soft May breeze riffled the dingy curtains.

"I'll make tea if the gas is still on."

"It won't be." Catharine appreciated his casual, easy comment, but nothing could still the excited beat of her heart. She crossed the tiny room to stand beside the card table next to the open window. The gentle sweep of air moved the pile of paper next to the portable typewriter.

She heard Jack close the closet door after hanging up their coats, but she stood unmoving, staring down at the sheet of paper in the typewriter. The page was half-filled, one word over and over again, run together, no spaces, no punctuation, nothing but catharinecatharinecatharine . . .

He stood behind her. "When I got back last night, I tried to write, but all I could think about was you."

He stood so close to her, but didn't touch her. In the distance, sirens still shrilled. A faint pomp-pomp marked the beginning of the AA fire; then it rolled across the city, louder and louder, the explosive bangs rocking the little room.

Catharine turned to face him. There were dark pouches of weariness under his eyes and lines of fatigue by his mouth. How long had he waited in the cold darkness last night, waited for a shout of success—or failure? That waiting was reflected in his eyes, which had seen so much savagery and despair that they expected nothing good; but, still, stubbornly, they hoped. She felt incredibly near to him, to this intense, taut man with the tough face, full, sensuous mouth, and vividly alive eyes.

They scarcely breathed as they looked at each other.

Catharine wore her hair in a soft bun at the back of her neck, but Jack knew that, if he loosened the pins, her hair would cascade softly down, rippling slowly like dark water. Her eyes, those incredible violet eyes, were the most brilliant color he'd ever seen.

His face softened. He reached up; his large, gentle hand touched the angry scratch across her face.

"You are all right." He said it like a benediction.

"You were there." There was still wonder in her voice.

"I'll always be there."

Tears burned her eyes. If only that could be.

"No tears," he said softly.

She reached up then, slowly, hesitantly, and her fingers touched his lips.

He cupped her hand in his, and his mouth pressed against her palm.

Then they moved together. Catharine felt the warmth of his breath against her face and the beating of his heart. Desire swept her, but it mingled with fear. It had been so long since she had loved. She felt frightened, uncertain, and, for the first time in so many years, desperately vulnerable.

"I'm not sure..."

His hand touched her cheek; a thumb brushed her throat. "Not sure of what?"

She bit her lip and looked away. "Of myself. I don't know, Jack. I haven't loved in so long."

"You haven't?" Surprise and delight lifted his voice. "Oh, Catharine, I'll help you."

She finally looked at him, met his gaze. She shook her head. "I'm not a... I've never been a very passionate..."

"But you will be." He spoke confidently.

His mouth closed over hers. It was a kiss unlike any other she'd ever known, not like Reggie's restrained and gentle kisses or Spencer's perfunctory kisses. This kiss was wonderfully, magnificently different, so deep and deliberate that it linked her to him, created in her a hunger that flamed alive within her.

His mouth moved across her cheek, touching the hollows of her eyes and the lobe of her ear. His lips and tongue found her mouth again. Finally, he drew away and looked down at her, smiling, his dark blue eyes alive with pleasure.

"Catharine." He said it jubilantly.

He took her arm, and they turned and walked toward the bedroom.

When they were undressed, she stood almost forlornly by the edge of the bed.

He reached out, took her hands, and slowly drew her toward him; then he picked her up, lifted her to the bed, and held her close. His lips again sought hers, joyously now, confidently. She responded naturally, with a quivering expectation, as his hands caressed her breasts and thighs, the long length of her body, gently, insistently, evocatively. Catharine felt a flood of passion, her breath came quickly, and she cried out for him.

They joined together in a plunging ecstasy, intense and glorious.

When they were quiet, she turned to look into his face.

"I have never felt such happiness, Jack, not ever before."

It was true. No matter what happened to them; whether tomorrow came or didn't, that lovely and love-filled afternoon would burn in her memory forever. It would shine in her heart because she had discovered for the first time the incandescent glory of passion. She would never be the same again.

Catharine stood in the center of the living room of the apartment she and Spencer had rented. It was a strange place; she wasn't accustomed to it, but the sense of alienation was stronger than that. She didn't belong. This was Spencer's home—and she no longer belonged. She dreaded seeing him. They'd been together only for short periods since the bombing. She had stayed with the neighbor and Spencer at the embassy. But tonight he was supposed to come home.

The telephone rang. Catharine drew her breath in sharply. She waited a moment, then realized with a sick feeling that she had waited for Fontaine to answer it. She crossed the bare floor, her heels clicking against the wood, and picked up the receiver.

"Catharine?"

It was a bad connection; she could scarcely hear Spencer.

"Yes, yes, I'm here."

His voice was faint and faraway. "I can't make it home tonight. Will you be upset if I don't come?"

Her heart lifted. "It's quite all right," she said quickly.

"Thank you, Catharine. I do need to keep after it, but if you need anything I'd be glad to come."

"No, oh, no." She burbled with words. "Everyone's been so kind. Alice Edwards brought over some clothes, and the Kendalls sent food. Really, Spencer, everyone's rallied 'round."

"Splendid. If you're sure you're all right, I'll keep after it."

"I'll be fine."

When she hung up the phone, she felt so incredibly relieved that Spencer wasn't coming home. Anyone would understand it—but not forgive it. She was being unfaithful to her husband, and she didn't want to see him. It was something she'd never expected to happen. To her, marriage was a commitment, and the fact that it was now an empty marriage was no excuse.

Catharine turned and walked slowly through the unfamiliar rooms. There was nothing here to remind her of Spencer, but she didn't need familiar furnishings or mementoes to remember her husband. She remembered only too well his disinterest in her, which had been made painfully clear these past two years. Of course, he worked so hard, put in such long hours. His work was more important to him than anything else. Still, if she cared, if they cared, there could have been more between them. They had moved so far apart after Charles's death, but had they ever really come together? She tried for a moment to recall those long-ago days in Paris, the diplomat and the art student. What had happened to them? What kind of people had they become?

She shook her head sadly. She knew what had happened to her, but it still shocked her. She'd fallen in love. She was a married woman but she had, for the first time in her life, fallen in love and experienced passion. She knew that she had permitted this to happen because no one could count on tomorrow.

The days slipped away. Catharine worked hard at the War Relief Society, and every day she met Jack. They greeted each other each time with a sense of triumph. They had survived another night, and now they were together again at least for these few hours. They walked in Regent's Park, pausing sometimes before cages emptied by the war to wonder where their occupants were and when they would return. They met at the Tate Gallery and at the British Museum. They met in little cafes. They met, laughed, talked, and plumbed each other's minds. Every day they ended their meeting at Jack's apartment.

One afternoon in early June, she stirred sleepily in his arms.

His arms tightened around her. "I wish we could stay here forever."

"Hmm. That would be nice. No more ersatz food or meatless pies, just love, love, love."

"Delicious love. It sounds better and better."

She reached up and cupped his face in her hands, loving the rough feel of stubble against her fingers. "Good enough to eat," she judged. She drew his face down; they kissed, a light, exuberant kiss.

"Do you know," Catharine said suddenly, "you are quite wonderfully male."

He quirked an eyebrow at her. "I should hope so."

"But you are," she insisted. Her hands slipped down to his shoulders, then pressed against his muscular chest. "Really good enough to eat."

"There seems to be a particular emphasis on food today," he said drily. "Hey, that reminds me. You aren't going to believe this, but I have a chocolate éclair in my fridge."

"No!"

"Cross my heart."

"I didn't think there was a pastry in London."

"It isn't from a shop. One of the girls at the office made it and brought it to me."

"Oh, she did," Catharine drawled. "Now why should she have done that?"

"Do I detect a note of jealousy?" His voice oozed satisfaction.

"Not really. But, who is she and, more important, why did she so favor you?"

Jack propped his hands behind his head. "That sounds like a Victorian assignation."

Catharine pushed up on an elbow and looked down into his laughing face. "Who is she?"

"Her name is Mildred. She's tall and slim, kind of like a blond Hedy Lamarr."

"A blond Hedy Lamarr," Catharine mused. "I can tell I have my work cut out for me." She leaned forward and her hair swept against him like a dark curtain. She kissed the edge of his mouth. Her tongue teased at his ear.

"Nice, nice, nice," he murmured approvingly.

Her lips moved against his cheek, his chin, down to his chest, and her fingers lightly caressed the hardness of his stomach.

"Catharine."

She pressed her face against the wiry hairs on his chest and felt the strength of his arousal against her breasts.

"Catharine." Insistent, demanding.

She lifted her face and asked lightly, "You don't even like chocolate éclairs, do you, Jack?"

He twined his hand in her dark, flowing hair.

"Do you?" she asked again.

"Oh, hell, no," he replied. "Come here."

She came.

Three days later, he called, his voice an excited, staccato burst. "I've got fantastic news."

"Jack, what's happened?"

"The Germans have invaded Russia."

"My God. Oh, my God, what luck for us."

"It changes everything. You know, we didn't understand why they hadn't bombed in more than a month. They must have been moving their forces to the east."

Catharine tried to take it in. Could it mean that the horror was over, that the bombers wouldn't be coming back?

"Do you really think they won't bomb anymore?"

"Yes. It means the worst is over, and England's hung on." Then he laughed, and the sound rumbled over the telephone wire. "Catharine, it's the funniest damn thing. You know how the Communists were picketing and screaming this was an imperialist war? Suddenly it's not an imperialist war after all. I've been interviewing the local comrades and boy, the tune has changed."

Catharine listened and nodded and felt a little lightheaded. No more bombing. That changed everything.

"Look"—he was suddenly rushed—"I've got to get this story on the wire, but I'll see you in a little while. The usual time, right?"

"Right."

But Catharine was frowning—suddenly, everything was changed.

7

atharine reached the apartment in Greenwood Courts first. Inside, she drew off her gloves and dropped them, along with her purse, on the table by the door, but she didn't take her hat off. Instead, she walked to the open west window and looked out.

It was a beautiful day, the sky a delicate, pale English blue—a Wedgwood sky. Catharine leaned forward, her hands against the sill. She saw Jack turn the corner, striding toward the entrance. His walk reflected the man; abrupt, impatient, determined. She took a deep breath and wondered if she could do what she must.

Jack took the stairs two at a time, all six flights. Key in hand, he hurried to the door, but it opened before him and Catharine stood there.

His usual gut-wrenching flare of excitement at seeing her was even more intense today. She wore a soft gray suit with a white silk blouse and a double strand of pearls at her throat. The modest, quiet gray emphasized the sleek darkness of her hair beneath the red cloche hat. She was extraordinary, beyond compare, and she loved him. Delight flooded him. She loved him. He could never doubt it because no one as reserved and fastidious as Catharine would open herself to another except for love.

Reaching out, he swept her into his arms and pushed the door shut behind them. He wanted to love her, to kiss her slowly and lingeringly until she cried out for him—but not yet.

He'd prepared what he would say, worked it out in reasonable prose; then he barreled into it with no warning, no preparation.

"I want to marry you."

She closed her eyes and looked as though she'd been struck.

He still held her in his arms, but the closeness was gone. He frowned as Catharine shook her head.

She broke free from his embrace and walked across the room to look out of the window.

Jack stood by the door and stared at her rigid back. For the first time in his life, his confidence failed him. "I thought . . . Catharine, you said you loved me."

Her head bowed forward.

"Of course, I couldn't give you the kind of life you've known." His voice was dull now, tired.

She faced him and tears streamed down her face. "Don't say that. You could give me the best life in the world."

He frowned now, a dark and angry frown. "For Christ's sake, what's wrong?"

She clasped her hands in front of her and stared down at them. Her fingers were so tightly entwined they hurt. "I don't know if I can explain. You see, Jack, I didn't think the bombings would ever stop."

In the midst of his own pain and hurt, he heard the bewilderment and torment in her voice. "What do you mean, Catharine?" he asked gently because he sensed the painful battle within her.

"I wanted to love you," she continued, so quietly he could scarcely hear. "I wanted to love you more than anything in the world and I wouldn't let myself think about someday because I thought we'd die, you know, that one day or one night the bombs would get us. Then it wouldn't matter; I'd be free, finally. Finally free. But when you said on the telephone today that the bombing was over, I knew that someday was here, and I had to face it."

"Face what?"

"Saying good-bye to you." She buried her face in her hands, and the tears merged into sobs.

Jack once again swept her into his arms, but protectively now, gently.

"Honey, you don't have to say good-bye. Not ever. I want you to be my wife."

She lifted her face, streaked with tears, agonized by pain. "I can't leave Spencer."

"You don't love him." There was anger now in his voice.

"No, I don't love him."

"Then, for God's sake, Catharine, this isn't the Middle Ages. You can get a divorce and . . ."

Once again she shook her head, hopelessly. She said harshly, "I told you from the very first that nothing could come of it. I told you I shouldn't meet you."

"But you did."

"I did." She reached up and touched his cheek. "I did and they've been the loveliest days of my life."

"We can have a lifetime of lovely days, Catharine."

"I can't leave Spencer."

"Catharine, why?"

"I'm very important to Spencer." Her voice was dull now, empty of emotion. "You see, if I left him, it would cause him great damage." She took a deep breath. "I can't do it."

"Because he loves you?"

"No, oh, no, Spencer doesn't love me. That makes it so much worse. He needs me for his career. A divorce would hurt him. It's unfair, of course, but life is unfair, isn't it?"

"You'd stay with him for his career?"

She understood Jack's reaction, and she flushed and looked at him angrily. "Damn you. Jack, it's not that. I've never cared about position or power or any of it, but I can't hurt Spencer. All he has is his career."

"And you," Jack said bitterly. His hands dropped away, and he stared down at her angrily.

Catharine moved blindly toward the door, reaching out for her purse and gloves.

"You could at least be honest about it," he said bitingly.

She turned and looked at him, her eyes enormous in a pale, tear-streaked face.

"Honest?"

"Sure. How dumb do you think I am? I'm all right to while away summer afternoons, but I'm not good enough for always, am I?"

"Don't make it worse than it is."

"That's the truth, isn't it?"

"No."

"Then you really do love him."

"No."

"Then what's the almighty hold he has over you?"

Her hands held her gloves, crushed them into balls.

Jack stood very still. Her anguish pierced his anger, and he moved toward her, reached out to touch her with gentle hands. He bent close to hear the faint, pain-filled sentence.

"You see, Charles died." A pulse throbbed in her throat.

"Tell me, Catharine." His voice was low and quiet.

Her lips trembled. "No one here knows about Charles. And I couldn't find his pictures, Jack. I looked and looked through the rubble of the house. They told me everything in the room must have been destroyed. I couldn't even find his pictures." Her eyes stared emptily into his. "Charles was very beautiful. But I suppose all mothers say that, don't they?"

Jack wanted so much to comfort her, but he knew without being told that this was sorrow he couldn't assuage. "Tell me, Catharine," he urged again, softly.

"That night our house was bombed, the girl, Priscilla, she'd asked me if I had any children—and I said no. I said no." Tears filled her eyes, spilled unchecked down her cheeks. She looked imploringly up at Jack. "It was a lovely day in April, and I told the nurse to take him to the park. I was busy." Her voice rose. "Oh, God, I was busy."

Jack gripped her shaking shoulders, but he knew she wasn't there in the room with him—she was in another room on an April day.

"He was in his carriage, and he laughed and waved at me. He had on his blue sweater with a soft cap that matched. He looked very good in blue, he was so blond and fair. We were giving a dinner that night for the Danish ambassador, so I told the nurse to take him to the park."

She stared past Jack; her hands convulsively squeezed the gloves.

"The storm blew up in just a few minutes." She looked at Jack then, her eyes pleading. "It was clear when they left for the park, but suddenly the clouds rolled in, and there was a cold, pelting rain. By the time they got back, Charles was drenched. I helped her bathe him, but he was cold, and he fell sick in the night."

Catharine's mouth twisted. "He called for me, and when I came and touched him, he felt like he was on fire. His hair was wet with sweat, and there were great patches of heat in his cheeks."

She raised one hand, pressed it against her mouth for a long moment, then said dully, "He died a week later. If only I hadn't sent him to the park, he wouldn't have been sick. Wouldn't have—died."

Jack shook her then, shook her roughly. "Catharine, it wasn't your fault."

"Oh, yes, yes, it was my fault. I didn't take care of my baby."

Jack picked her up and cradled her in his arms and buried his face against hers; his tears mingled with hers. "Oh, God, Catharine, I'm so sorry. I'm so sorry."

8

"Go right on in, Mr. Cavanaugh, the ambassador's expecting you."

Spencer nodded his thanks to the secretary and opened one of the huge double oak doors that led to the ambassador's office. Ambassador Winant insisted on working in his office even though most embassy papers and materials were stored belowground. The ambassador had permitted his staff to move his desk away from the immense windows, now boarded over, to a far corner of the long and elegant room. As Spencer entered, Winant rose and came around his desk to shake hands.

Inside Spencer churned with questions. Why did the ambassador want to talk to him? He knew he was on top of his job. The flow of Lend-Lease supplies was steadily increasing. Winant couldn't have any criticism to make there.

"Good morning, Mr. Ambassador." Spencer smiled, but his eyes anxiously scanned Winant's face. Did Winant know about Peggy? "Lovely morning, isn't it?"

"Certainly is. London in August is lovely, even now." The ambassador waved Spencer to a seat, then returned to his own red leather seat behind his gleaming oak desk.

Winant glanced down at a telegram on his desk, then said briskly, "You've done extraordinary work this past year, Cavanaugh, and it hasn't gone unremarked. The department is pleased, very pleased indeed."

"Thank you very much, sir." But this session wasn't just to commend him. Spencer felt very sure of that. There had to be something more, something major.

Winant nodded heavily. "A very outstanding job with a difficult, if not impossible, task."

Spencer waited and felt the smile on his face was going to crack.

Winant thumped his hand down on the telegram. "Now the department has another tough job for you."

Spencer was very alert. He tried hard to look pleasantly attentive, but he sensed trouble. He should be promoted in rank this year. He was counting on it. What assignment could possibly be as important as the one he held? Being sent anywhere else would surely be a demotion.

"We're at a critical point in the Lend-Lease program, sir. It could be disastrous to change staff at this time."

Winant leaned comfortably back in his red leather chair. "I know you're committed to the program, and that's admirable. I know the kind of hours you've put in. That's one reason you've been so successful of course, but the department needs those qualities of yours, that willingness to work whatever hours it takes, that single-minded determination to win out, in another theater."

"The Lend-Lease program needs the personal attention of the finance officer, sir. I have good rapport with several of the British officials and . . ."

"Of course you do," Winant said a little impatiently. "In fact, you have the program pretty well whipped into shape, and that's why it would be a good time to make a change. Fact of the matter is, you're needed for a new task, and it's damn important, Cavanaugh. State needs you in the Philippines."

Spencer stared at him blankly. The Philippines. Automatically, he pictured a string of various-shaped splotches in the midst of the vast Pacific Ocean. If not the end of the world, it was the next thing to it. How could anyone's career be enhanced by a move to the Philippines? The war in Europe was all-important, however much the Japanese postured and threatened in the Pacific. Spencer's mouth tightened to a thin line. It was a demotion, surely, and it must be tied to Peggy. That was the only possible explanation.

". . . damn important," Winant continued. His voice dropped.

"And very ticklish. It will require a supremely gifted diplomat. You see, we've got to get a handle on the gold and silver in the Philippines. If the negotiations underway in Washington fail, it may mean war, and all the military experts say the Japanese will take the Philippines if we come to war. We can't be caught napping. The department wants you to go to Manila to account for all the gold and silver in the islands and prepare it for shipment to the United States if war breaks out in the Pacific."

"Would I be sent out as finance adviser?" Spencer asked sharply. Surely he would at least have the same title he held in London, though no one, and certainly no one in the diplomatic service, would ever equate Manila with London. It was a demotion, of course. This was ridiculous, acting as though he'd been singled out for an honor.

Then Spencer heard Winant say, "Oh, no, this is too sensitive. It's a very critical task. You'll be sent out as a special envoy."

Special envoy. He would outrank the high commissioner who headed the U.S. mission to the Philippines.

"Of course," Winant said quickly, "you understand that your authority would extend particularly to the registration and shipment of the gold and silver."

Spencer understood the addendum. He would be expected to defer in all other matters to Francis B. Sayre, the high commissioner.

Special envoy. It would mark him as one of the most successful of all American diplomats. Short of a major ambassadorship, it couldn't be topped.

"Certainly, Mr. Ambassador, I would be both pleased and honored to accept the new post." He paused and smiled. "I want you to know I appreciate this vote of confidence, and I'll be delighted to accept the challenge. I'll do the very best job I possibly can."

"Of course, you will," Winant replied warmly. Then he frowned. "There is one point, Cavanaugh."

Unease stirred within Spencer. "Yes, Mr. Ambassador?"

"This is a sensitive post in a number of ways." Winant looked decidedly uncomfortable.

Spencer kept his face impassive. Was the ambassador going to mention Peggy?

"We need to go the extra mile to reassure the Filipinos of the depth of our commitment."

Spencer waited.

"As you may know, the president ordered all military wives home from the Philippines last spring, but State Department dependents are staying. This is a deliberate effort to show President Quezon that we aren't going to cut and run, no matter what happens."

Spencer waited.

"The point is, Cavanaugh, will your wife go to Manila with you?"

Relief made Spencer's voice expansive, relaxed. "Of course, she will." He even smiled a little. "After all, sir, Manila will seem like a holiday after London. You know our house was bombed, and Catharine was trapped for a while."

Winant nodded. "I know. I just hope it isn't a case of going from the frying pan to the fire."

Spencer's smile broadened. "I doubt it, sir. After all, the Japanese aren't an industrial people. None of the chaps I've talked to take their armed forces very seriously."

"I hope they're right." Winant's voice became brisk. "In any event, Washington will be pleased to know you've accepted. It will be an immediate transfer."

The ambassador stood and Spencer scrambled to his feet. They shook hands. Spencer turned to go, then paused and said casually, "There's one thing, sir."

"Yes?"

"If possible, I'd like to take some of my team here with me. Jim Donaldson and my secretary, Peggy Taylor."

"Certainly. Anyone you wish." Winant smiled. "Within reason, of course."

In the privacy of his own office, Spencer Cavanaugh stood stock-still for a long moment; then his mouth curved in a triumphant smile. Special envoy. Special envoy. Special envoy. There would be no stopping him now. He leaned over his desk and punched Peggy's buzzer.

When she hurried into the office, carrying her stenographer's pad, Spencer said, "Close the door." He smiled at her. When the door was shut, he crossed to her, his eyes electric with excitement. "Peggy, I've got great news!"

Catharine was in no particular hurry. It was such a lovely August day. Since the bombing had stopped in mid-May, London had seemed almost like her old self. Passersby no longer looked exhausted, their faces sunken from lack of sleep. There was a feeling of hope in the air.

Perhaps love could triumph in a world which gave so little time for caring. Ever since that difficult day when Jack had asked her to marry him and she'd told him about Charles, they'd met without discussion of their future. She knew he understood how very much she wanted to be his, that she would give her life to be his. And understood, too, that it had to be done with as little harm to Spencer as she could manage. She owed Spencer that much, at the very least. Thank God, Jack understood. Perhaps when Spencer received a new assignment, she could make the break, then permit him, of course, to divorce her.

She walked slowly up the street toward the flat where she and Spencer had moved after the bombing. She wished instead that she was on her way to Jack's apartment, but he was off on a story about coastal defenses and wouldn't return to London until next Wednesday. She pictured his small, plain apartment and the bedroom with a rather narrow double bed. She felt his presence so dearly, remembering the feel of his mouth and body.

She was reaching for her keys at the apartment door when it swung open. She looked up, startled.

"Spencer! It's midmorning. What's wrong?" She stared at him. She'd rarely seen him look so alive, so excited and buoyant. "What's happened?"

He held the door for her. "I had to come home to tell you. It's wonderful news, Catharine."

Something at the embassy, of course. The promotion he'd hoped for? Excitement touched her, too. If he'd received it, if it were certain and sure, perhaps he wouldn't need her any longer. Her heart began to thud.

"It's everything I've ever hoped for," he began.

Joy surged through her. It was happening, oh, God, it was. This could be the right time, perhaps the only time. He wouldn't be hurt if she left him, not if he had his future assured. She could even suggest some kind of settlement—that is, with particular care that she not offend him by suggesting he'd sought her out because of her wealth. She began to smile. "Spencer, you've received your promotion."

"Better than that. Of course, it isn't at all what I'd expected. At first, I thought it was a disaster—until the ambassador told me I'd be a special envoy."

Catharine understood his excitement. She'd been a diplomat's wife long enough to know what the title meant. A special envoy carried extraordinary power.

The president wouldn't appoint a special envoy to Great Britain. So where would Spencer be sent? But that didn't matter to her now because if he had reached the level where he was a special envoy, he no longer needed her—and she could easily say she was going home to spend time with her family.

She smiled at him, sharing his excitement. "That's wonderful, absolutely wonderful. I'm so happy for you, Spencer. I know this means everything to you, and I'm so delighted you've been recognized. This means your career is assured now, doesn't it?"

"Well, if I can do a good job."

"Of course, you'll do a good job. You always do a superior job."

He smiled at her gratefully. "Catharine, you're a sport. I've always said that. I've always told everyone that. No man could be luckier in his wife than I am."

Her heart twisted at his words. Oh, God, don't let him be grateful to her. Not now. Because she was going to tell him as soon as she could—not today so it wouldn't tarnish his happiness in any way, but as soon as possible—that she wanted a divorce. She honestly thought that he wouldn't care, not deeply. She felt certain of it. He depended upon her, and she'd been important to his career, to his progress up through the ranks, but they didn't love each other. If he'd reached the level of special envoy, it wouldn't matter if they were divorced. And he could put all the blame squarely on her. She would insist upon it.

"Where is the assignment, Spencer?"

"Hell of a distance," he said ruefully, but his voice was still ebullient. "And it will mean some danger; the ambassador stressed that, but I told him we expect to take risks. Everybody knows crossing the Atlantic's a chess game now, but torpedoes are no worse than bombs."

"Crossing the Atlantic?"

"We'll go back to the States on our way. I'll spend a week in Washington, being briefed. You can stay with Ted and Betty; then we'll be on our way to San Francisco. We'll ship out from there to Manila."

"Manila." She could scarcely take it in. They'd spent their lives in European capitals. She'd never been to the East, and she couldn't imagine what it would be like, but she smiled happily. It didn't matter to her. For the first time in years, she would make her own choices, her own decisions. No one in Manila would even remark about Spencer coming to his new post without his wife. After all, a stint as a special envoy was never permanent. It was a post assigned in response to a particular problem. The emphasis would be upon Spencer's skills, not his family.

He was smiling, too. It is odd, Catharine thought, how little we know one another. Spencer assumed she was happy because of his advancement.

He reached out and squeezed her shoulder. She realized it was the first time Spencer had touched her in a long, long time. He beamed at her. "You are a good wife, Catharine. The ambassador was worried that you might not be willing to go, but I told him there wouldn't be any problem."

Catharine felt a sudden, terrible emptiness. She listened to Spencer's bright, happy words, and her own happiness drained away as water seeps from a cracked vase.

"Of course, you'd come with me. You've always come, and this time it's essential. Winant said the Filipinos mustn't feel there's any danger of the Americans pulling out on them. As the ambassador said, what can be more reassuring than for diplomatic personnel to bring their families with them."

"The ambassador especially wanted to know if I would come?"

He heard the constraint in her voice. He looked at her sharply. "Yes. It's imperative, Catharine."

She stared at him, her face pale but composed. For an instant, happiness had seemed within reach. Images whirled in her mind, of Jack, his face dark with anger, of Spencer, sleek and satisfied, absorbed in the excitement of his future.

If she went to Manila, she would close the door on the only happiness she'd ever known. It had been such a short spell of happiness, days snatched out of fear, brief moments filled with life and love.

Spencer needed her.

Jack loved her.

But Spencer needed her. He didn't have Charles. He didn't have her love. All he had was his career.

She knew Spencer didn't love her, but could she shrug away his long-ago kindnesses to her in Paris when they first met, his gentleness after Charles's death that brought her back from black despair, and all the skeins of commitment between a man and a woman, whether they were in love or not? If Charles were alive, everything might be different, but Charles was dead and Spencer had nothing left but his career.

Deep inside, she heard her own cry of need. She would have nothing, nothing at all. With Jack there was life and the beginning of true healing with her willingness once again to love.

Catharine lifted her chin. "Of course, I'll come, Spencer." She heard herself speak as if from a long distance and marveled at how easy the words sounded, how simple. There was nothing in her tone to suggest that her heart was breaking. Oh, Jack, Jack!

Spencer heaved a sigh of relief. "God, Catharine, you had me worried there for a minute." He smiled again, his good humor restored.

"I know Manila sounds like to hell and gone, but this will only be the beginning. If I handle this one right, there'll be no stopping me." Then he glanced at his watch. "Look, Catharine, I've got a million things to see to, but I didn't want to spring this on you over the phone." He glanced around the apartment living room at the rented furniture. "I never thought I'd be glad we didn't have anything, but it's going to make our move a lot simpler." He gave a half-laugh.

She nodded numbly.

"So you can be ready to leave in the morning, can't you?"

"In the morning?" Her voice rose.

Spencer grimaced. "I know, it's short notice, but we're very important, Catharine. They've squeezed us onto a convoy that leaves tomorrow night. Isn't that something?"

"Yes. Yes, Spencer, that's really very impressive."

He was Spencer again, controlled, intense, but with the new, vital excitement flaring just beneath the surface. His face spread in a wide grin. "Dammit, Catharine, I still have trouble believing it. Me, a special envoy." He shook his head a little. "I've got to get back to the embassy. You'll see to everything, won't you? The packing won't be much."

The door slammed behind him. Catharine stood in the middle of the room where he'd left her. She still wore her hat and gloves. Slowly, she reached up, took off her hat, then slipped off her gloves.

Tomorrow.

Jack wouldn't be back until next week. She'd thought they'd be together on Wednesday. Her mind fumbled with thoughts; there was so much to see to, but none of it touched the core of pain within her.

She would never see Jack again. Never.

She moved then, one slow, painful step at a time, to the upright desk in the corner of the room. She sat down on a hard straight chair, pulled out a drawer, and lifted out note paper. She picked up a pen and stared down at the empty sheet.

"Dear Jack," she wrote.

Tears filmed her eyes so that she could scarcely see. Scratchily, unevenly, she began to write.

9

Ann's lips pressed together in disapproval. She stood with her arms akimbo and watched Peggy try to wedge a pair of shoes in one side of her bulging suitcase. Finally, Ann couldn't stand it any longer.

"Peggy, don't be a damned fool."

Peggy looked up at her roommate, then shook her head and pushed harder on the shoes. When they were jammed in, she smiled brightly at Ann.

"Peggy, you listen to me."

Peggy pushed down the lid on the suitcase. "I don't know how I'm going to shut this."

Ann marched across the room and stood beside her friend and the suitcase. "Peggy," she pleaded, "he's just using you, can't you see that?"

Peggy stiffened and turned away.

Ann felt a mixture of helplessness and anger. Her pleasant face settled into unaccustomed lines of determination. "Look, I know it's not any of my business, and maybe you didn't realize I knew, but, my God, anybody with half an eye would know. You light up when he comes into the room. You light up like a damned Christmas tree." She shook her head and wondered how in the world a girl as nice as Peggy could fall for a prick like Spencer Cavanaugh. "Peggy, you're too nice to get involved with a married man. A very married man."

Ann hated the look of pain in Peggy's eyes and the look, too, of shame and misery, but she was determined to speak out.

"Honey"—Ann's voice was soft now and cajoling—"tell him you won't go. He can't make you go."

"He doesn't make me do anything," Peggy replied. "I know what you think, Ann. You think I'm cheap."

"No, no, no," Ann objected furiously. "I don't think anything of the sort. You're not cheap. That's what makes me so mad. If he were involved with Louise or Candy, I wouldn't give it a second thought, but why does he have to pick on you? You're just a kid and he's not, by a long shot."

"It isn't like that," Peggy said quietly. "It isn't like that at all. Spencer's not just fooling around. He really cares for me, Ann. I know he does."

Ann bit her lip. Damn Spencer Cavanaugh, the good-looking, slimy, selfish, self-absorbed prig. Ann gritted her teeth, then said reasonably, "If he cares, why doesn't he divorce his wife?"

Peggy's blue eyes widened. "He can't do that. He just can't. It could ruin his career."

"So?"

Peggy looked utterly shocked. "You don't understand, Ann. Spencer's very important—his new post is so important we can't even talk about it." Her voice dropped. "It's just really, really secret and special. He's so excited, and he'll be wonderful. I know he will."

Ann sighed, but she didn't give up. "That nice boy in the code room, Tom Biggers—he wants to go out with you."

Peggy looked down at the suitcase and once again pushed hard on the lid. This time it snapped shut.

"He's really nice," Ann continued. "Why don't you give him a chance?"

Slowly, Peggy stood. Her round, cheerful face was serious and determined. "I'm going with Spencer, Ann. You see, I love him."

Jack's fingers jabbed at the typewriter keys. He used two fingers on each hand, and they attacked the machine in short, erratic bursts as he punched out the stories from his five-day tour of coastal defenses.

"England's coastal defenses are all in place, barbed wire, dynamite, mines, but the best guess now is they won't be necessary because of the German push to the East."

Jack paused, took a deep drag on his cigarette, then continued; but in the back of his mind, behind the words so carefully arranged in the story, a refrain sang; I'll see Catharine in only a little while, I'll see Catharine in only a little while . . .

Finally, he ripped the last sheet from his typewriter and took the pile of copy to the bureau chief. "There you go, Sam. Everything you ever wanted to know about coastal defenses and more."

Sam took the copy, then looked up at Jack. "Getting bored? Not hot enough for you here?"

Jack shook his head quickly. "No complaints, Sam."

"Is this the Jack Maguire I know? I thought you'd be pressing me to be on the next boat to Africa. You getting old?"

Jack understood Sam's surprise. There was a day, not so long ago, when he would have pushed to be in the thick of the action. Part of him still wanted to be in the Western Desert right now.

But Catharine was in London.

"There are plenty of stories in London, Sam."

"Sure." There was still surprise in Sam's voice. "How about a drink, Jack?"

"Rain check, Sam. Got a date."

He knew Sam looked after him with sudden interest, but he didn't care. Catharine would be at the apartment—surely she would. She knew he was returning today.

He took a cab and all the way to Greenwood Courts he thought of her and what they would do and say. He felt a mixture of tenderness and passion. There had been many women through the years, but there had never been anyone in his life like Catharine. Her cool, distant beauty masked a passion equal to his own.

That first time he'd seen her, he'd wondered about the dark and beautiful woman he'd glimpsed in the shiny surface of the pillar. Now, he knew. He knew her long, soft black hair could fall forward, its silky strands brushing against his skin, framing their faces as their lips touched, screening out the world. He'd wondered how she would love. Now, he knew, but he knew more than their love; he knew that each time they came together it was a unique union of passion and delight. He knew her love, and yet he knew that never, not if they loved a thousand years, would he be able to define the depth and range of her love.

Was it this complexity that fascinated him, that made their encounters so magical and distinct? He smiled and wondered how she would love him today. Gently, with the faraway look of a wood nymph? Passionately, with a bawdy light in her eyes? Slowly? Or quickly, desperately, hungrily?

When the cab nipped into the curb, he handed over his bill, then pushed out, impatient now. He didn't wait for the slow, creaking elevator. He'd had only three hours' sleep the night before, ridden a jolting troop carrier back to London, and hunched over his typewriter for five hours, but he ran lightly up the steps, two at a time, his heart pounding with anticipation.

He was hungry to touch her hair, to frame her face with his hands. He wanted to make her a part of him, hold her so closely and tightly that they breathed together and he would feel the thudding of her heart against his chest. He jammed his key into the lock and banged the door open.

"Catharine . . ."

The window that looked out to Regent's Park was closed. The curtains hung limp. The room was hot, stuffy—and empty.

Jack stood in the doorway; the eagerness died. He frowned. She knew he was coming back today. He looked down at his watch. It was almost five. He walked inside and shut the door. Then he felt a quickening again. She'd be here soon. He'd open the window, freshen things up a bit so the place wouldn't be stale when she came. Catharine liked things to be bright and lovely.

Jack was pulling up the window when he saw the note on the card table. He'd never seen Catharine's handwriting before, but he knew at once the fine, looping script was hers. The cream-colored stationery with his name on the envelope looked cool and remote. Slowly, he reached out and picked it up. It had a film of dust on it.

His mind registered all these things. A sense of impending disaster welled up inside him. He didn't open the envelope. He reached out, yanked up the telephone, and dialed. Finally, after several rings, he hung up the receiver.

The envelope wasn't sealed. He slid out the single sheet of note paper.

Dear Jack,

When you read this letter I will be in the mid-Atlantic . . .

Jack read the first sentence, and the words moved in his mind like heavy stones falling through dark water, down, down, down. His chest ached as if he'd run miles and miles, but the end wasn't in sight and there was no more breath left in him. The next sentence was smudged and uneven.

Jack, please don't hate me. I couldn't bear it if you hated me, because I love you so much. This is the first time I've ever written those words to you. I love you, Jack. I love you. I can see you now, standing by the table, holding this letter, and I can feel my heart breaking. Silly words, aren't they, words people use casually, meaninglessly, but now I know what they mean and how it feels to have your heart in agony. Spencer has been posted to Manila. He came in just a little while ago to tell me. He is to be briefed in Washington, then travel to Manila. At first I thought this would be my opportunity. I listened to him, and I practiced the words in my mind, how I would tell him that I wanted to be free. He was so excited about the posting. It is a promotion, an important one. I thought it would mean he no longer needed me. I listened and waited for the moment, but the moment didn't come. The ambassador made it clear. I had to come as Spencer's wife to reassure the Filipino government that Americans can be counted on, that they are coming to Manila and bringing their families. So, I have to go—because I am Spencer's wife. That hurts, but so many people hurt around the world today. I can't claim special privilege. I don't know if you are still reading. I don't know if you are terribly angry. Please, Jack, don't be angry with me. Let's remember our wonderful days together. I will remember them always. And perhaps someday, if we have very great fortune, we will be together again.

All my love,
Catharine

The paper was crumpled. A tear had splashed down upon those last lines, and the words were smudged.

Jack licked his quivering lips. Catharine was somewhere on the Atlantic Ocean, on her way to the Philippines. He clenched his teeth until the muscles in his face ached.

Somewhere in the mid-Atlantic a convoy thrust its way west.

Peggy fished a piece of spearmint gum out of her purse. She slipped it into her mouth, and the mildly minty flavor eased the queasy rumblings in her stomach. It had been an exciting find, the box of gum in the ship store, a decided treat after months of rationing, and so welcome now. She could take the up-and-down plunging of the ship, but the long, slow roll from one side to the other threatened to make her sick.

She took a deep breath and stared down at the empty sheet of note paper in her lap. She couldn't decide what to do. The answer should be simple. She hadn't been home to Stone Mountain for three years—not for three years, two months, and eighteen days. She should go home during the week's leave she would have.

But Rowley would be there.

She didn't have Rowley's letters—there wasn't room to bring them—but they'd come regularly every week to London. Last year the letter telling of his mother's death had come. Now he was free to marry, and he wrote and told her so.

She smiled, thinking of him. Tall, thin, serious Rowley. He was thirty-four, too old to be drafted. His automotive repair shop had to turn business away. There were no cars to buy for the duration, and everybody brought their old cars for Rowley to fix. The war had improved his finances so much that he told her proudly they could buy a house after they were married. He knew, without saying, that she wouldn't want to live in the old house where his mother had spent so many years of illness.

Peggy's smile slipped away. Rowley was kind and gentle. A good son, everyone stressed, taking care of his invalid mother.

Peggy knew that if she went home to Stone Mountain, Rowley would press her to marry him. She'd written him several times that she would never marry him, but each time, patiently, he wrote back, saying he knew she'd come home to him someday.

The ship wallowed heavily. The bow came up then, sickeningly, the long, slow roll began. Peggy's bottom bunk tilted slowly out, then back.

She wished to God the voyage would end. But, when they docked in New York, she would have to make her choice. Spencer would be going to Washington for a week of briefings. Peggy shot a furtive look across the narrow cabin. Catharine rested in the bottom bunk. She held a book of poetry loosely in her hands, but she wasn't reading. Peggy hated being so near Catharine. Even in the dull light of the gray cabin, Catharine was beautiful, her black hair glossy and fine, her eyes such an incredibly vivid violet. Throughout the voyage, she'd smiled gravely to the others—she was always courteous—but Peggy had no inkling of what she thought or felt.

Peggy had dreaded sharing a cabin with Catharine. She had only

glimpsed her at various embassy functions, so she had no idea what
Spencer's wife would be like. Fortunately, the ship was crammed full
of men and women housed separately, ten to a cabin. She and Catharine shared a cabin with a German refugee family, the mother and three
children. The two teenage girls chattered constantly, which was irri-
tating but made it impossible for Peggy and Catharine to talk.

But Peggy didn't want to talk to Catharine anyway. She didn't
want to see her or be around her because it reminded Peggy, forcibly
and bitterly, that Catharine was Spencer's wife.

Spencer never spoke of Catharine. He never said a word about his
marriage. In the quiet of one night, he'd told Peggy about Charles, and
Peggy mourned inside because she would never be able to give him a son.

Now Catharine slept in the bunk across from Peggy, and Catharine
was on her way to the Philippines as Spencer's wife.

Spencer had explained it. "Catharine's got to come. If it weren't for
the department, I'd leave Catharine in New York."

He looked down at Peggy then. "You don't have to come," he'd said
quietly, "but I want you to come."

Peggy moved restlessly in her bunk. She felt suffocated and miserable. She hadn't seen her family in three years, but Spencer would be
alone in Washington because Catharine was going to visit her brother
in New York. If Peggy went to Washington, she could be with Spencer.

She took a deep breath and began to write.

Dear Mom and Dad,

I was so close to home last week. I thought about you and I
would have come if I could have, but I was only on a brief stop
in Washington on my way to San Francisco.

She stopped writing and thought about her mother, her russet hair a
little dulled now with age but her face youthful and loving. Peggy wanted
to see her so badly—she and her mother had always been very close.

But her mother would know there was someone. She would want

to know all about him. She'd be excited and would want to plan a wedding.

Peggy gripped the pen and bent back to her letter.

The gray metal walls of the bulkhead felt cold and clammy. For a moment, Catharine pictured the convoy in her mind, eighteen ships in two staggered rows, all of them a misty gray, plunging heavily through the rough Atlantic water. At dawn and at dusk the ships looked ghostly, but that was the point, of course. German submarines liked to attack at dawn and at dusk, sending torpedoes in white-capped rows toward their hurrying prey. Catharine wondered coldly just what their odds were. But anyone who could get on a convoy to America went because it meant they were going to a country that wasn't at war. People ate well in America, and the cities glistened without fear after dark. America was more than an ocean away from war. The passengers on this converted peacetime liner didn't mind the cramped quarters or the blacked-over port holes or even the fear, because they were on their way to America. A pervasive eagerness underlay the passengers' speech and manner.

Except, Catharine thought drily, the passengers in this particular cabin. She glanced at the German family. She'd talked with them several times, and they were pathetically grateful to find someone who spoke German. They were going to America because they were refugees—refugees with some hope left, but with little eagerness or joy.

The frail, thin mother wore her gray-streaked blond hair in a tight coronet braid. She clucked nervously after her daughters. They were going to live with the mother's cousin in Chicago. Mrs. Eberhardt asked Catharine what Chicago was like. Catharine smiled and said quietly, "I've not been there, but a friend once told me that it was very alive, very exciting." The old woman nodded, a little frown between her eyes. Catharine knew she was frightened. The Eberhardts escaped Berlin when Jews were being rounded up. They fled to France, but when France fell to the Nazis, the call for Jews once again went out.

The mother and daughters escaped through the underground, but Herr Eberhardt and their son, Emil, were captured by the Gestapo in Paris. "They were sent by train to a place called Dachau. And people say, they whisper that it is awful there."

Greta Eberhardt knitted as she lay in her bunk. The two younger daughters chattered. The oldest girl lay in her bunk, unmoving, her face turned toward the bulkhead.

Catharine's glance moved on to touch Peggy. Catharine had never paid much attention to Spencer's secretary, but she was really a very pretty girl, with a fresh round face, eager blue eyes, and lovely golden-red hair. But Catharine detected something wrong there, too, some kind of deep unhappiness.

A man, of course.

What else but love or the lack of it can cause such sorrow.

Catharine felt suddenly guilty. She'd been so absorbed in her own loss, in coming to terms with her separation from Jack, that she'd had no time or energy to share with anyone else. It didn't matter with Spencer. He was deep into a mass of papers that had been sent to prepare him for his mission to Manila. He and Peggy spent most of every day in a far corner of the old saloon, which had been transformed into a combination mess-cum-office and lounge. Spencer smiled absently when they met at meals and inquired if everything was all right, her accommodations satisfactory. He'd laughed once. "Not quite the way we traveled home the last time." He'd certainly kept Peggy busy, but perhaps that was best. Catharine wished she had something to absorb her thoughts, to pull them away from the never-ending circle of pain and regret.

Catharine turned a page of the book she held in her lap, but she was watching Peggy. Yes, there was some story there. Otherwise, why was she so stiff and distant when you could tell by looking at her that she was generally happy and friendly? And she was looking decidedly ill. The best thing, of course, would be to get up on deck. Catharine opened her mouth to speak.

With a hideous clang, the warning klaxon blared and a tinny voice shouted over the PA, "Battle stations! All hands to battle stations!"

The German woman, her face pale and pinched, looked frantically at Catharine.

"They must have sighted a submarine," Catharine said huskily in German. She knew the sudden tightening of her throat revealed her fear, but they were all afraid, she knew that. All of them shared the tight, quivering throb of fear because they were trapped and waiting, once again helpless, passive victims. Neither fear nor hope nor tears would affect the path of torpedoes. Catharine reached down for her life jacket. She looked across the cabin and saw Peggy strapping on her life jacket.

The ship lurched far to the right. The bunks across from Catharine swung crazily upward. Everyone reached out to grab onto the nearest support.

A dull crash that sounded like thunder reached down into their below-water cabin, but they all knew it wasn't thunder. Mrs. Eberhardt cried out and her younger daughter ran to her.

The ship heeled abruptly in the opposite direction.

Catharine knew then that a sub had been sighted, and their ship was desperately swerving to avoid being struck by a torpedo. Would the accompanying destroyers sink the sub before it succeeded in its mission? Or would a torpedo strike home and would the strike hit their ship or another? Who would live and who would die?

Peggy spoke out harshly. "Mrs. Cavanaugh, tell that girl to put on her life jacket. She's just lying there."

Catharine turned. The oldest German girl lay in her bunk, face to the wall. Her mother spoke in rapid German.

"Doesn't she understand what's happening?" Peggy demanded irritably.

"I imagine she understands," Catharine said quietly. "I don't think she cares. Her mother told me she was very much in love." Catharine took a deep breath. "She saw the Gestapo drag him away."

"Oh, God," Peggy said wearily.

Clutching the edge of the bunk for support as the ship continued its plunging effort to avoid torpedoes, Catharine worked her way closer to the girl, then spoke softly in German. "Please, Marlene, put on your jacket. Please do it for your mother."

Slowly, the girl's head turned. Catharine knew she'd never seen emptier eyes, but, finally, like an automaton, Marlene pulled herself upright in the bunk and slid unresistingly into the bulky life jacket. Then she rested back against the bulkhead, her eyes staring blankly ahead.

The steel plates beneath Catharine's feet suddenly quivered. The women looked at each other with frightened eyes as depth charges exploded far beneath them, and the concussion waves rippled through the great ship.

Catharine reached out for Marlene's hand and then for Peggy's. They clung to each other. The Eberhardts softly cried. No one spoke as the enormous explosions continued. The strained hull of the ship creaked. Catharine tried not to picture the water outside, but in her mind she saw black-nosed torpedoes slicing keel level through the ocean.

They huddled together, silent and frightened, but beyond the moment, beyond the fear and the strain, Catharine felt Jack's presence almost as if he stood beside her with his lively, dark face and sardonic courage.

Her lips curved in a soft smile.

Whatever happened, she had loved a man.

10

"Goddammit, Jack, I'm sorry, but New York says no."

"Screw New York."

"Look, man, take it easy. It doesn't do any good to get mad." Sam looked exasperated. "Why the hell should they send you to Manila? They've got a man in Manila."

"Who?"

"Freddy Phillips."

"Phillips couldn't cover a fire if it burned his ass." Jack leaned forward, spread his big hands across the top of Sam's desk. "I've got to get to Manila."

Sam lit a cigarette, blew a thin curl of smoke, and looked at Jack speculatively. "Why?"

"There's a story out there. I want to go after it."

For the first time, Sam was interested. "What kind of story? What are you on to, Jack?"

"No deal. It's my story. Top secret, but I'm on to something big."

Sam sucked the hot smoke deep into his lungs and coughed a little. "I've got to give New York more than that."

"Tell them they'll be damn sorry if they don't send me."

Sam shrugged. "I'll lay it on, but don't hold your breath." He reached for the phone, placed the call, and, in a moment, looked up at Jack. "It will take a couple of hours to get through. I'll let you know."

Jack nodded. He moved restlessly back to his desk, but in a few minutes picked up his cap, jammed it on his head, and hurried down-stairs and out into the September night.

The cab dropped him at the Savoy. Once inside, he stopped for a moment at the top of the stairs leading down into the River Room. The soft, easy notes of Carroll Gibbons's piano flowed over him, the melancholy strains of "I'll Be Seeing You." He joined a raucous group of correspondents, ate dinner, and drank three scotches. He kept looking at the pillar next to the table and its silvery, shiny covering. He could see Catharine's face, her fine, distinct bones, deep-set eyes, and sleek midnight-black hair.

When he got back to the office, he walked to his desk and found the note tucked in the carriage of the typewriter:

"New York says no, sorry."

Jack took the note and scrawled a reply, "That's okay. It's been good to know you. I'll write from Manila. Jack."

The train clacked through the star-spangled night. Catharine was glad they didn't have a compartment. She didn't want to share such a small space with Spencer. They had berths, she and Peggy two lowers and Spencer an upper. Catharine raised herself up on her elbow and peered out the window. The train would be coming into Chicago soon. She knew she wouldn't be able to see much, but Chicago was Jack's home and he'd promised to bring her there someday.

The train began to slow. She strained to see through the darkness, but it was an anonymous landscape, nothing more than rows of dimly seen dark houses. She would write Jack and tell him she'd been in Chicago, if only fleetingly, and that she'd thought of him. Oh, God, yes, had she thought of him.

She thought of him during the long days as the train rumbled across America. She thought of him during the hours they waited on sidings as troop and equipment trains took the right-of-way. She thought of him every day and every night and accepted the truth with a dull, never-ending pain—every mile on the train carried her farther and farther away from Jack.

The thought remained with her on the gray, chilly day that the U.S.S. President Harrison moved slowly out from San Francisco Bay. She stood at the railing until the last glimpse of the orange-red Golden Gate Bridge was lost to view. She was going farther and farther away from Jack.

Jack picked up his duffel bag. Huge patches of sweat marked the sides and back of his crumpled khaki shirt. The line of moving men stopped again. Jack dumped the duffel bag to the ground and pulled a battered pack of cigarettes from his pocket. He waited patiently in the broiling sunlight until, finally, it was his turn to step into the ramshackle tin office. A harried sergeant snapped, "Where are you bound?"

Jack pulled out his correspondent's papers. "INS to Singapore."

"Singapore, Singapore," the sergeant muttered. Then he yelled across the room, "Hey, Frankie, has that Lancaster left yet?"

"Due to lift off in ten minutes."

Jack's casual demeanor fell away: "Hey, that's for me. Hurry, man, I've got to make that plane."

The sergeant nodded irritably and finished scanning Jack's papers. He picked up an official stamp, slapped it twice on a mimeographed sheet, which he handed to Jack along with his papers. He jerked his head to the left. "Out that door. First plane in line."

Jack hefted the duffel bag and pushed through the door. He began to run, his eyes squinting against the merciless Egyptian sun. There it was. The propellers were beginning to spin, but the aft door was still open. He put on a burst of speed. A sergeant began to pull away the steps.

"Hold up!" Jack yelled, waving his travel pass.

The sergeant nodded and waved him aboard.

Jack hurried up the steps and over the coaming.

Straining to see in the dim interior, he stepped over bags and boxes to take an empty bucket seat near the wing. The hatch slammed shut, and the Lancaster began to taxi up the runway.

A slouched figure in the next seat turned. "Who're you with?"

"INS."

"UP. Tom Carson."

"Jack Maguire."

They shook hands, then settled back forcibly as the plane accelerated and lifted off the field with a rough, jerking roar, turning slowly to the East.

Next stop: Singapore.

One city closer to Manila.

A military band waited on pier 7. As the U.S.S. *President Harrison* pulled slowly into its moorings, the band began to play "The Stars and Stripes Forever."

Catharine and Spencer stood on the promenade deck with the captain, who pointed down at the band. "That's in your honor."

The familiar, stirring march affected Catharine oddly. She had seen the American flag fly in many foreign capitals, but today the band looked small as it stood stiffly below on the sun-drenched pier. The march sounded peculiarly American and out of place on the steamy tropical air. The heavy, moist heat carried a fishy seaweed odor mingled with that of rotting garbage, tropical flowers, and sewage. Catharine looked beyond the seafront at the glittering white of Manila's new buildings, the soft gold and tans of the older Spanish section, and far away at the purple-black peaks of mountains.

Spencer tugged at her elbow. "They're ready for us to debark, Catharine."

Catharine moved forward with Spencer to the gangplank. Spencer smiled and looked pleasant and approachable, an incoming diplomat with far-reaching powers who was aware of his importance but didn't wish to emphasize it. The manner and attitude were impeccable, but Catharine knew he was exulting in this stately arrival and display of rank.

As she started down the gangplank, Catharine saw the party of four waiting on the pier—two men in tropical whites and two women in light, summery dresses, picture hats, and white gloves. Each woman held a white-gloved hand to her hat, steadying it against the hot wind.

"It's the high commissioner himself," Spencer said in a low, delighted voice.

They reached the bottom of the gangplank, and introductions were made.

The high commissioner's wife, Mrs. Sayre, beamed at Catharine. "My dear, we're so delighted you've come. We're quite a small circle since the military wives went home last spring. You'll be a very welcome addition, and we'll hope to show you the Manila we love." Then she gestured to the woman beside her. "And I'm happy to introduce you to Amea Willoughby."

Catharine smiled and held out her hand. She knew the name, of course. Amea's husband, Woodbury Willoughby, was the finance officer. His cooperation would be absolutely essential if Spencer were to succeed in his assignment. Would Willoughby resent Spencer's being sent in as a special envoy with extraordinary powers? Amea's warm, welcoming smile held no reserve. As Catharine well knew, wives often reflected their husbands' feelings as accurately as barometers. Catharine glanced at Willoughby pumping Spencer's hand, beaming with pleasure, and saying, "I am very relieved you've been sent to us. That shows State means business and understands our problems. You'll be able to cut through some of the obstruction at the central bank and . . ."

Catharine felt a wash of happiness for Spencer. Everything was going to turn out beautifully for him. Then, quick on the heels of that relief, came the quicksilver thought: When this assignment was over, somehow, someway she would find Jack.

A tiny, pale green lizard darted across the ceiling. Amea looked up at it and smiled. "They bring good luck, Catharine."

Catharine looked at the lizard with some reserve. She had no particular aversion to lizards, but the small creature seemed typical of Manila, moving smoothly across the white walls to the sixth-floor apartment, defying logic to explain how it traveled to that height. But its quick, darting progress reminded her that everywhere the tropical growth was barely held at bay, all the crawling, swarming denizens pushed to take over man's structures. Catharine shuddered. She felt alien in this overpoweringly lush land.

"You are finding it very different here, aren't you?" Amea asked perceptively.

Catharine looked at her with interest. Amea didn't say much, but Catharine decided that she saw a very great deal.

"It's very beautiful," Catharine said carefully.

Amea laughed. "It's all right. The walls don't have ears. You've been here three weeks. What do you think of Manila?"

Catharine slowly smiled. "It's the oddest place I've ever been," she responded, enjoying the frankness and feeling of friendship. She liked Amea, liked being able to say what she thought without fear of being misunderstood. "The air-conditioned stores and the billboards are so American, but underneath it all there's that languor of the tropics. I'd read about it, but I didn't understand. The Americans who're still here live like kings. Even privates have maids. And I have a houseboy, a cook, and two servants for a two-bedroom apartment, and we aren't spending a particle of what we spent in London."

Amea's face sobered. "Was it very dreadful in London?"

Catharine thought of the battered gray streets and the smell of old dirt and clay thrown up by the bombs and of Jack. "Not all of it," she said quietly.

"I suppose the destruction is awful."

Catharine nodded. They talked of landmarks no longer there and of the dreadful night when it looked as though St. Paul's would go. But Catharine couldn't help thinking of Jack, of the way he smiled, the way his full mouth could curve up so slowly into a wide and marvelous grin that laughed at the world. She thought of his hands, strong hands with blunt fingers stained by carbon. She thought of his eyes, those piercingly blue eyes that looked at her so directly and honestly. Would she ever see that smile again or feel the touch of his hands or rejoice in the warmth and longing in his eyes?

She came back to the hot white room, the undistinguished rattan furniture, and the whirr of the overhead fan as Amea made motions to go.

"It's been such a pleasant afternoon," Amea said cheerfully.

Catharine smiled as she walked to the door with Amea. "I'm so glad you could come to see me."

Amea slipped on her gloves. "You know, we'd love to have you join our Red Cross group. We're rolling bandages now. We have some first-aid classes going, too."

"I'll think about it," Catharine said pleasantly.

Amea paused in the doorway. "It does help to keep busy," she said in her gentle voice. "I know Spencer's been working day and night, just like Woody. The Red Cross helps fill the days."

After she was gone, Catharine wandered slowly to the broad west window. So Amea Willoughby thought Catharine was lonely. Was it that apparent? The wives of the State Department officials were a tight-knit group in Manila. They'd been friendly and welcoming to Catharine. She'd gone to teas and played bridge, but she hadn't plunged into their day-to-day social life.

Catharine appreciated Amea's intent, but Amea was wrong about one thing. Going to the Red Cross meetings wouldn't fill the void in Catharine's life. For a moment, Catharine wondered how shocked Amea would be if she knew the real reason for Catharine's aloofness.

This was the first time in all the years of her marriage that she hadn't plunged wholeheartedly into an active social life in the American community wherever they were posted, but this time she couldn't bring herself to participate. Spencer was so totally absorbed in his work he hadn't even noticed. Catharine couldn't bear the light, social afternoon gatherings, the inconsequential chatter. That was why she spent long, dull afternoons in the muggy apartment, sometimes remembering London and sometimes forcing herself to forget. But she would go to the Red Cross meetings. Those bandages might be needed.

The front door opened. Manuel came in, carrying a basket of groceries, smiling and bobbing and nodding and holding out in one hand a stack of mail.

Catharine felt an instant of breathless expectation. She'd written Jack and sent him her address. She'd waited ever since hoping to hear from him. She hadn't been able to resist the deep, visceral need to contact him. She'd made it clear in her letter that she knew she had no claim on his time or thoughts, but she'd always love him.

She reached out eagerly for the stack of mail and skimmed through the envelopes, then saw, sickeningly, her own handwriting and the address, "Mr. John Maguire, 50 Greenwood Courts, London." A careless hand had scrawled "Addressee Unknown."

The petty officer looked up. "You again?"

Jack nodded.

The sailor hesitated, then motioned Jack to come nearer. "Look, this is on the qt, but if you'll show up early tomorrow I can get you aboard the Repulse"

"Where's she going?"

"They say the Philippines."

11

Peggy frowned in concentration. It was so hard to type the long, detailed list of gold holdings without making any mistakes. The lists were marked over with insertions and corrections. She sighed wearily. There was list after list after list.

"Peggy."

Peggy stiffened. She knew it was Catharine before she looked up. Peggy's hands paused on the keyboard; then she forced herself to smile.

"Hello, Mrs. Cavanaugh. Mr. Cavanaugh's in conference with Mr. Sayre and Mr. Willoughby."

Peggy's face felt stiff and unnatural when she tried to smile. Catharine Cavanaugh was as immaculately groomed and lovely as always, but today she looked strained, worse than she had during the Blitz. Peggy sensed the incongruity of it, but the thought was swept away by a rising tide of unhappiness. How could Catharine be unhappy? She was Mrs. Spencer Cavanaugh. She was so lucky, Peggy thought bitterly.

"That's all right," Catharine said softly. "I'm here to see Mrs. Sayre, but would you give Spencer a message?"

"Of course, Mrs. Cavanaugh."

"Remind him that tonight is the ball at the Japanese embassy. Since he usually spends the night here at the Residence, he may have forgotten."

Peggy looked sharply at Catharine and wondered if anyone nearby had overheard that comment, but the low hum of the air conditioner and the clatter of typewriter keys made it unlikely. What if Catharine talked to Mrs. Sayre about Spencer staying nights at the Residence? Of course, Mrs. Sayre probably wouldn't give it any thought. A number of the State Department officers stayed in the extra rooms on occasion and certainly often did so these days.

Peggy said woodenly, "I don't believe he's forgotten, Mrs. Cavanaugh, but I'll give him the message."

Catharine smiled. "He'll be irritated. He won't want to go. No one does, the way things are now, but he must."

When Catharine had gone, Peggy still sat, her hands limp on the typewriter. Tonight Spencer wouldn't be coming to her apartment. He would be dancing with Catharine, with Mrs. Spencer Cavanaugh.

Peggy bit her lip, then angrily began to type the lists of gold.

The long pastel dresses swirled gracefully as the women danced. Catharine thought of butterflies wheeling and turning in the sunset. White uniforms stood out in sharp contrast to the yellows and blues of the gowns. The reception was just another diplomatic party except that it forced her to remember a particular party, a reception at the German embassy in Paris in the spring of 1939. That cold and hostile evening in Paris the representatives of certain countries stood carefully on opposite sides of the ornate room. Tonight, the English diplomats stood with their American counterparts. Spencer was deep in conversation with the British military attaché. Catharine looked across the ballroom floor at the Japanese officials ranged along the opposite wall. Consul and Mrs. Yoshida stood in the center of the room in a formal reception line to greet arriving officials. Japanese serving women in bright kimonos offered tea and cakes.

The British military attaché stood just to Catharine's right.

"Mark my words, Cavanaugh, it will be over in a matter of weeks if the Japs do anything foolish. Why, those little brown Johnnies are a joke as fighters. We'll mop them up with no problem—and, of course, Singapore is impregnable."

"They have their hands full in China," Spencer offered. Then he frowned and said worriedly, "But things look bad. If the Japanese commission in Washington doesn't accept our terms, then I'm afraid . . ."

The orchestra began to play a stately waltz. Catharine looked away from Spencer and saw a tall, slim Japanese in the uniform of a colonel walking purposefully toward their corner. Spencer and the British major stopped talking.

The Japanese colonel ignored them, walked up to Catharine, and gave a slight bow.

"Do you remember me, Catharine?"

Her eyes widened in surprise; then she smiled and held out her hand. "Tom, of course I remember you." Still smiling, she turned to Spencer. "Spencer, this is Tom Okada. He was at school with my brother, Ted, at Stanford. He often came home with Ted." She turned back to the Japanese officer. "Tom, this is my husband, Spencer Cavanaugh."

Colonel Okada bowed. Spencer stiffly nodded his head.

They didn't shake hands.

"I knew your wife when she was a little girl, and she was as lovely then as she is now."

Spencer nodded but didn't respond.

The colonel turned back to Catharine. "May I have this dance, Catharine?"

She hesitated for just an instant. The Japanese and American diplomats treated each other with punctilious courtesy but no friendliness these days. This had been the norm ever since Roosevelt applied the embargo and the Japanese continued to insist upon their right to expand and the future of the Greater Asia Co-Prosperity Sphere.

Would it really be appropriate for her to dance with a Japanese military officer?

But this was Ted's friend and hers.

Lifting her chin a little, she said quickly, "I'd love to, Tom."

He took her hand, and they walked out onto the dance floor. She could feel Spencer's disapproval. As she and Tom circled the dance floor, she saw the tight, closed faces of the other Americans. Tom, of course, saw them, too. He laughed a little.

"Consul Yoshida looks as though he's eaten something disagreeable. Isn't it absurd, Catharine?"

"Yes. Yes, it is." She looked up at her old friend. "Tom, do you think there's going to be a war?"

He shrugged. "Who knows? But there's nothing you or I can do about it." Briskly, he changed the subject. "Have you seen Ted recently?"

"Yes, when we came through New York. Ted's still with Mercantile General. He and Betty live in Scarsdale and have four children."

"Four!" Tom exclaimed. "It seems funny to think of Ted as a family man. When we were in school, he was a ladies' man." Then he looked at her quickly.

Catharine laughed. "You don't have to protect my brother's reputation with me. Ted always loved and left the ladies until he met Betty, but now he's thoroughly domesticated. How about you, Tom? Are you still a gallant bachelor?"

He shook his head. "No. My wife and I have two sons. I suppose the years catch up with all of us." He looked at her quizzically. "And you, Catharine, do you have any children?"

Despite the years since they'd last met, he knew her well, and he saw the pain in her face.

"I'm sorry, Catharine. I've said the wrong thing, haven't I?"

She shook her head quickly. "You couldn't have known." She steeled her voice. "We lost our little boy just past his first birthday." She forced a smile and asked brightly, "Is your wife here in Manila with you, Tom? I'd love to meet her."

"No. She's at home in Osaka. I'm not permanently stationed here. I'm on a special mission."

She started to say the same was true of Spencer, but caught herself. There was between them, abruptly, a constraint. He, too, didn't seem to know what to say.

The waltz ended, and they walked back across the floor to where Spencer and the British major waited, their faces impassive.

Tom bent down and said softly, "I'm glad, Catharine, that you haven't turned against your old friend."

She smiled and felt at ease again. "I'll never do that, Tom."

"Would you like to see the consulate garden? It is one of the love-liest in Manila."

Catharine could see Spencer, waiting stiffly. "I wish I could, but I'd better rejoin my husband now."

"Of course." Just before they reached Spencer, he said, "Perhaps I'll see you again before I leave Manila."

She gave him a quick, warm smile. "I hope so."

When they reached Spencer, Tom bowed formally, then turned away.

Spencer waited a moment, then said through clenched teeth, "That was an incredible performance, Catharine."

"Was it?" she asked indifferently.

"For God's sake, Catharine. Polite but formal, that's how the high commissioner told us to deal with the Japanese. Don't you understand, there's a damn good chance there's going to be war?"

She looked at him coolly and was somewhat surprised that his reprimand didn't touch her at all. She wasn't even sorry he was upset. She already hurt too much to let this petty argument cause her any pain.

"Spencer, I am a perfectly loyal American, but until the day we are at war, I have no intention of turning against a very old and very dear friend."

Spencer's anger was still evident the next morning at breakfast. He didn't speak as Manuel served their fruit and toast.

Catharine ignored Spencer equally and read the Manila Tribune. Headlines told of worsening relations between Washington and Tokyo. Catharine skimmed the stories, then turned to an inside page. She didn't look up as Spencer pushed back his chair.

"Catharine."

She looked up. "Yes?"

"You are not to have anything to do with this Okada."

"I'll see."

He hesitated and almost spoke again, but she turned back to the paper. She heard him walk across the room. He paused at the door.

"I'll be staying at the Residence tonight." The door slammed behind him.

Catharine remembered his angry face several times during the day as she went through the motions of being Mrs. Spencer Cavanaugh. She attended a luncheon at the British Club and spent the afternoon at the U.S. Residence attending a first-aid class, in part to please Amea. She watched the earnest women in their summery frocks practicing how to splint broken bones and apply tourniquets. The American women ranged in age from their early twenties to their late sixties. Catharine thought they had absolutely no inkling of what war was like. She thought of houses after a bombing raid open to the street like stage-set scenes; the terrible quiet of a heap of rubble; the slow, tenacious efforts to find survivors; the bloodied, dusty bodies carried off in mortuary vans; the death notices in the London Times, and the rank, raw, hideous smell of destruction. These pleasant-faced, confident women talked earnestly about what to do in case of attack. Her heart ached for them.

Amea Willoughby turned to Catharine. "You've just come from London. What is it like to be in an air raid?"

Catharine looked thoughtfully at Amea.

Amea misunderstood Catharine's silence. "Forgive me," she said quickly. "I shouldn't have asked. Someone told me you'd actually been bombed and lost all your things."

"I don't mind answering," Catharine said slowly, "but it's hard to explain. I think it's the helplessness that's the worst." She paused and frowned. "It's the waiting, sitting there, night after night, waiting. You never know where the bombs will fall or what they will do. It's so completely fortuitous." She smiled wryly. "I suppose it's arrogance to believe we can control our destiny. That's the first thing you lose in a bombing raid, the sense of control and rationality. Nothing matters but chance. It's as if you're playing a gigantic, cosmic game of chance, and your life is the chip if you lose."

Amea nodded toward Catharine. "Is any of this going to help us if it happens?"

"It can't hurt," Catharine said gently.

Amea reached over suddenly and patted Catharine's hand.

When the meeting was over, Catharine moved ahead of the others and out of the Residence into the heavy, throbbing heat. She waved for a calesa for the journey back to downtown. She sat in the gaily painted cart pulled by a plodding pony and looked out across the glittering blue bay. The cool, fresh breeze off Manila Bay swept over her, and the sticky dampness of her dress was uncomfortably cool. When the cart stopped in front of her apartment house, she handed the driver fifty centavos. He reached up to help her step down.

She hesitated for a moment on the sidewalk, but it was almost four o'clock. Too late, really, to go shopping. Moreover, there was nothing she needed or wanted. She stood irresolutely, then turned and walked into the lobby.

She had nowhere to go, no one whom she cared to see, nothing to look forward to. She rode up alone in the slow, rickety elevator.

She let herself into the quiet apartment and stood in the center of the unbearably warm living room. The heavy whirr of the overhead fan, the standard brown rental drapes, the tropical rattan furniture made her feel alone and alien. She was shaken to her core by a wave of despair.

Catharine clenched her hands tightly. She mustn't give way. She must not.

But why not? Who cared?

No one. No one anywhere in the world.

Jack had cared, but that was over, gone, done with. She knew he was angry and hurt. She'd left him without even saying good-bye. How could he possibly be anything but bitter? He hadn't even seen the letter she'd sent.

The longing was sharp, painful, deep. Unendurable. Oh, God, she wanted him so much, she loved and needed him so much.

Somehow, no matter what effort it took, she had to find him. She had, at the very least, to know where he was and that he lived. She had to know.

The doorbell rang.

Manuel hurried from the kitchen to the front door. He bowed and smiled to Catharine, then opened the door.

In the hall beyond him, Catharine saw a delivery boy holding flowers.

When Manuel brought them, she fumbled eagerly for the card. She opened it and, through tears of disappointment, read the message: "With all best wishes from your devoted friend, Tom Okada."

Catharine handed the flowers to Manuel. "Find a vase for them, please."

In a moment, he returned and placed the spray of tiny, glistening white orchids on a table by the window.

Catharine held the card in her hand. Funny, she'd hoped for a crazy moment when she saw the delivery boy that the flowers would be from Jack. That was crazy. He didn't know where she was, had no way of knowing her address. Besides, Jack would still be furious.

She stood in a shaft of sunlight by the window, but it didn't melt the sadness inside her. She looked down at the card. "Your devoted friend." Funny. Everything was funny these days. The only warmth she'd received in this alien place came from the gentle wife of a diplomat who understood something of the horror of an air raid, and from a Japanese colonel in Manila on a special mission.

Yes, everything was damned funny. Tears slipped down her face. If only she knew where Jack was.

The staccato rattle of typewriter keys was punctuated every few seconds by the slam of a carriage. The noise reverberated in the small, hot room and spilled out into the dingy hall. The smell of cigar smoke hung heavily in the thick, steamy air. Catharine's white-gloved hands tightened on the handles of her woven purse, and she stepped purposefully forward.

The man behind the desk glanced up irritably. Then his eyes bright-ened and he stopped typing. "Yeah. What can I do for you?"

"Is this the office of the International News Service?"

"Right the very first time. Kuyk Logan at your service."

"I have a friend who works for INS in London. Is there a way I could send a message to him?"

"Sure." Logan's light brown eyes studied her. He scribbled an address on a sheet of yellow copy paper. "This'll get it," and he handed it to her. "Who's your friend?"

"Jack Maguire. Do you know him?"

"Maguire." Logan frowned. "Yeah, I've heard of him. I don't think he's still with us. If you'd like, I can check and see."

"Would you please? I'd appreciate it."

"No trouble. Drop back by tomorrow."

Catharine returned at the same time the next day.

Logan looked up through cigar smoke curling lazily in the still, hot air. He stopped typing and leaned back in his chair. "I checked. Maguire quit his job and nobody's seen him since early September."

Catharine had been so certain she would be able to get in touch with Jack. She'd counted on it. It was as if she stood facing an abyss and had nowhere to turn.

"Sorry."

"They don't know where he went?"

He looked at her kindly. "Not an idea. He might as well have stepped off the edge of the world."

It was a cruel week. Without mentioning the evening at the Jap-anese embassy, she and Spencer settled back into their polite, con-strained pattern. He was courteous; she was passive. The long, steamy days held no focus for Catharine. At odd moments, she would hear the correspondent's light voice, ". . . might as well have stepped off the edge of the world," and a sickening feeling of emptiness and despair swept through Catharine. Nobody knew where Jack was; now she would never know what happened to him. She didn't know anything of his family except they were named Maguire and lived in Chicago. She had no way of finding out his father's first name.

He might be anywhere in the world, but she would never see him again, never again feel his gentle and so loving body next to hers.

She moved through the days with a distant, pleasant smile, trying to cope with the emptiness and the sorrow. Now, she had no hope. Deep in her secret self, she'd looked forward to the end of Spencer's assignment with the hope that she would leave him then. She'd thought that even if she couldn't go back to London because of the war, she would write Jack and offer to join him anywhere he could go, anywhere in the world. She would go anywhere and wait for however long it might take. Perhaps that had always been nothing more than a dream, but now she didn't even have the dream.

Manuel handed the telephone to Catharine. "Ma'am, it's your husband."

Catharine took the receiver. "Yes."

"Catharine, are you free tomorrow afternoon? Woody wants to know if we can attend a polo match tomorrow at the British Club."

"Of course. Shall I meet you there?"

"That would be perfect. I appreciate it, Catharine."

"I'll be glad to." Her voice was colorless and even.

"Is anything wrong?" Spencer asked.

"Oh, no. Everything's fine."

"You don't sound fine."

Even in her distant, uncaring mood, she was touched. That was perceptive of Spencer.

"It's all right, Spencer."

"Catharine, I'm sorry things are so difficult. I know this isn't very pleasant for you, to be stuck here with nothing to do and no real friends, but we're making a lot of progress. We may be able to go back to the States by January."

Once, she would have been so excited at the prospect. She would have braced herself to tell Spencer that she was leaving him, but now it didn't make any difference. Manila. New York. Now or January. What difference did it make?

"Catharine?"

"Yes, I'm here. And I'll count on the polo match tomorrow."

The horses thundered down the field. Catharine recognized an American officer leaning low out of his saddle, swinging his mallet. The *thock* as it struck the wooden ball echoed across the field. Someone in the stands yelled, "Good shot, Brewster!"

Catharine stood beneath the intertwining branches of a banyan tree and watched the match without much interest. It was cool and shady beneath the tree, and she felt she'd done her duty for a while. She'd left Spencer in the reviewing stand and circulated through the tent set up near the field and visited with the wives of players and spectators. She'd met several nurses from Fort Stotsenburg Army Hospital, some pilots from Clark Field, and a naval officer from Cavite Naval Base. Now she leaned against the tree and watched the people standing beside the field, men in uniform, women in swirling summery dresses. She watched dreamily. Everyone looked especially attractive today. Funny to think they were eight thousand miles from the States. And how many miles farther was it to England? She could work it out, of course, but it didn't matter now because Jack wasn't in England, or, if he was, she didn't know where.

Then she jerked upright; her breath caught in her throat. She stared through the dimness beneath the tree out into the brilliant, harsh sunlight.

It couldn't be. Not possibly. It was her imagination creating familiarity out of the set of broad shoulders, the wave of thick, curly black hair. Then the man turned and looked across the emerald-green lawn. Her hand rose to her throat, her heart began to pound, and she felt as if she were going to faint.

12

She was thin, too damn thin. Had she been sick? Then Jack knew she'd seen him. Her hand went to her throat. Her eyes widened in shock—then joy softened her face. A shout rose behind him. Someone had scored. There was a rush of movement and noise, the thunder of clapping hands. Everywhere there was a sense of movement and excitement. Only he and Catharine stood still, staring at each other through the thick, hazy heat of the November afternoon.

He wanted to hold her, yet he stood with leaden legs. He was afraid. She'd gone with Spencer and left only a note behind. He knew she cared, but how much? Still, it was absurd to stand here, only yards from her, and look with longing eyes. He'd crossed oceans and continents to find her, yet he hesitated. For a damn certain man, he felt very uncertain. Would she be angry that he'd come? He stared across the grass and found it hard to breathe as he looked into her violet eyes. No color ever anywhere was so vivid as Catharine's eyes, not bluebells in Scotland nor a mountain lake in Switzerland nor the deep purplish haze that twilight brings to a Caribbean sunset.

He was walking toward her now, not even aware he'd taken a step. A gentle breeze molded her soft pink dress against her. She looked lovely and unapproachable, as exotic as the flowers that trellised the bamboo fence behind the spreading banyan tree. He ducked to step beneath the low-slung branches of the banyan.

She stood waiting, her hand still at her throat, her eyes enormous in a pale face.

He stopped just in front of her, stared down, and couldn't find the words he needed.

Catharine's mouth trembled. "I thought I would never see you again," she said huskily. Then she said it again, her voice rising and harshening. "I thought I would never see you again."

Jack knew then.

Her voice ached with pain, buckled with pain, and he knew why she was so thin and pale. He knew with a rush of gratitude and happiness that she did love him, that she had never stopped loving him, that she stood in the shadow of the banyan tree and struggled for composure. She was his whether he belonged in her world or not, forever and always.

"It's all right." He reached out and took her hands in his, held them hard and tight, and he knew he was a lifeline.

Tears brimmed in her eyes, those glorious, vivid, magnificent eyes. "I wrote you. The letter came back addressee unknown. Oh, God, Jack, I didn't know where you were. I didn't think I'd ever see you again."

"It's all right," he said again.

Gravel crunched as a couple passed along the path beside the banyan tree.

"Hello, Catharine," a woman's light voice called.

Catharine looked blankly past Jack and nodded; then she pulled her hands free.

When the couple was past, Jack said abruptly, "Let's get out of here."

She nodded, then said breathlessly, "I must leave word for Spencer." She found a pad in her purse, wrote a short note saying she was tired and leaving early with friends, and gave it to a steward to deliver. Then, her face alight with happiness, she took his hand. "I can't believe you're here."

He smiled down at her, wanting so badly to hold her that he had to clench his hands at his sides. He wanted to take her in his arms and kiss her, feel her strain against him. He smiled and knew with a surge of triumph that she wanted him just as much.

His car, a two-seater Ford convertible, picked up speed when they reached Dewey Boulevard. Manila Bay sparkled to their left. The sea breeze blew against their faces.

Catharine leaned back against the brown leather seat and smiled. Her face almost hurt, the smile felt so unaccustomed. She'd never expected to feel this kind of exuberance and delight again.

"Where are we going?" she shouted against the hot rush of wind.

He turned to look at her.

She loved the way the wind whipped his thick black hair and the way the sun shone on his strong face. He looked wonderful, absolutely wonderful. She loved, too, the puzzlement in his voice when he answered. "Hell, I don't know. I just got to town. Where can we be alone?"

A tiny flush moved in her cheeks. "There's a headland about five miles out of town, and there's an abandoned sugar mill . . ."

She watched his profile as they drove. The coast was a blur beyond his face. She didn't care how lovely the great expanse of bay was or how the silver tips of the waves glittered in the sunlight. All she cared about was Jack.

She bent forward, reaching out to brush his cheek with her hand.

His head turned. His eyes were dark and warm, full of love and desire.

"I love you," she said simply. Then she cried out sharply, "Jack, watch out, that cart!"

He jerked the wheel and the Ford careened dangerously near the far edge of the road, just missing the cart.

"I'm going to wreck this goddamn car if we don't get there pretty soon," he said urgently.

She laughed shakily. "It's not far now. There's a turn-off. See, up there, at the top of the hill."

He swung the car off onto a narrow, rutted dirt road that was scarcely more than a track. Dust rose in swirls behind them as they bucketed along through a curling green tunnel of jungle growth.

Catharine swallowed. She knew the hunger that drove him because she felt it, too. She wanted to love him. Now. This minute. They didn't need words. Not now. They needed each other.

The car burst out of the tunnel of growth and into a sparse, dusty, deserted clearing. Jack jammed on the brakes, then turned off the motor. In the sudden quiet, they turned slowly to each other. Monkeys chattered high in the trees above them. A blue and red macaw squawked angrily.

"There's no one here." Catharine's voice was high and breathless.

"This isn't what I'd planned." Jack's voice was uneven, too.

"What had you planned?" she asked gently.

"A perfect night. A moon, soft music, champagne." He reached out and touched her shoulder. "You'd wear a silver negligee."

"Not the front seat of a Ford convertible in a jungle thicket?" There was laughter in her voice, laughter and love. She lifted her hands, cupped his dear, brown, worried face. "You're a fool," she said dreamily, "a damn fool. Don't you know that doesn't matter? I love you. I love you here or in a silk-sheeted bed or in a buffalo wallow or behind a throne. Oh, Jack, love me, love me now."

He moved then; they both moved. His arms came around her like steel bands. Suddenly there was no more thought, only feeling. They sought each other, their lips moving and touching, their hands urgent. It only mattered that they were together, and their urgent, fiery, hungry need couldn't wait. They came together in a rough and thrusting union as hot and explosive as lava rolling down a mountainside to plunge into the sea. Not neat or tidy. But monumental and wonderful.

When they rested together, his arms around her, her head on his shoulder, Catharine's mouth curved in a small, amused smile. Of all the times she'd ever made love, this time was at once the most awkward and the most satisfying. She would never have imagined herself, Catharine MacLeish Cavanaugh, locked in passion in the front seat of a shabby two-seater convertible parked in a jungle clearing. She lifted her face and looked up at Jack. Her smile widened.

He was watching her, but there was no laughter in his eyes—only a kind of tenderness that made her want to cry.

"You're so lovely," he whispered.

"Even now?" she asked drily. "In a crumpled dress, my hair falling down . . ."

His mouth closed over hers; his kiss answered all questions.

There are only a few moments of sheer happiness in each life. Catharine knew that, knew it as well as any woman living. This was one of those moments for her. She framed his face in her hands and felt closer to him than she ever had been to anyone in all her life. "Jack, I want to tell you something."

He tightened his arm around her shoulders.

"I want you to know," and she spoke simply and openly and every word came from her heart, "that this is the loveliest, most perfect afternoon I've ever known."

Pain and happiness both moved within him. He felt an uneasy sense of life's evanescence, coupled with delight in Catharine. But that was why he'd come. He'd come for Catharine. He was determined that she would be his forever. He knew that life was fragile and human hope more fragile still. They could never count on tomorrow, but they could, while life and breath lasted, count on each other, whether that time would be measured in moments or in years.

"We're going to have hundreds of perfect afternoons. This is just our beginning, Catharine."

She didn't smile. Her eyes were dark with sadness. "I've learned not to count on tomorrow, Jack."

He tangled his hand in her thick, dark hair. "I'm going to prove to you that you can count on tomorrow. I'm going to love you every day, and one day you won't have that haunted look in your eyes. You won't be afraid." He smoothed her hair; then his hand reached into his pocket. "Look, Catharine."

He pulled a letter-sized manila envelope from the inside pocket of his uniform jacket. He opened the envelope and took out two tickets. "The S.S. Galveston sails for Honolulu next Saturday. These tickets are for us."

Catharine stared at the tickets. Two tickets on the S.S. Galveston. Two tickets back to the United States, two tickets to happiness.

She wanted to go. She wanted desperately to take Jack's hand and go, the two of them together, no matter what the world would say.

She could see the date written on the outside of the ticket. Saturday, November 29,1941. Less than a week away.

She looked up and knew that he could see the anguish—and the refusal—in her eyes.

His jaw muscles tightened. Suddenly, frighteningly, he looked angry and formidable.

"Goddamn it, Catharine, I came for you."

She reached out and touched him. His arm was hard and rigid.

"Please, Jack, don't be angry with me. I love you, and I will go with you—"

His face began to change.

"—as soon as Spencer's tour is over."

Slowly, stubbornly, he shook his head. "Saturday, Catharine."

Peggy stared somberly down at the black and white photograph. She tried to remember Jill's coloring. Jill had been such a pretty baby, silky golden hair and dark, dark blue eyes. Funny, she could scarcely see a trace of that baby in this photograph of a gawky, solemn ten-year-old with pigtails and braces and eyes hidden behind heavy glasses. It was so hard to believe Grace's baby was now ten. She'd been four the last time Peggy had seen her. Jill was her only niece.

Pain twisted inside Peggy. She would love babies, too. She knew she would. To hold a tiny life in her arms. To hear the high, mewing cry a new baby made. To see a tiny baby's hands open and shut, little pink fingers beginning to explore and learn. The smell, feel, and wonder of new life.

She was never, never going to have a baby.

Peggy put the photograph down on the tabletop beside the box of packages her family had sent for Christmas. They'd sent them long ago, of course, to be certain they would arrive in time. It took seven weeks for the ships to sail from San Francisco to Manila. Grace, her mother, and Jill must have braved the thick heat of Georgia in August to do their shopping for Peggy. It was evidence of love and caring. Peggy could feel the hot sting of tears in her eyes. She blinked the tears away and looked again at the photograph. Grace's daughter. Her niece.

Peggy looked slowly around the dingy apartment. The thick, heavy heat pushed against her, and she felt weary and depressed. Everyone had been so cheerful this afternoon at the Thanksgiving dinner at the Residence. All the staff was there, the high commissioner and his wife, the diplomats and their wives.

Spencer and his wife.

And children, of course. Children of all ages played on the lawn after dinner, running, shouting, having a wonderful time.

She'd sat at a different table from Spencer and Catharine's, but that didn't help. Catharine was at his side, his wife. She would always be his wife.

Again a physical sensation of pain moved in her chest.

Usually, she didn't allow herself to think about it, to look ahead and see the passing years and herself following Spencer from post to post, Peggy Taylor, the efficient, successful secretary. Her mother's friends remarked that Peggy sure did have an exciting life, all those foreign places, but when was she going to come home and marry Rowley? Why, surely that pretty little Peggy wasn't going to be a spinster?

Tears burned behind her eyes. She knew how they talked in her little Georgia town. She knew how the bright, curious eyes probed her mother's face.

This afternoon, she could see, a touch of sickness in her throat, the long years passing, the apartments here or in other cities—and Spencer.

Spencer loved her.

She knew that was true, knew it with certainty.

But he didn't love her quite enough.

That was the thought she'd never admitted to herself—the thought she'd buried, refused to face and think about. But today it slid out from the dark recesses of her mind and throbbed with an angry, aching pain.

He loved her, he needed her, he wanted her, but he loved his career more.

Peggy once again put the photograph on the table and picked up an unopened letter that had arrived yesterday with the package of gifts. She hadn't opened it because she knew what it contained. Rowley had such a distinctive hand, small, neat printing in block letters.

She could go home to Stone Mountain and Rowley and one day there would be babies.

But Spencer . . .

She heard his key in the lock. She hadn't expected him to come this holiday evening. Usually, she jumped up and moved eagerly toward the door when he came, but today she sat in the wicker chair, her shoulders slumped, Rowley's unopened letter in her lap.

The overhead light flickered on.

"Peggy, why are you sitting in the dark?" He hurried across the room and looked down at her with concern. Then he bent forward. "Honey, are you all right?"

She bit her lips to keep them from trembling. She couldn't say a word to him or she would cry. Was she all right? No, she was all wrong; her life was all wrong.

Spencer reached out and touched her shoulder. "Honey, what's happened?"

She shook her head. How could she tell him it was the Thanksgiving dinner with sets and sets of husbands and wives, the sound of children playing on the front lawn, a picture of a solemn ten-year-old girl, and an unopened letter from a man who loved her in a steady, quiet way? She shook her head again. Tears spilled down her face.

Spencer knelt beside her and took her hands in his. "Peggy, tell me what's wrong."

She swallowed jerkily, her lips trembled, and she could scarcely see him through the blur of tears. "Spencer, I want to have babies."

He went rigid, as if an electric shock coursed through him. His face looked suddenly drained and white. Slowly, he stood, pulling her to her feet. They faced each other, but he didn't speak.

She broke the taut silence. "I'm going to go home."

She hadn't planned to say it, hadn't even thought it before. The words came without warning. Deep inside, she waited for Spencer to say no, to say he loved and needed her, to insist that she not leave him.

He looked down at her and said nothing.

Peggy made a noise, a deep animal noise of hurt. She turned away, jerking her hands free, and began to walk blindly across the room, one hand outstretched as a blind woman might.

Spencer fought tears, too. His throat ached as he watched Peggy blunder across the room. She bumped into a table and fumbled with the knob to the bedroom door. Her shoulders heaved and he knew tears ravaged her face, that she was choking for breath. Still he stood, unmoving. The bedroom door slammed, and he was alone in the hot, still living room. He could hear the hard, racking sounds of her sobs through the thin wooden door. He wanted to go after her, to comfort her, to take her in his arms and to love her.

But if he did, she would stay, and he felt a deep, primal conviction that she should go back to the United States as soon as possible. Manila had received the alert this morning, a war alert sent to all United States naval and army forces in the Pacific. A war alert. The Japs might attack anywhere in the Pacific within the next two weeks.

He'd had friends in Nanking when the Japs invaded there. He knew what the Japanese did to conquered women.

The harsh, broken sound of her weeping battered him. Tears filmed his eyes. He began to move toward the door, one halting step at a time. He reached the door and touched the knob.

If Peggy went home, if she left now, she would be safe.

There wouldn't be any light or laughter left in his life, but he had to stay in Manila and complete his assignment. It was the best assignment of his career, and it mattered, it was very important. Who knew where he would be sent from here if he succeeded, and he was succeeding. He might be returned to London at a higher rank, or perhaps he would be attached to the secretary of state's personal staff in Washington. He would have proven his worth—if he finished the task here, if he meticulously accounted for all the gold and silver in the islands and made provisions to have the treasure safely removed should war occur.

He couldn't ask Catharine for a divorce until this task was completed. His wife had to be here, had to be part of the effort to reassure the Filipinos.

If he told Peggy he would get a divorce, she would stay here, but once again that primal instinct flared. Get Peggy away. Get her out of the Philippines. He'd reserve a berth on a ship to San Francisco, take the first vacant cabin.

His hand dropped away from the knob. He walked stiffly across the room and opened the front door, carrying the sound of her tears in his soul.

13

Dust swirled in an orange-red haze. Jack pulled himself up to look over the convertible's windshield at the traffic stacked up ahead of them. "Damn, this is going to take hours. I guess we won't go to Baguio today."

Catharine shaded her eyes against the metallic, blistering sun. The long line of dun-colored tanks stretched as far as the eye could see. The hatches were open and the crewmen draped over the copings, waving and whistling to the spectators. Filipinos by the hundreds lined the road and waved tiny American flags.

"Where are they all going?" she asked.

"Fort Stotsenburg. They're from a convoy that landed yesterday." He looked at Catharine soberly. "They're another reason I want us to leave on the Galveston tomorrow."

"The tanks? What do they have to do with us?"

"Washington didn't send those tanks out here to cut the grass, Catharine. That's just another sign that war's coming."

He maneuvered the car so it was half-turned now. With a final twist, the convertible nosed around and headed back for Manila. "There's a nice beach out past Cavite. We'll go there."

Catharine laughed. "You've only been in town for a week, but you already know the good beaches, the best restaurants, and the bars that serve the best whisky."

He grinned lazily. "You bet. An advantage of living with a newspaperman."

"Not the outstanding advantage," she said demurely.

He shot her a quick look, then exploded with laughter. "For a woman who looks like the epitome of the prim and reserved American, you have quite a bawdy mind."

"Do I shock you?"

"You shock me. You delight me."

They chattered happily all the way down the narrow two-lane road to Cavite. They spoke lightly, but their eyes were soft and warm. There was so much between them that was unsaid, that didn't need saying. Catharine didn't even mind the usual blazing sunlight or the ripe jungle growth that crowded against the roadway. She didn't worry about tomorrow or regret yesterday. She was existing for this very moment, for now, for being with Jack.

When they reached the end of a sandy trail that led down to the beach, Jack hired a Filipino in a vinta to take them to one of the deserted islands that lay close offshore. When they stepped out of the boat, Jack arranged for the boatman to return at sunset.

Catharine carried the picnic basket, and Jack carried the blanket. They went to the bay side of the island, the tiny, deserted island, and spread a patchwork quilt on the hot white sand.

Catharine smiled at Jack then and said softly, "When we're together, everything is wonderful."

He looked up at her and slowly smiled, but said nothing. Her heart sang in gratitude. Let them have this afternoon, and, if it were going to be the last afternoon, let it be a happy one without any quarrel. He'd made it clear last week. She was to come with him tomorrow. All this week, when they'd met and loved in the afternoons, it had been implicit, unstated. Now they were together the day before the S.S. Galveston was to sail.

She couldn't go.

Jack would argue that she shouldn't feel guilt, but she did and she would. She had to balance it out in her own mind and heart. What did she owe Spencer? There were the years they'd spent together, there was Charles, and there was the importance of this assignment to Spencer. Moreover, if she left, it could be a signal to the Filipinos that the Americans were wavering.

She couldn't go.

She watched Jack with hungry eyes. She watched the way his soft cotton shirt stretched across his shoulders as he bent forward to lift their sandwiches out of the hamper.

"Hungry?" he asked.

"Starving."

"How about a turkey sandwich? This will be our Thanksgiving."

She'd spent yesterday at the Residence, at the marvelous Thanksgiving feast for the diplomats and their wives and the staff, but she'd picked at her food and talked desultorily.

This afternoon, the sandwich tasted wonderful. Jack opened two bottles of beer and handed one to her. It tasted wonderful, too, dark and slightly acrid.

They ate hungrily, talked eagerly, and drank their beer, then stretched out on the red-and-white quilt—and still they talked. There would never be enough time in the world for them to say everything.

Catharine propped up on one elbow and looked at him quizzically.

"What are you going to do when you get back to the States?"

"Go by Chicago; then I think I'll hit Washington."

"Why Washington?"

"Somebody ought to need a newspaperman."

She stared at him, not understanding. She knew, of course, that he'd left INS, but she'd assumed he was with another news service. For the first time, it occurred to her that he didn't have a job.

"Jack, aren't you working for somebody now?"

"Nope."

"Do you mean you don't have a job at all?" She looked stricken. "Did you quit your job to come here?"

"Sure."

"Oh, Jack. I assumed you'd gotten a job with one of the other news services." She frowned. "Didn't you come here by military flights and then on the Repulse,"

He nodded.

She was still puzzled. "How could you do that if you weren't working for a news agency?"

His grin stretched all the way across his face. "Easy. I flashed my correspondent's papers. Nobody asked if I still worked for them. The military PIO offices are so swamped they don't know which end is up."

"You came all that way illegally?"

He was still laughing. "It could be so described."

She began to laugh, too. "Jack, you're awful." His delight was contagious, irrepressible.

"Yeah."

"You think it's a joke."

"Sure."

Slowly, her smile faded. "If you don't have a job, how can you afford to be here and how did you buy those tickets?"

"Oh, one way or another," he said evasively.

"And the car," she pressed. "How did you buy it?"

"You want to know?"

She nodded.

"You really want to know?"

She nodded vigorously.

He rolled over on his elbow, too, and their faces were close together.

"There was this joe on the flight to Singapore," he said confidentially.

She waited.

Jack shook his head a little. "He thought he knew how to play poker." He began to grin again. "Actually, he has a lot to learn and lessons are expensive."

"You gambled?"

"That's what poker's all about."

Catharine pushed herself up and stared down at him, amazed.

"My God," she said simply. "You hook rides on fake papers, and they'd probably shoot you for it if they found out. You don't have any money so you gamble. Jack, you're crazy."

"Yeah."

"I love it." And she did. In all of her life, she'd never met anyone with Jack's insouciance. He was stronger than any man she'd ever known. He didn't need security or station or any of the supports others clung to. He wasn't afraid to dare or challenge or risk. "You're a madman—and I love you."

He grinned. "And you'll run away with me tomorrow."

She'd known they couldn't skirt the issue forever She knew this moment had to come. She reached out, took his hands in hers, and clung to them tightly.

"I won't come with you tomorrow, but I will go anywhere in the world you want me to go when I am free."

He looked up at her somberly, the happiness gone from his face. "When will you be free?"

She leaned down toward him, her eyes pleading.

"It won't be long, it really won't. Spencer's assignment may be finished as soon as January. It will be February by the latest. Don't you see. Jack, that's hardly any time at all. Next week is December. So it's only a matter of weeks. As soon as we leave Manila on our way back to San Francisco, I'll tell Spencer. When we dock in San Francisco, I'll go directly to Reno. Six weeks later, I'll be divorced and then I'll come to you, Jack, anywhere in the world that you want me."

"Why don't you tell him now?" Jack demanded.

"It isn't going to be easy." Then, quickly, as Jack's face hardened, she continued, "No, I don't mean it that way. I don't care. It would be easier if I did; perhaps then I wouldn't feel so guilty, so . . ."

"Catharine, stop that. You don't have any reason to be guilty. If he loved you, I wouldn't say that, but he doesn't love you."

Catharine looked away, looked out at the brilliantly blue water and, far away, at the thumb-shaped smudge that was Corregidor.

"He doesn't love me," she said slowly, "but he's counted on me all these years—and now I'm going to desert him." She swallowed. "And he doesn't have Charles."

Jack reached up, pulled her down, and held her tight. He pressed his mouth against her hair. "Don't, honey, don't."

Tears rimmed her eyes. "But I'll come to you, Jack. I'll follow you. I'll . . ."

"Oh, shut up," he said gruffly. "I'm not going to go off and leave you. I cashed in those damn tickets yesterday."

"Yours, too?"

"Both of them."

She began to shake her head. "But you need to get back to the States. You need to find a job and . . ."

"Shut up, Catharine." But his voice was soft now.

His lips moved gently across her cheek, and he molded her body to his.

She could feel the fire of desire, but still she had to talk, had to insist that he look to his own future. "Wait," she said breathlessly. "I can't let you sacrifice for my sake. You laugh, but I know you care about what you do."

He pulled back just far enough to look down into her face. "You're damn right I care, but I care more about you. They can take all the jobs, all the wars, and all the columns ever written and stuff them into a sink-hole, and I'll still love you."

She stared up at him, her eyes wide.

"Yeah, you're right. I'll write. I'll always write. I have to. I have to take the world, all the wonderful and horrible bits of it, and put it into words, make my own sense of it, give it some structure and meaning. I'll write whether I'm here or in London or Reno or wherever the hell. That's part of me, but, most of all, I've found you, and I'm not going to lose you. There'll be a job for me somewhere. I don't worry about it— but I'm not going to lose you."

She smiled even though tears filmed her eyes, and she couldn't see him very clearly. She slipped her hands behind his neck and drew his face to hers. They kissed, and she felt the flare of passion, the swift hot sweet ache that only he could ignite and only he could satisfy. As their tongues touched and tasted, they slipped free of their swimsuits, and their skin was warm and soft as they moved together. She welcomed the touch of his hands, and she pulled him hard against her and within her. There was the pulsing warmth of union and the wonderful surging ecstasy as they moved together in an explosion of delight.

When, finally, they lay quietly and waited for their thudding hearts to ease, Catharine smoothed his thick dark hair and rested her cheek against his face. Jack wasn't going to leave her. It was going to be all right. She had quit believing in tomorrow, but now tomorrow was hers again, a wonderful and certain tomorrow. She could see the days spinning by. Next week it would be December and, as sure as the stars moved in the heavens, the days would pass and it would be January.

14

Through her closed bedroom door Catharine dimly heard the shrill peal of the telephone. She fought her way up through heavy sleep, reached out, and switched on her bedside lamp. She blinked and came further awake. The clock read three fifty-four. Who could possibly be calling at this hour? Her heart began to pound. It had to be bad news. Something bad must have happened.

Her bedroom door swung open, slammed open. Spencer stood in the doorway, his hair tousled, his face slack with shock.

"The Japs have bombed Pearl Harbor."

She stared at him, not understanding. Pearl Harbor. Was that in Hawaii?

Spencer shook his head, a man struggling for control.

"They got almost the whole fleet. Oh, God, almost the whole damned fleet." He shook his head again. "I've got to get out to the Residence. You'd better get up, pack."

She fixed coffee while Spencer shaved. War with Japan. Despite the war alert of the past week, she'd never really thought it would happen. At least, not this way. Who would ever have predicted that the Japanese would attack without warning and attack at the heart of the American fleet? How had they done it? How had an armada possibly slipped across the Pacific undetected?

Spencer took time for only a few quick swallows of the freshly brewed coffee; then he was at the door.

"I'll call you as soon as I learn more," and he was gone, his chin nicked from the hurried shave, his tie awry.

When the door shut, she hurried to the telephone. Dawn was just touching the clouds in the east with shafts of crimson when she dialed Jack's apartment.

No answer.

So he already knew. She replaced the receiver. He must already be at the USAFFE Headquarters in Victoria Street. He would keep on top of it, of course, whether he had a job or not, and, probably, INS would be glad to take him on now.

Back in the kitchen, Catharine poured a second cup of coffee. She felt very alone. The orange glow of the sunrise spread over the old walled city and glittered against the glass of the new skyscrapers. People would be rising now, beginning another day, Monday, December 8, and yet she knew that this day would be like no other. How many knew what had happened? And who could have any idea what the future would hold? She knew what the diplomats expected if war came. If war came, the Japanese would invade the Philippines, and the American forces would fight to keep them offshore as long as possible. Then the Americans would withdraw to the peninsula of Bataan and hold out until help could come. They called it War Plan Orange.

Catharine drank deeply of the hot, strong coffee.

Were the Japanese invasion troops en route right now?

She carried her coffee to the bedroom and dressed in tan slacks, riding boots, and a cotton blouse.

The phone rang.

She dropped a stack of underwear, ran to the living room, and yanked up the receiver.

Spencer was hurried. "The wives and staff are ordered to the Residence. Pack necessities and come at once."

Peggy answered on the first ring. Spencer told her what had happened; then his voice broke. "Oh, God, I knew it was coming but I thought you'd be on your way home first. I wanted you to be safe."

Peggy clasped a hand to her pounding chest. "Is that why you wanted me to leave?"

"Yes. I wanted you to be safe."

"Spencer, you love me? You really do?"

"I love you. I always have. I always will."

Catharine packed as fast as she could, but she tried twice more to reach Jack. When she was ready to leave the apartment, she called the INS office.

A hurried voice answered. "Logan here."

"May I speak to Jack Maguire?"

"He's at HQ. Sorry, gotta go." She was left holding a dead line.

So Jack was back with INS.

Catharine stood uncertainly in the middle of the living room. Had she remembered everything? Their passports, of course. Sunburn cream. Mosquito oil. Soap. Aspirin. Toothbrushes and toothpowder. She wondered suddenly if this were how the refugees had felt when they fled Paris ahead of the invading Nazis. Catharine knew what it was to be bombed, but this was her first time to be a refugee.

Refugee to where?

The question turned coolly in her mind as she wrote a note to Manuel and the other servants. She didn't know what to say, what advice to give. Finally, she left them two months' salary and wished them Godspeed.

Refugee to where? Hawaii was five thousand miles away. Australia was fifteen hundred miles distant.

The doorman flagged a cab, and the cabbie talked in sibilant, broken English all the way out Dewey Boulevard. Catharine answered occasionally, but she was looking at the familiar wide sweep of street and the brilliant gleam of the bay and seeing it all with new eyes. It looked so ordinary, familiar, and impervious to change, but she knew so terribly well that buildings which had survived for hundreds of years collapsed in smoldering heaps in London.

The cabbie slowed and started to turn into the big circle drive that curved in front of the Residence, but an MP waved him to a halt and looked grimly inside.

Catharine leaned forward. "I'm Mrs. Cavanaugh. My husband is the special envoy. He told me to come."

The MP nodded. "You'll have to get out here, ma'am. The drive's closed to traffic. Leave your bags over there. I'll have them sent up in a while."

Catharine nodded and paid the cabbie. She started up the curving drive. Sweat beaded her face, began to slip down her back. The hard glare of the sunlight, even this early in the morning, reflected off the harsh whiteness of the Residence. A plain black iron grille fence separated the grounds from Dewey Boulevard. Past the sea wall, she could see the deep blue of Manila Bay.

At the entrance to the Residence, MPs stood on either side of the door, checking identification. Once inside, Catharine hesitated. It was like being plunged into a nightmare. The mass of people crowded into the lobby reflected fear, horror, and shock. There had been so much talk of war, but no one actually believed war would come. Men and women, some of them holding fretful children by the hand, were lined up three abreast in front of an improvised counter, clamoring to know if ships could carry them away. Catharine looked closer and recognized piles of gas masks on the counter.

"Catharine."

The voice sounded pleasantly over the din of the crowd. Catharine turned and smiled at Amea Willoughby.

They struggled through the frantic crowd to meet.

"I'm so glad you've come," Amea cried.

Catharine reached out and squeezed Amea's hand, then bent close to ask softly, "Have you heard any news?"

Amea's voice dropped, too. "The news is very bad. The Japanese struck on Sunday morning when almost all the ships were in port."

"Sunday morning," Catharine repeated blankly. But the attack had been only a few hours ago and this was Monday.

"Hawaii's over the International Dateline," Amea reminded her. "It's Sunday there, Sunday, December 7. The bombing started just before eight in the morning there, about 2:00 A.M. Monday our time. Apparently, the casualties are very heavy." She bit her lip, then said quickly, "Have you had your inoculations yet?"

Catharine shook her head. "No, I just got here."

Amea led her to the line for anti-tetanus shots. Catharine took her place at the end. As the line inched forward, she watched the intense but controlled activity. There were guards everywhere. MPs bustled about, taping and covering the exposed windows and placing sandbags in the rounded archways of the patio.

After her shot, she felt rather dizzy, but she dutifully stood in another line for her gas mask and one for Spencer. Finally, she climbed the curving stairway to the third floor and the ballroom. She said hello to other wives she knew, took a place at one of the trestle tables, and began to roll bandages.

They were eating lunch when word came that the Japanese were bombing Clark Field and Fort Stotsenburg. They could hear the heavy sound of the bombs. Catharine knew about bombings. She knew about the mindless visitation of death, the fortuity.

Where was Jack? Oh, God, was he safe?

Every imaginable kind of vehicle moved at a snail's pace toward Manila, away from the twin columns of thick smoke that hung like sooty black plumes against the bright enamel-blue sky over Clark Field. Filipino families walked behind laden carabao, all their possessions balanced atop the buffalo or packed on their own backs. Buses, two-wheeled carts, Ford coupes, and a Packard limousine jolted forward, then stopped, jolted forward, then stopped, time after time.

Jack guided the half-horsepower motorcycle onto the graveled shoulder past stalled cars, then back to the narrow two-lane blacktop. The nearer he got to Clark Field, the worse it looked—huge, hot columns of fire and smoke twisting hundreds of feet into the air. He narrowed his eyes and tried to make out the silhouette of the field against the flat Luzon plain, but there were no familiar landmarks. Waist-high, thick-stalked stands of cogon grass blazed like burning straw around the perimeter of the field. Oil and gas supplies burned with an angry orange-red flame. No building was untouched. Jack leaned the motorcycle against a chain link fence and stared in disbelief at what had been only hours before a major military airfield. The roar and crackle of the ignited grasses surrounding the field underscored the sense of desolation and devastation.

Amid the burning fury of the fires, men worked to free those still alive. The dead bodies were in rows not far from the bombed mess hall. A bus loaded with wounded set off for Manila. Blood seeped from the bus, spattering the road.

Grim-faced, Jack began his search for a ranking officer. How many casualties were there? Was the USAFFE air arm destroyed? If it was, how the hell had it happened? How had the Japanese found the major portion of the Far East air fleet on the ground hours after the war began? On the ground and parked wing tip to wing tip, because that was clear from the jumbled wreckage. How in the hell?

Jack leaned against Logan's desk. He was exhausted, but determined. His eyes glinted with anger.

"Goddamn it, that's what happened! A complete surprise. A blow out. A goddamn massacre."

Logan tilted back in his swivel chair. "I don't doubt you, Jack, but we'll never get the story past the censors." He looked down at the yellow sheets Jack had just handed him. There was more than a newsman's interest in his voice. His voice was thin with shock. "Is it really that bad?"

"It's bloody awful. They've got maybe four planes left, and however many B-17s they'd sent to Mindanao earlier."

"How the hell?" Logan asked.

"They'd been up since they heard about Pearl, but they came down to refuel. That's when the Japs attacked. Maybe three P-40s took off. Five more tried, but it was like ducks in a gallery. Whoosh."

Logan picked up a cigar, carefully cut off the end, lit it, and inhaled deeply. Then he looked up at Jack. "You know what that means, don't you?"

"Yeah. I know." Without airpower, the islands would fall.

There was a weary silence for a long moment. Logan smoked some more, then, his voice a little high, said, "Why don't you check out civilian morale tomorrow and see what you can pick up around the banks? There was a run today."

Jack nodded, then turned and walked out into the night. Back in his apartment, he didn't even take time to wash the smoke stains from his face or to get a drink for his parched throat. He dialed Catharine's number. The phone rang and rang.

No answer.

He yanked up the phone directory and found the number of the U.S. Residence.

It took a long time to get an answer. He asked for Catharine and, again, waited for a long time. Finally, a distant voice said, "I'm sorry, but we are unable to connect you with Mrs. Cavanaugh. May we take a message?"

"Tell her Jack Maguire called. Tell her to call me at noon tomorrow at my apartment."

"Jesus, it's hot," a man muttered in the thick darkness.

Catharine lay quietly on her mattress and wondered how many others bedded down for the night on the patio were awake and miserable. Probably almost everyone out there. Mattresses were arranged in groups of five, then enclosed by three-foot-high scaffolding draped with mosquito nets. The thick netting blocked any breeze, though it would have taken a gale to cool the sweltering temperature. She lay in pools of sweat, but it was better to be hot than to be exposed to the malarial mosquitos. She was hot and painfully thirsty, but the fear which had permeated her day was gone—she had her message from Jack. Somehow, she was going to see him tomorrow.

As she thought of Jack, her body relaxed, and she felt the beginnings of a smile. Unexpectedly, sleep washed over her.

The air raid siren woke her. Her heart thudded almost in concert with the hollow thump of exploding bombs. She struggled up on her elbow and listened and knew the bombing wasn't too far away. People began to struggle out from beneath the netting and to call out excitedly.

"The bomb shelter's in the cellar," someone shouted.

Catharine stayed where she was because the bombs weren't coming nearer, but her feeling of ease and happiness was gone. Once again, she tasted the metallic edge of fear. Where was Jack? Where was he now?

The raid continued almost until dawn. Catharine got up as it ended, rolled her mattress up, and went inside to freshen up.

Amea hurried up to her. "Where have you been? Why didn't you come down to the shelter?"

Catharine shook her head. "It wasn't that near."

"I suppose you can tell, after London."

Catharine said drily, "You'll be an expert soon enough."

After breakfast, the women gathered in the third-floor ballroom. This morning they worked swiftly and grimly rolling bandages. Mrs. Sayre made it clear they were badly needed.

"They've opened another hospital at the jai alai courts," Amea said. "There have been so many casualties."

Jack rolled a fresh sheet of paper into the Royal and began to type, his blunt fingers jabbing at the stiff keys. Occasionally, he paused and took a drag from the cigarette. It was hard to figure what the censors would let through. He couldn't describe the almost complete destruction of the air arm, but they couldn't squash the news that Clark and Iba had been bombed. He finished the wrap-up on casualties and an interview with a doctor at the jai alai courts, now converted to a military hospital. Then he glanced down at his watch. He'd called in and told Logan he would be writing at his apartment this morning, that he'd come into the office later in the day with a pile of copy. He shook his head and started another story, but while he wrote and the sentences crackled into life, he was thinking of Catharine. Was she frightened? Of course, she was. She knew what war was like. She'd lived through the Blitz. Now, she might have to face worse. He looked absently at the window, obscured by a driving rain. They should be grateful for the rain. At least the Nips wouldn't bomb right now. But it was time for the dry season. When the rain stopped, the bombers would return, and ultimately Japanese troops would come. If only he'd been able to convince Catharine to leave last week.

He was in the middle of a sentence when he heard the light knock at the door. He shoved back his chair so quickly it tipped over. He reached the door in two strides, jerked it open, and pleasure flooded through him. He reached out and pulled her into his arms despite her wet raincoat. She clung to him as he closed the door.

"It's all right." He said it over and over again until she stopped trembling, looked up at him, and managed a smile.

"I know. I'm a fool," she said huskily. "I make it worse than it is. Every time I hear a bomb drop, I'm afraid for you."

His hand gently touched her cheek. "Hey, that's a waste of good emotion. You know about bad pennies."

She looked up at him, her violet eyes dark with sadness. "You aren't a bad penny."

"Sure I am. But the point is, the Irish never lose. You know why?"

She began to smile. "Why?"

"Because we're too handsome and wonderful. So don't worry about me, Catharine. I'm going to survive this war—and so are you."

"I don't think so," she said slowly, quietly. "I have a feeling . . ."

He broke in sharply. "Don't have feelings like that. It's bad luck."

She looked at him steadily. "I've not had much good luck, Jack, and I've certainly never brought luck to anyone else. Now it's your turn. If it weren't for me, you wouldn't be trapped here. You'd be in England. You'd be safe." Her eyes were enormous now, enormous circles of pain and suffering.

"Stop it, Catharine," he said harshly. "You carry around too much guilt and you aren't going to add me to your burden. I came because you were here, but the Japs would never keep me away. I haven't spent my life playing safe. I do what I want to do, and I want you more than anything else in the world, and I always will."

"I've put you in danger."

He gripped her shoulders and shook her. "Listen to me. I don't give a damn about safety. I never have. I never will. If it weren't for you, I'd be in the middle of the Western Desert right now, and the fighting's bloody awful there."

Catharine licked her lips. "This may be worse than the Western Desert."

"Yeah, it may be, but you know what will make it worth any pain, any price, any risk?"

She waited.

"You," he said softly.

"Jack, oh, Jack, I do love you so."

They moved together, their lips touched, they tasted each other, and they were warm and alive and afire.

The phone rang.

Catharine started to pull away, but his arms tightened around her. "Forget it." His lips moved across her cheek, her temple, nuzzled her hair. Then he turned her toward the bedroom and closed the door against the continuing peal of the telephone.

When they were undressed and lying together, Jack loved her slowly, so slowly, his lips soft against her skin, his hands stroking, searching, caressing. There was no world but the sensual seeking between them. Nothing else existed or mattered. They were perfect and complete in themselves, and soon, like sparks crackling deep within an intense fire, their passion exploded in a tumultuous, exquisite union.

15

I t didn't rain Wednesday, and the Japanese onslaught began. As Catharine and Amea rolled bandages, they listened to the radio announcer, whose voice crackled with strain.

"... the air is full of planes, full of them. Bombers ... fighters ... They are attacking Cavite ... a Japanese convoy, hundreds of ships, has been sighted near Aparri."

New bulletins carried increasingly worse news, and they could hear the faraway sound of exploding bombs. The bombing was over by one o'clock. When they went outside and stood on the lawn, they saw to the south twisting, bulbous clouds of oily black smoke marking the destruction of the immense naval yard.

"It's dreadful," Amea said. "Dreadful."

Catharine nodded, but she didn't answer because she knew this was only the beginning.

In the darkened garden, Spencer and Peggy clung to each other.

"If I'd left you in London, you'd be safe." He said it softly against her hair.

"Don't, Spencer. You didn't know. And you tried to make me go home."

"But not in time."

She lifted her face to his. "Let's love each other—for whatever time remains."

The bombers came every day at noon. Two Japanese convoys were sighted on December 22. In the south, Japanese troops landed at Lamon Bay. The race was on from south and north to reach Manila.

Catharine stood in line in the lobby of the U.S. Residence, waiting for another chance to use the single telephone allotted for private calls. She had been there since shortly after breakfast. Each time she reached the phone, she dialed the INS office, then Jack's apartment. It was almost five o'clock when she finally caught him.

The connection was very bad.

"What, Jack? What did you say?"

". . . into effect . . . WP03 . . . the troops are . . . out . . ."

Catharine understood. The diplomats had talked grimly of it all day. MacArthur had ordered all the Allied forces to withdraw from the main part of the island onto the peninsula of Bataan.

The line cracked again and his voice came clearly.

"I'm going south tonight to cover the retreat up through Manila."

He was going to the fighting.

"When will you be back?"

"I don't . . ." Static drowned him out. He raised his voice. "Catharine . . ."

"Will you be at your apartment this evening? I'll come . . ."

"No, don't try it. It's too dangerous. It would be dark before you started back."

She knew he was right. It was madness these last days to be out in Manila after dark. Trigger-happy militia shot first and asked questions later.

The marine at the desk interrupted reluctantly. "Ma'am, your time is up."

The receiver crackled with static. Catharine called out, "Please, please, take care of yourself . . ."

The day before Christmas dawned bright, clear, and hot. A good day for bombing, Catharine thought. Would Jack be back in Manila? She would call. If he were, then somehow she was going to see him. She hurried downstairs to breakfast and was almost finished when she saw Spencer standing in the doorway to the dining room. When he came toward her, she realized with a shock that he looked ill, his face drained and white. She had scarcely seen him since Pearl Harbor. He was at the Residence, of course, but he worked from early morning to late at night on the gold lists. As he came nearer, she knew he was working far too hard. And what difference, for God's sake, could those interminable lists of gold make now? There were no ships leaving Manila. Every ship that could get underway left the week after war began. Many of them never cleared Manila Bay, victims of Jap bombers, and dozens of listing hulks still burned. Why did Spencer continue to work so hard? It was foolish, idiotic of him. Then she felt ashamed of herself. Spencer was just doing his job, trying to do what he thought was right. But inside, a clear, cool voice whispered, *Oh, yes, Spencer always does what's right and particularly when he is observed.* He was Spencer, trying to succeed and impress, even when his world teetered on the edge of extinction.

He stood before her and looked down, his eyes dulled with exhaustion. His voice was hoarse and scratchy. "I need to talk to you for a moment. Will you come out on the patio?"

Nodding, she took a last swallow of coffee and followed him outside. It was already hot. Spencer took her arm, and they walked toward the sea wall. The deep blue water sparkled in the bright sunlight. Only the twisting coils of smoke rising in the south destroyed the atmosphere of tropical perfection.

When they reached the sea wall, he offered her a cigarette.

"Odd way to spend Christmas Eve." He took a deep drag on his cigarette, then said bluntly, "We're pulling out at noon. Get your stuff ready, but do it unobtrusively."

"Pulling out?" She looked at him blankly. "Where? Where are we going? Where can we go?"

He gestured out into the bay. "Corregidor."

Catharine looked south and west across the sparkling water at the low, dark island of Corregidor. She knew it was a fortress, a small island thirty miles from Manila that sat squarely in the mouth of Manila Bay. Its value lay in the immense guns which faced out toward the South China Sea. So long as U.S. forces held Corregidor, no enemy ships could enter the bay.

"The troops are withdrawing into Bataan," Spencer explained. He broke off a frond from a palm tree and squatted down to scratch out the big island of Luzon. Manila sat in about the center of the great sweep of Manila Bay. About forty miles to the north, a narrow road led through sugar country to Bataan, the peninsula which poked down into Manila Bay.

"What good will that do?" Catharine asked.

Spencer leaned back on his heels. "The troops can hold out for months if they can reach Bataan. That's wild country, huge mountains, ravines, rushing streams. It's practically impassable. If the troops get to Bataan, it will take a hell of a lot to dislodge them."

"If?"

"The troops in the north are going to have to hold off the Japs while the southern troops move up through Manila and into Bataan. It's all started, but it's going to be touch and go."

Catharine looked again across the bay at the dark dot that was Corregidor. "Why are we going out there?"

"It's better than being captured," Spencer said grimly.

A chill of horror moved in her. "Is the army giving up Manila?"

"Yes. It'll be an Open City."

Catharine looked across the patio at the Residence. "What's going to happen to everyone?"

He shrugged.

"How many of us are going to Corregidor?"

"A couple of dozen."

Catharine looked horrified. There were several hundred in the Residence.

"I know," he said angrily, "but I can't help it. Just be grateful we're on the list. And don't tell anyone. Have your stuff ready and be out at the drive by noon." He grimaced. "I've got to get back to work." He took a step, then paused. "I've got to see about transferring the gold."

As usual, there was a line for the one available phone. Catharine took her place, waited and prayed as the line slowly inched forward.

There was no answer at Jack's apartment. She left a brief message at the INS office which she hoped he would understand. Then she wrote a note and took it to one of the young MPs guarding the drive.

"Would you do me a very great favor?"

He looked at her and smiled. She knew it was the first time he'd smiled in days. "I will if I can, ma'am."

She gave him her note and he promised that if he got into Manila, he would take it to Jack's apartment.

Catharine looked up at him, then stood on tiptoe and kissed his cheek.

"It's all right, ma'am." His voice was both gruff and gentle.

She saw the MP again when she walked down the drive just before noon. He lifted his hand to her.

She felt terribly conspicuous with a suitcase. People knew. They looked—then their eyes slipped away. Their faces were not judgmental or angry, just carefully vacant.

Catharine looked down at the ground and followed the line of people carrying suitcases. The buses waited at the foot of the drive.

Amea was holding a seat for Catharine when she climbed aboard the second bus. "Come sit with me. Woody and Spencer will meet us at the pier."

"I know."

They didn't talk on the drive. Both of them looked grim-faced at the shattered intersections and gutted buildings, and at the steady stream of refugees interspersed among the jeeps and trucks, all moving north.

Two PT boats waited at pier 7. The VIP party boarded first. It included High Commissioner and Mrs. Sayre; President Quezon, his wife, Aurora, and their three children; and General Douglas MacArthur, his, wife, Jean, and their son. Catharine had only a brief glimpse of MacArthur before he ducked below decks. His son, Arthur, stayed above with his nurse. Spencer and Woody were on the pier, directing the loading of the odd assortment of trunks and boxes which contained the gold and silver. Finally, Catharine and the rest of the party were waved aboard. Catharine looked back at the sprawling city cupped in its semicircle of low hills.

Just as the boat began to move, a disreputable yellow Ford convertible pulled up and the door was flung open.

She began to smile even as tears blurred her eyes. Jack had found out she was leaving. She didn't know how. Perhaps he'd received her message. Perhaps the news had burned across Manila like a grass fire that the American leaders were fleeing to Corregidor. Somehow, he'd known and here he was. She raised her hand and waved.

Jack waved back.

She clung to the railing of the bucketing boat and waved until she could see him no longer.

Once past the breakwater, the PT boats idled and the escaping VIPs transferred to an interisland steamer, the Mayon, for the three-hour trip across the bay. Catharine was standing amidship when MacArthur, his wife, and little Arthur went down the central stairway. She watched curiously. She'd seen MacArthur before but never so near. He was imposing, his posture ramrod straight, his uniform impeccable. She'd seen so many unshaven, exhausted officers these past weeks. MacArthur might have stepped from a July Fourth reviewing stand. He walked briskly, his wife and child following; then he was out of sight down the stairs.

A steward brought around sandwiches and Coca-Cola. Catharine shook her head. She put her suitcase with the others in the main lounge, then returned to the deck. The steamer was passing by the burning ruin that had once been Cavite Naval Base. The smell of burning oil overlay the scent of the sea.

Catharine stood by the railing and stared across the water. She was cold, but she didn't want to go below decks. She stayed by the railing and watched the dark blur of Corregidor grow larger and take shape. She thought how odd it was that she should be on a steamer in the middle of Manila Bay, fleeing from the Japanese. War caused such strange things. It took lives that had been planned and tossed the plans to pieces. What a peculiar twist her life had taken. During her childhood years in Pasadena, she had never even heard of the Philippines. All those long years ago, life had seemed reasonable, a happy equation. She'd discovered when Reggie's plane nosed down into rolling English hills that equations sometimes didn't prove out. She'd learned that reality more bitterly when Charles, breathing stertorously, lay heavily in her arms and slipped beyond recall. Now Jack was in Manila and the Japanese were coming.

The steamer slowed. Two PT boats from Corregidor nosed closer, and the passengers gathered up their belongings. The MacArthur party made the first transfer. Arthur MacArthur laughed as his mother swung him up to carry. Catharine's heart ached for the MacArthurs. How dreadful to hold your child, your only son, in your arms and know that death and destruction lay ahead. At least Charles was safe now. Nothing ever again could hurt or frighten Charles.

"Catharine, come along."

Catharine managed to turn and smile at Amea. As they walked together toward the crosswalk, Catharine looked beyond the PT at Corregidor. Back in Manila, when all she could see was a dark dot on the horizon, Catharine had imagined a cattish, rounded island, but Corregidor flung itself out of the water, an enormous chunk of volcanic rock with sheer five-hundred-foot cliffs at its head. The island glistened with lush vegetation, including thickly branched fir trees that covered the rugged terrain in green.

Amea pointed at the middle hill. "That's where we're going."

"Are there quarters there?"

Amea didn't answer directly. "Woody and I came over to visit once. We played golf and lunched at the Officers' Club; then they took us on a tour." She took a deep breath. "We saw Malinta Tunnel."

Tunnel. Catharine thought of a subway tunnel; rounded brick walls, narrow, constricting, dark space.

She followed Amea across the plank to the PT boat. As soon as they were aboard, the PT roared to life. A few minutes later, the boat docked at a concrete pier. They were herded off, this time to board a rickety bus. Spencer and Woody stayed behind to supervise the unloading of the gold and silver.

The bus chugged and wheezed up a narrow dirt road that clung to the edge of Malinta Hill. It stopped in front of what Catharine would come to know as the east entrance.

Once again, the refugees gathered up their belongings and slowly filed off the bus, then walked toward the huge mouth of the tunnel.

Malinta Tunnel.

It was like nothing Catharine had ever seen before.

16

The enormous mouth of the tunnel arched twenty feet high and was wide enough for four cars to drive abreast. Railroad tracks ran down the middle of the tunnel. As far as the eye could see, wooden crates and boxes lined the concrete walls in stacks six to seven feet tall. Men in uniform moved in and out of the tunnel in a constant stream.

Catharine felt very aware of her sex. Men were everywhere. Then, with a feeling of relief, she saw two army nurses in khaki pants and combat boots. The nurses looked surprised at the straggling group of women in civilian dress.

Catharine immediately disliked the tunnel. The air was unpleasantly damp, the kind of damp found in cellars or mausoleums. There was a graveyard smell of wet rock and other unpleasant smells, too: diesel oil fumes, urine, sweat, creosote, medicine, disinfectant.

She followed her group into the main tunnel. A black-and-white sign announced "Hospital," and the group turned right into a smaller tunnel. The smells of medicine, blood, and disinfectant grew stronger. Smaller tunnels opened to the left and right off the hospital lateral. The women were taken to tunnel number 11, which housed the medical detachment. They walked down a narrow aisle between neatly made cots for the doctors. Midway down this side passage, sheets were draped over a rusty metal screen which marked off the nurses' sleeping area. This was to be their new home.

"Home sweet home," Amea said drily.

The three Quezon children giggled and laughed as they dumped their things on their cots. Mrs. Quezon looked around the cramped, bleak, smelly quarters, then smiled brightly. Mrs. MacArthur and Arthur weren't included in the group of women and children to be quartered with the nurses.

Catharine and Amea chose neighboring cots. They tucked their suitcases beneath the cots, then looked at each other.

"Shall we explore?" Catharine asked.

"Of course."

The hospital lateral was about half the diameter of the main tunnel. As they walked back through it, they passed the laterals opening off to each side, each marked by a sign: Surgical, Respiratory, Dental, Clerical, Dispensary. For privacy, sheets were draped over the lateral entrances. The main hospital corridor was about one hundred yards in length and broken by two slight bends. Double-decker beds were lined up on each side of the main corridor for the patients. Their passage created a wash of silence as the men—officers, soldiers, patients—watched them walk by.

"I feel rather conspicuous," Amea murmured.

Everyone noticed them. The glances were apparently interested, but always polite.

The main tunnel swarmed with activity. Keeping close to the crate-stacked wall, Catharine and Amea walked the length of the tunnel. Every glimpse and sound reinforced the reality of war. Soldiers sweated as they maneuvered handcars along the rails. Men hunched over desks or clustered by map boards. Telephones buzzed. The overhead neon lights bathed everything in faintly blue light. Catharine had never thought of all the paperwork and logistics involved in men killing one another.

"Let's go outside," Catharine urged. The noise and the penetrating, heavy smell sickened her.

They walked back down the main tunnel to the east entrance and came out onto a narrow road. Trucks climbed up in low gear and exhaust fumes choked them, but there was also the sweet scent of frangipani and hibiscus. They followed a narrow path and struggled up the steep side of Malinta Hill until they stood at the crest and looked back across the bay at Manila.

Catharine knew she should be happy to have reached the island safely. She was safe here, at least for now. Manila would fall quite soon. MacArthur intended to declare Manila an Open City to save it from further bombing, but that didn't mean the inhabitants would be safe when the Japanese took over. The smoke that hung over the city looked dark and sooty like rain clouds. Catharine turned and looked to the north at Bataan, the mountainous and vividly green peninsula just across the channel from Corregidor. That was where the American and Filipino troops were going to make their stand. It looked wild and forbidding. She turned to look again in the direction of Manila. Whitecaps glittered on the bay. Jack was across the bay. He was somewhere in Manila, somewhere beneath that thick and ugly pall of smoke. Perhaps he'd already left Manila. Perhaps he was covering the withdrawal and was on his way to Bataan.

God, please don't let Jack be hurt, she prayed.

Bullets and bombs didn't discriminate between soldiers and civilians. There was no safety for Jack and no safety for the soldiers he was covering.

But she said her little prayer over and over again.

The acrid smoke curled into the sky, eddied near the ground. Flames crackled in every quarter of Manila. Heated clouds of smoke dumped occasional swaths of artificial rain, leaving oily black smudges on everything it touched. Every so often. Jack took a grimy cotton cloth and reached over the windshield to wipe a clear space. It was late on New Year's Eve when he reached the INS office; not surprisingly, it was deserted. He wondered briefly what had happened to Logan, then he sat down at his desk and began to pound out the story. He could have written for hours, but he knew he only had minutes. When he completed the story on the withdrawal of the southern troops toward Bataan, he dialed Western Union. The telephone rang and rang.

Artillery fire rumbled from the south.

Jack stuffed the copy into his canvas pack. He was on his way to the door when an enormous explosion rocked the room. He was lifted from his feet and flung backwards. As he came up against the cracking wall, he knew this was more than bombs or artillery shells. He scrambled to his feet, ran outside, and stared up at the roiling columns of black smoke. Flames danced in great blazing sheets. He knew the army had blown up the Pandacan oil storage tanks. Even from the distance of several miles, he could hear the roar and whistle of the fire. Explosions erupted to the east as the fuel supplies at Fort McKinley were fired. What was left of Nichols Field went up in smoke and fire. Flames ringed the city.

The Japanese troops must be near, Jack thought. He had to move fast, for they would intern any Americans they found in Manila. He damn well didn't intend to spend the rest of the war in a Japanese prison. He ran to the convertible, gunned it to life, and swung the wheel toward the harbor. If he could find a boat, any kind of boat, he'd head for Bataan.

When he reached the deserted yacht club, he swung his flashlight across the basin and spotted a rusty motorboat. He scrambled down the ladder and climbed aboard. The motor sputtered to life, but it almost immediately died. It was out of gasoline. No wonder the owner had left it when almost anything that could move or be moved was being utilized by those escaping from Manila. Gasoline. He hit the pier running, hoping the little yellow convertible was still parked in front of the club.

He found the car and searched the glove compartment and the trunk, but there was no rubber tubing. He ran back to the club and looked in a storage shed which no one had locked. The garden hoses were too big and heavy. He moved to the back door of the club, grabbed up a loose brick, and broke in. It was ghostly inside, the tables set for dining and no one there. He found the kitchen and rummaged through the drawers. He picked up a siphon bottle and a length of rubber tubing attached to a sink.

Back at the car, his improvised siphon worked beautifully. He filled the bottle and, returning to the kitchen, searched until he found several gallon-size empty jars, which he filled, too. When he'd emptied the car's tank, he grabbed some food from the kitchen and transferred his precious fuel supplies to the motorboat.

Gunfire rattled on Dewey Boulevard. The militia or the Japanese?

Jack jumped into the boat. He pulled the cord, and the engine came to life. He maneuvered the boat slowly out of the yacht basin. He moved cautiously, skirting the masts and funnels of sunken ships.

Another explosion erupted; Jack twisted to look back at Manila. The city lay silhouetted against the brilliant orange-red fires that glowed around her.

As the sounds and smells of the burning city faded behind him, Jack sprawled on the seat, his hand steady on the tiller. He fished a cigarette and lighter from his jacket pocket. The cigarette tasted sharp and fresh. This was his last pack of Lucky Strikes. As he smoked, his eyes skimmed the dark water. Occasionally, he looked up at the night sky, with its incredibly bright, shimmering stars. The dark and soft night reminded him of the lovely sweep of Catharine's hair. The first night he ever saw her in London he'd seen her face reflected in the bright sheen of a pillar, and nothing was ever the same again.

Catharine. Her eyes were the deepest violet, richer and deeper than amethyst, eyes fringed magically by long, soft, dark lashes.

He'd wanted to know what she was truly like. She was so aloof that night in the River Room, so far from him and his world. Was that what drew him? Perhaps, but it wasn't what held him now. He knew her now; he knew how she loved and how she cared. He knew the feel of her lips, how her hands touched him, how her dark hair felt against his face. He knew her touch, her body, soft and rounded, straining to him, but he knew so much more. He knew the gentleness of her spirit. He knew the darkness in her heart, the pain and anguish she'd suffered. He knew that she'd lost hope, that she didn't believe in happiness. More than anything in his life, he wanted to be the man who gave Catharine the faith that life could be good.

He lit another cigarette, drew deeply on it, and smiled. Love was wonderful, wasn't it? Here he was, on his own, somewhere in Manila Bay, aiming for Bataan. He raced against the night to make landfall before daylight exposed him to attack from Japanese planes. Yet, he felt a great sense of peace and contentment, and it was all because of Catharine, because of his memory of her, because she loved him and he loved her. All his life, he'd struggled and fought, never really knowing why. He'd battled through loneliness, despair, and discouragement, keeping on in a world filled with cruelty and horror. He'd done it all on his own, no one to look deep into his eyes and smile for no other reason than his existence. None of that was true now. It didn't matter that Catharine was isolated on a volcanic island he couldn't reach. It wouldn't even matter if she were still in London or he were in Chicago, because their love was independent of time or place. It existed so long as they both lived, and it was strong enough to carry them through anything.

Jack lounged against the seat, steered the little boat to the west, and remembered their happy hours. The contentment stayed with him through the night. About three hours out of Manila, hard, choppy waves slapped into the boat. He shook his head wearily and peered into the darkness. He turned into the wind and headed for the tip of Bataan to avoid the minefields around Corregidor. The first streaks of dawn appeared ahead of him. Directly ahead, looming high against the sky, was the purple peak of Mount Mariveles.

Bataan lay dead ahead.

17

Catharine sat near a gardenia bush on Malinta Hill and watched Manila burn.

Where was Jack?

Had he been captured by the Japanese moving up Luzon from the south? Could he possibly have caught up with escaping American and Filipino troops and reached Bataan? Or was he still in Manila among the marooned Americans waiting for the Japanese troops to arrive?

As she huddled there, her eyes straining to see through the luminous tropical night, she clung to one certainty. Jack was alive. She knew it because her heart would know if Jack were dead.

She began to smile, a soft smile. He was such an outrageous man. He was wild, crazy, and wonderful. But he was also gentle and vulnerable. He was a patchwork of many conflicting qualities. Knowing him had added a depth and color to her life that she had never imagined possible. He made her realize that there was more to her than she'd ever understood.

A vivid pulse of light rose in the east. She knew some cataclysmic explosion had rocked Manila. She buried her face in her hands, but she knew he was all right.

Oh, God, please, let Jack be all right.

His name was printed in block letters on the chart at the foot of the bunk: DENNIS RALPH WILSON. Catharine squeezed into the narrow space between two rows of bunk beds and looked down at the boy in the bottom bunk. Most of his face was in shadow.

"Are you Dennis?"

She could barely make out his features: a thin, pale face, a strand of blond hair drooping down on his forehead. His eyes stared straight ahead and didn't move when she spoke. She waited a moment, then said briskly, "Are you called Ralph?"

No answer.

Catharine bent down. "Could I write a letter home for you?"

"Leave me alone." His voice was dull and empty.

Catharine didn't want to stay. It was so alien to her to force herself upon anyone. She'd never been officious, never taken it upon herself to decide what was good for others. She valued freedom, but that morning a nurse had talked about Dennis Ralph Wilson at the outlet, the gathering spot where the hospital tunnel opened into the road. "He's going to lie there and die," the tired young nurse told Catharine, "and I don't have time to help him. It breaks my heart. He's just a kid, and he's going to lie there and die." So Catharine agreed to try to befriend him. God knew that Catharine had time, too much time. She crouched beside the boy's bunk and tried to find the right words to break into his cocoon of despair.

"Dennis. It is Dennis, isn't it?"

He nodded slightly, a nod that said yeah, so what.

"Dennis." She repeated his name gently. "That's such a nice name. I'll bet you have a girlfriend who's told you that."

The garish blue glow of the neon lights allowed Catharine to see the way his mouth quivered.

"Do you have a girlfriend, Dennis?"

His face turned toward her. Light blue eyes looked up at her with enormous pain.

He said suddenly, violently, "Why didn't they let me die? Why didn't they?"

She had many answers, but Catharine didn't offer one. Instead, she said simply, "You weren't supposed to die."

His mouth quivered again. "They should've let me die." Tears brimmed in his eyes. He jerked his head, trying to flick the tears away, trying to pretend they weren't there.

"You can get well," Catharine said. "That's what the nurse says."

His mouth twisted. "What for?"

Catharine felt the hard ache of unshed tears, but she knew she mustn't cry.

"Because people love you, Dennis."

Those despairing eyes blinked. "Not like this." His voice was weaker now. He was tiring.

"That's not true," Catharine said steadily. "If you love someone, no matter what happens, you still love them."

His eyes looked old in his young, white face. "Sure, lady. Tell me how you'd love a man who didn't have any arms or legs," he said sarcastically.

Catharine struggled to breathe. What would she do, how would she feel if a bomb did this to Jack? How could she bear for him to be hurt like this, to be made helpless? It would be dreadful beyond belief. She would grieve for his pain, his loss, his helplessness, but if he could be alive . . .

She bent forward and touched Dennis's cheek. Tears slipped down her face. "I would cry, and I would love him just as I do now."

The boy lay very still. Something moved in his light blue eyes. He looked at her intently. "You love somebody?"

"Yes."

"And you wouldn't care if he was just a body? No arms. No legs. No hands. No feet."

"I would care terribly, and I would work hard to help him learn how to walk again with artificial legs and learn how to use artificial arms." She paused; then she said softly, and there was no mistaking her meaning, "And I would love him every day in every way I could."

A touch of color stained Dennis's cheeks. "You love him that much?"

"I love him more than anyone or anything in the world. Thinking of him makes me feel that the ugliness and the horror can't touch me, because deep inside I have something that nothing ever can destroy."

Dennis licked his lips. "Do you think . . . do you think Cindy could feel that way about me?"

He had no hands for Catharine to reach out and hold. Instead, gently, lightly, she put her hand on his thin shoulder. "Of course she could."

He began to talk, jerkily, in broken phrases; a girl's face and charming spirit took shape in Catharine's mind. But Dennis's pride and eagerness told her more. Catharine saw beyond Cindy's charm; she saw vanity, selfishness, and heartbreak for Dennis.

"You see, she liked me best because we won all the dance contests. Every time. We can . . . we could jitterbug better than anybody in town." The light died out of his eyes. "She likes to dance better than anything in the world."

Once again, Catharine fought back tears.

"I've got some of Cindy's letters." He moved his head toward the end of the bed.

"Would you like for me to read them to you?"

He nodded shyly.

Catharine found the pitifully thin pile. The letters were worn and creased from repeated handling. She read them to him, and the vacuous phrases rasped in her mind. Cindy didn't care about anyone but herself; what would she do or say when she learned about Dennis? It didn't bear thinking about. When she'd finished, Catharine forced herself to say brightly, "Would you like to write her, Dennis?"

His head slumped back against the pillow. Slowly, he shook his head. "No. Not today. I'm tired now."

Again, Catharine touched his shoulder gently. "You rest now, but I'll come back and see you again. Is that all right?"

"Yes. That would be nice." He closed his eyes and turned his face away.

Catharine steeled her face until she was out of the ward, but tears burned the back of her eyes and her throat ached. Threading her way through the clutter of desks and supplies, she welcomed the bustling activity at the outlet. As always, groups of convalescent patients clustered around the radio or sat in the wooden chairs ranged on either side of the road that wound sharply down the steep hill. The outlet, which was at the end of the hospital tunnel, opened out about midway down Malinta Hill; the road was a bit wider there. All day long, despite air raids, trucks ground in low gear down the hill.

Despite the racket of the trucks and the constant smell of diesel oil, Catharine loved the outlet, loved being outside in the sun, away from the dim bluish light in the tunnels.

The early morning heat pulsed down from the bright, hard orange disk of the sun. Shading her eyes, Catharine gazed out at the North Channel, at the incredibly blue water, a blue so brilliant it made her eyes hurt. Across the channel, the huge peak of Mount Mariveles dominated the end of the Bataan peninsula. The rugged, upthrust land was dense with vegetation.

Catharine turned and looked back up Malinta Hill. When they'd arrived on Christmas Eve, Corregidor was glistening green, dark and verdant with the luxuriant growth from the rainy season, but now . . . The bombing had started a few days after Christmas. As the weather dried, the bombs ripped and cratered the island. Sharp ravines separated the hills. Now the dusty ground, burned-out hulks of buildings, and shredded trees baked beneath the blazing tropical sun of the dry season; the island shimmered in a haze of heat. Every bomb that crashed into Corregidor threw up swirls of choking dust. The dust permeated everything, sifting down into Malinta Tunnel and all its laterals, pulled down in hot, brown clouds by the machines that pumped air through the tunnel's depths.

The sun beamed overhead. Catharine lifted her hand to shade her face. The Japanese bombed at noon. She wondered if they ate their balls of rice in their airplanes or waited to get back to their mess hall. At least they probably had lunch, which was more than anyone on Corregidor could say. Rations had been cut to breakfast and a slim dinner at four.

Catharine smelled the heavy, unappetizing odor from the steaming kettles. Her stomach knotted—she was so damned hungry. She turned away and walked toward the edge of the road, where a canvas bag of drinking water hung from a low branch of a tree. She picked up a cup and turned the spigot. She drank the faintly warm water very slowly, but her stomach still wanted food. Breakfast at seven was stewed raisins, rice, and a cup of weak coffee. Dinner would be at four in the afternoon. Then there were the long hours to pass until she could sleep. Sometimes she played bridge. Sometimes she helped roll bandages. Sometimes she came to the outlet, sat with her back to the hill, and listened to a soldier play the harmonica and people sing. Someone was always ready to sing. The songs were the same, "Harbor Lights" and "Stardust" and "Deep Purple." Why were they always songs from a life so far away it seemed impossible that it could still exist? But maybe that's what the singers liked—to remember when life hadn't been sitting and waiting to die.

Catharine lit a cigarette and noted that her hands shook. Hunger again. She moved them slowly through the air as if they were foreign matter. The minute she relaxed, her hands began to tremble again, but at least the cigarette helped dull the hunger.

Catharine crossed the road again and walked up to a table beneath an awning where State Department wives sat and rolled bandages. Amea Willoughby looked up with a welcoming smile, and Catharine marveled at Amea's unfailing good humor. She was so small, slightly built with a delicate face. When they'd first met, Catharine had noted Amea's consistent pleasantness and thought little of it. It was expected of State Department wives, but Amea's cheerful demeanor never wavered, not even among the dirt, flies, and fear that existed on Corregidor.

Amea beckoned to Catharine. Over the noise of a nearby radio turned up full volume, Amea called out, "Come help with the bandages." Then she pointed at the radio, "And listen to our daily ration of buck-you-uppo."

Catharine grinned. MacArthur dubbed the island's local radio the Voice of Freedom, but the broadcasts lacked subtlety. They seized on the very occasional successes of the few remaining PT boats and repeated them in glowing terms ad nauseam.

As Catharine joined the group, the radio announcer intoned, "Spirits were never higher on Corregidor than after successful survival of yesterday's raids. Quick responses minimized damages, and the island population continues to look forward to the arrival of reinforcements . . ."

A young soldier sitting nearby turned to a friend. "Hey, Pat, did you hear that?"

The State Department wives were suddenly very quiet. Not one of them looked at her neighbor. They all stared at the bandages on the table, because these wives knew the truth. No help was coming. They were here and here they were going to stay until they were killed or captured.

Jenny Bishop said bitterly, "Snake oil."

The woman beside her shot a warning glance.

Jenny flushed, then said defiantly, "I understand that announcer's been nominated for a DTC."

Everyone laughed, and the laughter helped ease the somber knowledge they shared.

"That's right," Jenny continued. "A Distinguished Tunnel Citation. He hasn't poked a nose out for three weeks."

Amea was too softhearted to be rough on anyone. "Oh, well, he's just doing his job, and I'd rather listen to him than to Manila."

Station KZRH in Manila played soft, seductive music. A woman announcer who spoke English very well asked her listeners, "Don't you miss your homes? Why are you here so far away from home in a war that doesn't concern you? Asia is for Asians. If you put down your arms, you can go home again."

Home.

Catharine finished one cigarette, lit another. Every time she heard the word home, she thought of Jack. Yet, neither of them had a home anywhere in the world. Not anymore. But to be with Jack, that was going home.

She drew deeply on the cigarette; tears burned again behind her eyes. Dear God, she mustn't cry again. She seemed to want to cry all the time now, about the boy in the hospital, about Jack, about the numbing horror of the hot, dusty, frightening days and nights. Part of it was hunger, part fatigue, and part was contending with the never-ending pocket of fear that festered deep inside her. It was almost noon. The bombers would come at noon. Everyone would dash into the tunnel; then the concussions would rock them, no matter how far or how deep they went. The dust would sift through the tunnel, carrying the smell of blood, unwashed people, stale food, and fear. Worst of all, every racketing, faraway boom meant death or suffering. They would see the mangled bodies of the gun crews after each raid when the wounded and dead were brought into the tunnel.

"Catharine, let's go see how Woody and Spencer are doing." Amea's voice was light and cheerful.

Catharine looked at her numbly. Catharine had seen very little of Spencer since they'd arrived on the Rock. He was billeted with the other State Department men in a different lateral with Woody and Peggy. They worked, of course, on the lists of gold.

Catharine felt laughter rising inside her like the uncontrolled bubbles in a newly opened bottle of champagne. "The king is in his counting house counting out the money," she said jerkily.

For the first time in their acquaintance, Catharine felt Amea draw away. "It's their job," she said quietly.

"And so important." Then Catharine felt a rush of dismay. She didn't want to offend Amea. She drew strength from Amea's unwavering good humor, her quiet bravery. "I'm sorry. Please . . ."

Amea smiled. "It's all right. None of us are on an even keel these days."

"I'd like to go see them," Catharine said quickly.

They went single file through the narrow entrance to the outlet, squeezing by the pile of sandbags. They turned sharply to get in, then passed the reserve generator with its huge warning letters in bright red: KEEP OFF—DANGER—2,000 VOLTS.

As always, the hospital tunnel hummed with activity. Filipino enlisted men swabbed the gritty concrete floors with disinfectant. The thick, cloying smell of bug spray hung in the air, part of the unrelenting and unsuccessful effort to kill bedbugs and ants.

Outside the men's sleeping lateral, Spencer and Woody hunched over battered desks. They looked up as Catharine and Amea approached.

Woody smiled and waved a welcome. When Spencer looked up, Catharine was shocked at his physical change since their arrival. Red-rimmed eyes looked at her blankly out of a thin, white face.

"Time for a break," Amea called out. She smiled at her husband.

Woody clapped Spencer on the shoulder. "Amea's right. Let's play hooky for a while."

At Spencer's quick frown, Woody continued, "We can combine business with pleasure. Let's take the girls to see the vault. We need to check on those trunks from the Central Bank."

Spencer hailed a marine corporal and ordered a car. Soon the four of them bucketed along a narrow, unpaved road on the way to Middleside, a five-minute drive. This was Catharine's first foray to this part of the Rock since the bombing began. The utter devastation appalled her. All the trees were dead, their branches splintered, the leaves ripped away by blasts. Craters pocked the ground. Nothing remained of the glistening white wooden buildings which had once topped Middleside.

The jeep jolted to a stop near a low stone building surrounded by a grove of shriveled trees. Spencer led the way, unlocking the heavy wooden door. It swung inward on creaking hinges. Naked light bulbs hung on dangling cords from the low stone ceiling. Old whisky crates, wooden boxes, tin trunks, and steel lockers were piled haphazardly on the hard-packed earth floor. Spencer and Woody studied a diagram on ruled paper which gave the provenance of each container. As they moved about, talking in low tones, Catharine stared at the motley assortment of boxes and at other loose mounds of gold. She moved closer to a pile of gold in one corner. Some of the dirty yellow bars were the size of butter cubes.

Spencer finished his tour of the rooms and came up to Catharine. He wore an expression she knew well: confident, satisfied, supremely arrogant.

"We did it," he said simply. He waved his hand around the room. "There it is, Catharine, more than forty-one million dollars' worth of gold and silver. We got it away from the Japs and when we get it back to San Francisco, I've got the lists to show who every bit of it belongs to, without question."

"Back to San Francisco," she said slowly. For a moment, she wondered if he was mad, if the long hours in the dank, dusty heat of the tunnel had snapped his reason. This gold was seven thousand miles from San Francisco, seven thousand miles across an ocean controlled by the Imperial Japanese Navy.

Spencer bent down and struggled to pick up a dark brown lump of gold. "I know who this belongs to." He smiled. "When the gold arrives in San Francisco, they're going to know we did this job right."

"San Francisco." Her voice rose. "Spencer, we're cut off, we're marooned here."

He looked at her in surprise. "Don't you understand how important this is?" Once again, his hand gestured at the boxes, crates, and piles of gold. "They're sending a submarine for the gold, of course."

A submarine. She'd seen one once, moored at Cavite, a dark, rounded hull, sloping deck, and conning tower.

A submarine for the gold.

Horror curled inside her. They were going to rescue the gold, but not the people—not the men who stood by their guns and died every day, not the nurses who tried to keep life flickering in a world where mutilated bodies happened before breakfast, in the middle of the afternoon, in the dark watches of the night.

She said nothing as they walked back to the waiting jeep. She carried with her the picture of the dark little rooms and their piles of treasure, but superimposed were other pictures: a nurse with pale, drawn face bending over a stretcher, a pail filled with amputated limbs, the strain on gray and dusty faces when the tunnels rocked with concussion.

The jeep was almost back to the east entrance when the flight of Zeros screamed across the North Channel. Bombs glinted against the sun like pieces of silver. The jeep squealed to a stop. The four of them and the driver jumped free, ran for the ditch, and flung themselves down. Catharine pressed her face against the grit, closed her eyes, and felt her body draw in upon itself as if she could make herself small and be safe. Heavy, thrusting noise as a coming bomb exploded, and enormous pressure pummeled her body and her mind.

18

Jack finished sharpening the pencil stub with his penknife, then looked at it wryly. No typewriters, no ink, no telephones, nothing but jungle and the erratic but vicious battles that exploded without warning in bamboo thickets or groves of banyan trees. It was like blindman's bluff with a deadly goal as the Japanese soldiers slid up and down steep-sided ravines and hacked their way with machetes through the ferns and vines that formed almost impenetrable barriers. The fighting was bitter, but the Americans and Filipinos had already fallen back from their first line of defense from Moron to Abucay. The Japanese surprised them by scaling what the Americans thought to be an impassable mountain. The Japanese slipped behind Allied lines to form pockets behind the defenders. The Americans and Filipinos withdrew again by the end of January, taking up a line midway down the Bataan peninsula along the fifteen-mile cobblestone Pilar-Bagac road.

Jack shaded his eyes against the blistering midday sun. Sweat burned in the stubble of a three-day growth of beard. His clothes were sweat dampened and board-stiff from dirt and earlier sweat. He wrinkled his nose in distaste. He was smelly, hungry, and tired. He willed it all away and concentrated on a half-filled sheet of paper. He had a half ream of paper stuffed into his backpack, the sheets crammed with his small, precise printing. He'd recorded what he'd seen this past month on Bataan. Would anybody ever read it? He shook his head. There was no point in worrying about that. He was recording a monumental struggle of gallant, stubborn, frightened men fighting fanatical attackers, malaria, dengue fever, yaws, and starvation . . . a struggle foredoomed to failure.

As he wrote, his face puckered in concentration, artillery shells crumped monotonously in the jungle a half mile ahead. The Japanese were saturating the area. Jack paused to light a cigarette, then wrote with renewed vigor, the words spitting onto the page.

"The battling bastards keep on fighting . . ."

Correspondent Frank Hewlett's bitter doggerel had become the byword of the men trapped in the sweltering jungle. Hewlett captured the aching hurt of the defending troops: We're the battling bastards of Bataan; No momma, no poppa, no Uncle Sam; No aunts, no uncles, no nephews or nieces; No rifles, no guns, no artillery pieces, And nobody gives a damn.

Jack wrote fast, trying to tell it all: the captain who choked back tears when he described his men—riddled with malaria, cramped with dysentery, yet struggling to their feet to meet another Jap charge; the nurses who ignored bombing aircraft to protect their patients; the doctors who donated their own blood when the plasma ran out; and the love and reverence of the troops for gaunt, gangling, sunburned General Jonathan M. Wainwright.

Jack stopped when the sheet was full and lit a new cigarette from the stub of the old one. He wiped his face with a grimy handkerchief. It was late March, the hot season. The jungle steamed during the day and was sharply cold at night. He stared down at his paper. There was so much else to write: the Japanese soldiers who fought blindly, scrambling over barbed wire and using the bodies of fallen comrades as a bridge; the American wounded who lay in blood and filth for twelve hours, twenty hours, forty-eight hours; the mess sergeant who scrounged in the jungle for his desperately hungry men and served them carabao, wild pig, iguana, and monkey stew.

Jack drew deeply on his cigarette. He had private thoughts that no one shared. Very private thoughts. Every night the deep velvet darkness reminded him of Catharine. He could trace her profile in the spangle of stars glittering above him. He thought of Catharine when he stared across the North Channel at Corregidor. He'd written to her; in the letters he tried to fashion words gentle as a touch. He'd written about the way he carried the thought of her as a talisman to see him through each day's fear and horror. He could feel the syllables of her name on his tongue and in his heart. He understood Tennyson's gentle wisdom. To have loved Catharine for even a moment in time made his life so much richer. He'd touched the deepest mystery of existence and knew now that the healing properties of love couldn't be explained or understood—but love was the only reality in life.

He wanted desperately to see Catharine. He'd ranged the front lines ever since he'd reached Bataan, but now, before the new attack began, he was going to take his accumulated stories to Corregidor for radio transmission to the United States—and he was going to see Catharine.

He hadn't seen her since Christmas Eve. Now it was late March. For a moment, his throat tightened. Everyone knew how heavily the Japanese had bombed Corregidor. Determinedly, he pushed the thought away.

Catharine would be there.

Shuddering explosions rocked the tunnel. Dust wavered in the dim bluish light. The wounded men ignored the noise, the choking swirls of dust, and the whining scream of the diving airplanes audible even so far below.

Catharine willed herself to look relaxed. She bent forward. "How do you feel today, Dennis?"

He responded to her now. She came every day to visit. Sometimes they talked about baseball. He'd told her five times about the day he saw Babe Ruth. Sometimes they talked about digging for clams and how quick you had to be. Sometimes they talked about Cindy. But he still wouldn't let Catharine write a letter.

Dennis smiled up at her. "I'm fine, Mrs. Cavanaugh. Are you okay?"

"Just fine, Dennis."

Another tremendous explosion thundered above them. The lights flickered.

Catharine swallowed, then spoke quickly. "I'm the letter express this afternoon." She held up a stack of letters. She'd been up and down the aisles, helping several men write home.

"Maybe they think we'll get out of here pretty soon, and they don't want the folks at home to be mad because they didn't write."

Catharine didn't answer. So many of the soldiers and sailors and patients still believed help was coming. "When the convoy gets here, we'll go home." That's how they started so many conversations. Catharine and other State Department wives listened, smiled, and nodded, but their insides shriveled in pain because they knew the truth: no one was coming—no help, no convoys, nothing.

"Listen, Mrs. Cavanaugh, somebody told me, and this is pretty secret. They said the word was that they'll come by April. What do you think?"

April. The cruelest month.

"I don't know," she said quietly. "I haven't heard. Oh, Dennis, the other night at the outlet I was listening to KGEI, and I heard your song."

He looked surprised.

"Don't you remember? You told me it was your favorite, yours and Cindy's." She began to hum.

His expression changed, and she knew he was no longer thinking about the convoy. He smiled. "Oh, yeah, yeah. 'Harbor Lights.' Yeah, that was our song." His face crinkled. He looked like a puzzled child. "I never thought about what it said, not then. But it's true. Harbor lights mean good-bye, don't they?"

Catharine plunged into a recital of the other songs beaming in from San Francisco and what happened at the outlet and who she'd talked to, but when she left him lying there, the mournful lyrics echoed in her mind. What had possessed her to mention the song to Dennis? But did it really matter? Any of the songs would cause an ache now. Happy songs brought back times that were lost, and sad songs threatened to loose emotions just barely held in check.

Everyone was hungry, frightened, worn down by the bombing that always came again. At any hour of the day. The long, hot, horrible nights were worst of all—the uneasy rustle of others lying so near in the close air, the erratic muffled explosions, the quivering flicker of the lights.

Sometimes, she slipped off her cot, walked into the hospital lateral, and saw the night nurses bending over beds, carrying pails, giving injections. She envied the nurses. They were exhausted and strained, but they were needed.

Whereas Catharine had never in her life felt so useless, so unimportant, nothing but a burden, a mouth to feed when food was so precious, a body taking up room but giving nothing back to the beleaguered community. Oh, she read to the patients, wrote letters home. She rolled bandages every day and helped with the records. She even assisted in the dreadful, heartrending task of tagging the wounded when they arrived after each bombardment, mangled, maimed, hideously disfigured. One night as she knelt beside a stretcher and looked down at the young marine's legs, or what was left of them, she didn't think she would ever find strength to rise again.

Catharine shook away the images and tried to see through the thick fog of dust to find her way to the outlet. She felt a rising tide of hysteria. She couldn't bear any longer being trapped in this choking, fetid haze, feeling the shuddering of the earth above as the bombs exploded. She walked faster and faster, brushing by the sullen groups of men who lounged along the sides of the tunnel. As she neared the outlet, the sounds of the explosions grew louder, harsher, almost deafening, but she didn't care. She had to be out in the air. She was almost to the end when an arm reached out and grabbed her.

"Mrs. Cavanaugh, wait, there's a raid on."

She looked up and recognized a chaplain from the hospital wards. She tried to pull away.

His grip tightened, but his voice was gentle. "Oh now, my dear, wait here a moment. You're like a moth flying blind. I know how you feel. It's too much for all of us sometimes, but you can't be going outside just yet. It would be worse. That I know. I've just come from there. It's a scene from *Dante's Inferno*."

Her tongue licked dry lips. "I can't bear being trapped any longer."

"Ah now," and his voice was cheerful and soothing, "it's not so bad as all that. You know these tunnels are truly a miracle. They can bomb us forever, and these tunnels will still stand."

The chaplain's arm came around her shoulders; she felt herself being turned away from the end of the corridor. "I've some coffee in my thermos. That will be soothing for both of us."

She permitted him to guide her to his desk, and she accepted a cracked mug filled with steaming coffee. She managed a smile, but the horror inside her was very near to bursting. She drank the coffee, and they talked pleasantly. Finally, she returned to the women's lateral and lay awake until morning.

All that next day, she could feel the tight quiver. She couldn't bear it, not another night.

She ate a spare serving of canned weenies and sauerkraut for dinner outside the outlet. She stayed as the hours slipped away. She didn't want to go in. She didn't know if she would be able to force herself to go in. The sun began to go down, and it would be dark in just minutes, the swift, velvety darkness of the tropics. She knew she was gambling because the shelling from Cavite might start at any moment. At least with the bombs, they would hear the planes first. A shell was upon them instantly with only a high shrill whine to announce the arrival of death. Tonight, Catharine didn't care. She knew she was close to breaking.

She looked up incuriously as a group arrived from Bataan. There were new arrivals every evening, usually with messages for HQ command.

And Jack walked out of the group.

She scrambled to her feet, her heart thudding, and felt such a tumultuous wash of feeling that she knew that he was life itself to her. The flood of joy transformed her, took a flagging, beaten spirit and suffused it with strength and happiness.

When they stood face to face, she saw her joy reflected in his face.

Catharine didn't know where they found the strength to stand apart.

Then dusk made its swift transition to the luminous tropical night. She reached out and took his hand.

"There's a path behind me, Jack. Sometimes at night I walk up the path and reach the flame tree on the point; then I climb down to a cove so that I can be alone."

They found their way with the aid of the fat golden moon, a bomber's moon. It was a difficult descent, but Jack held firmly to her elbow. At the bottom, the surf boomed and the moonlight threw the jagged boulders into relief. They walked around a huge boulder, and Catharine led the way to a small sandy patch protected from above by an overhang.

They came into each other's arms; Catharine clung to him. She held him with all her strength; then roughly, raggedly, she began to cry, her shoulders shaking, her body trembling.

"It's all right, love," he said gently. "It's all right. I'll always come, love. Believe in me. No matter what happens, I'll be there for you."

She wanted to believe. She wanted to feel confident that Jack was invincible, but she knew that no one had immunity. The handsome captain who laughed while playing bridge one night would be dead the next. The smiling corporal with the carroty hair kidded the chaplain at breakfast and died before dinner. She clung to Jack all the harder.

He whispered to her, stroked her hair, and dried her cheeks with his handkerchief; then he held the damp handkerchief up in the moonlight. "This proves what I've been saying."

She looked at him blankly.

Laughter bubbled in his voice. "I'm the only son of a bitch on Bataan with a handkerchief, so that means I'm fated to care for a damsel in distress. That's fate. You can't quarrel with fate."

She choked back a sob. "Oh, Jack, it doesn't help to joke about it." But she was almost laughing, too, and she loved him, loved his bravery, his gallantry, and his absolutely pigheaded conviction that he, Jack Maguire, would always come out on top. "Oh, Jack, you're a crazy fool." But she wasn't crying any longer. "A crazy, wonderful fool—and I love you desperately."

"I love you desperately, too." There was no laughter in his voice now. He touched her cheek with his hand. "I think of you, and it makes everything all right. At night, I look up into the sky, and I see your face. Catharine, I love you and knowing that you care for me has been God's greatest gift."

"Care for you? That's such a pale, lifeless way to say it. I love you. I love you more than anything in the world."

"Catharine, Catharine." He said her name with such a lilt that it was almost a song. His hands cupped her face, and his lips found hers. At first, it was such a gentle kiss. Then, like fire sweeping down a mountainside, the passion between them ignited, their tongues touched, and his hands slipped down her back. She strained to be close to him. He picked her up and carried her back into the sandy curve beneath the overhang.

When they lay together, he kissed her face and neck; his lips touched her softly, and his hands caressed her. Catharine murmured his name over and over again. They loved each other, delighted in each other. Catharine gloried in the feel of his skin beneath her hands. To be with him, to love him, to offer herself, to bring him pleasure, to reaffirm their love was a glory so great it transcended the war-torn night. As the enormous artillery shells screamed across the South Channel and exploded, she and Jack were lost in feelings so sweet and so deep that fear couldn't separate them. Their love had a pent-up energy, a desperate need too long denied, a sensuous response to their deepest desires. They loved joyously, coming together in a wild and glorious union as incandescent as the heat of a melting star.

19

Dust swirled through the women's lateral but the jarring thuds were over. The raid had ended for the moment. The planes would return. The shells would scream across the channel again, but, for the moment, they could move about, talk, poke their heads aboveground.

Catharine stood irresolutely at the entrance to the women's lateral, her hands jammed into her pockets, her face tight in thought. She had made up her mind. The world would say she was in the wrong. The world would call her an unfaithful wife. So she was. Yet, and the thoughts and emotions moved in her mind, she'd intended her actions for the best. She'd intended to stay in Manila for Spencer because it was important to his career. She owed him that even though there was nothing now between them—no spark, no love. She'd intended to see this assignment through. When they were en route to the United States and her presence was no longer essential, she was going to tell Spencer that she wanted a divorce. Hurtling bombs at Pearl Harbor on December 7 changed all that.

Now the hours were slipping away. Everyone knew what was coming; she wanted desperately to be honest, to spend with Jack what moments they could manage together. There was so little time left now. The lull had ended on Bataan, and the fighting began again with a ferocity that made the foreordained end clear to all. No matter what cheerful words unctuous radio announcers voiced, no help was coming. The battling bastards, sick, hurt, and starving, were keeping on without hope, without help, without anything but raw courage and desperation. It was a courage which saw the coming horror, yet continued to fight. Hollow-eyed and gaunt, American soldiers died by the hundreds now. On Corregidor, the bombing and shelling reached such magnitude that the mind couldn't assimilate it. The bombing raids had long since passed the hundred mark; the shells came without warning, day and night. Those belowground were filthy, exhausted, and hungry. Those aboveground existed in a nightmarish world of burnt, blistered ground, shriveled trees, and continuing explosions.

Catharine ducked through the opening into the hospital tunnel; then she stopped. Did she have the right to do what she planned? No. She had no rights. She knew that, felt it, but she was driven to speak; she could no longer continue without speaking. She couldn't love Jack on those rare and wonderful nights when he crossed to the island from Bataan if she didn't speak. Perhaps she didn't deserve to have peace in her soul, but she had to speak now because there was no more time.

She began to walk, then paused again to fight away the wave of dizziness. These recurring bouts of weakness made her impatient. They had so little to eat. Their bodies demanded food every waking moment and even in sleep. Catharine dreamed of steaks and fresh fruit. She could picture mounds of oranges and shiny, bright red Delicious apples. She shook her head impatiently and moved uncertainly up the hallway. She had to face the unpleasant task.

When she reached Spencer's desk, he wasn't there.

Woody Woodbury looked up and smiled. His eyes were dark with fatigue. He looked fine-drawn and worn but, as always, he was genial and kind.

"You just missed him, Catharine. He's gone over to the vault."

Catharine chatted with Woody for a moment, then moved on down the hospital tunnel toward the main tunnel. She felt a burning impatience to see it through.

She walked out of the east entrance. She hadn't been to this entrance in several days, and she noted the changes—more jagged humps of debris, more burned and shriveled trees, more sheered-off slopes. One day a tree or rock was a landmark; the next day it was gone.

Catharine hesitated for a moment, then walked purposefully to a jeep pulled up next to the trolley tracks. A private slumped behind the wheel. When she walked up, he sat up straight and his eyes widened. So many of them hadn't seen an American woman in months. It always made her ache inside, that reverential look, that look of remembering another world.

She asked for a ride up the hill.

He looked eager but said reluctantly, "The shelling may start any time, ma'am."

"I know. That's all right."

She rode beside him in the bucketing jeep up the twisting, narrow road. The incredible devastation sickened her. Everything was pulverized, reduced to particles of dust, to heaps of blackened debris. She wondered how the gun crews continued to survive. Some of them didn't. There was Battery Geary and the enormous loss of life when a shell crashed directly through an embrasure and fell through to detonate the ammunition. They'd all died, and so horribly. Fragments of shell did terrible things to the human body. She'd helped that night as usual in the hospital, but there was nothing usual in the frenzied efforts to save lives.

The jeep turned off the main road and dropped down a dusty track into the gully where the vault building stood in the remains of a grove of trees.

Catharine thanked the private and told him she'd walk back. She turned toward the vault. An MP recognized her. Nodding, he held open the heavy door.

Catharine stepped inside, squinting to adjust her eyes to the dimness. Then, from the far room, she heard voices. Soft voices. One belonged to Spencer. She hadn't heard that tone in his voice for years. She moved slowly toward the second chamber, then stopped and stared when she reached the open door.

Spencer and Peggy stood locked in a tight embrace, oblivious to her arrival. Spencer's face was pressed against Peggy's shining red-gold hair; his eyes were shut.

Catharine whirled around, moved blindly to the door, pushed it open, and slipped through, her mind and heart in turmoil.

Spencer and Peggy?

All those nights he hadn't come home—and she'd been so sure he was working. She'd been so easy to fool. Oh, God, if only she'd suspected. But was that her fault, because she'd had so little empathy for Spencer, what he felt, what he needed. She hadn't even cared enough to wonder.

Still, she felt shock and betrayal. Oh, dear God, if Spencer loved Peggy, why hadn't he told her? If only he had spoken. There was anger and hurt but, for the first time, a lightening of the heavy load of guilt which she'd carried for so long.

The noise was always there, like a summer thunderstorm that wouldn't end: the heavy rumble of artillery fire on Bataan. Reddish streaks exploded in the night sky.

Catharine waited tensely at the outlet. Jack had said he would come. She stared at the uneven, jagged flashes of light over Bataan. The heavy, numbing rumble meant death was abroad, rounding up his new recruits. And there was no magic circle of safety around Jack. His correspondent's tabs didn't set him apart. No one was safe. Artillery shells splintered into thousands of deadly fragments; everyone behind the lines on Bataan was prey to the Japanese guns.

She clenched her hands. Would this be the night he wouldn't come, that she would wait, huddled beside the outlet, until dawn streaked the sky, knowing that her reason for being had ended in the blood and dust of Bataan? As always, being apart from Jack caused her pleasure and pain—pleasure in recalling him, in recreating in her mind his lean, hard body, his tough, sometimes angry, always sensitive face; pain in knowing how easily in this violent world he could be destroyed.

Tonight, if he came, she would tell him a submarine was coming. She had to tell him because she would not lie to Jack, but she had made up her mind. Nothing he could say would persuade her to leave him behind.

Blue-shaded flashlights winked up the path from the shore. Catharine pushed up from the ground, and sheer happiness surged through her. She was struck anew with awe that love could work such wonders.

They clasped hands and moved away from the outlet toward their path. They weren't the only dimly seen figures that moved quietly through the night, seeking space to be alone. They moved cautiously, but their own shallow scoop of sand was untenanted.

No moon shone this night. Catharine could see his face dimly in the star glow. They moved into each other's arms. She raised a hand and touched his face, his cheeks bristly with a beard. He was here now and hers, and she knew he wanted her as he always did. She could feel his desire in the pressure of his body.

He spoke her name softly. His lips brushed against her cheek. She moved her mouth to meet his; they kissed sweetly and deeply as if they had all the time in the world, as if there were nothing that could separate them, as if they had a lifetime to love. When they lay on the sand, it didn't matter that artillery fire rumbled like distant thunder over Bataan. They knew that the Japanese rarely changed their range, and tonight the shells crashed several hundred yards to the south. Nothing mattered at this moment but the two of them, the love they felt for each other, and the warmth and pleasure as they touched.

Jack smoothed her long black hair away from her face, traced the shape of her cheek and the line of her throat. His hands cupped her breasts.

Catharine felt the strength of the muscles in his back. She caressed him and knew he responded as his touch increased in urgency. His mouth left a trail of fire over her body, igniting a passion she couldn't contain. She called out to him, and they moved together. As always, their love was fiery and magnificent, melding their bodies so completely for that long, magic moment they were a single unit of delight.

When they lay quietly together, she could feel the shape of a smile as his mouth moved against her cheek, and she smiled, too.

The thought darted through her mind then, bright and quick as a meteor's brilliant progress: she had loved a man. Whatever the future held, nothing could destroy that reality. She had experienced that greatest human communion, the joining of bodies suffused with love; nothing that happened could alter that glory.

"Thank you," she said softly.

His arm tightened around her shoulders, and Catharine knew their interlude was over. The barrage seemed louder, but she knew it was her perception that changed. Their magic circle of peace and love was gone. Catharine sighed, shivered, and reached for her clothes. They dressed in silence.

A sharply vivid streak of scarlet laced the night sky over Bataan. Catharine winced and reached for his hand.

"Do you have to go back?"

"Yes."

"It's almost over, isn't it?"

He took a deep breath. "Catharine," and his voice was grim, "I want you to promise me one thing."

She waited.

"If you can get out," he said gruffly, "and I don't care how—whether it's an outrigger or a seaplane or a sub—promise me you'll go."

"Not without you."

"Catharine, listen to me. I can't lose you."

The tremor in his voice brought tears to her eyes. She understood. She felt the same. He was all that mattered to her. To have him, to love him, meant more to her than life itself. She knew she would never again love this way, commit herself so completely to another man.

"I can't lose you either," she replied.

"Then listen to me." His hands cupped her face. "I'm a survivor. I'll make it, Catharine, I promise you. I don't care what I have to do, what I have to endure, I'll survive, and I'll come home to you if I know you are safe. I have to know you are out of this hell." His hands slipped to her shoulders; his grip tightened. "There's a sub coming for the gold, isn't there?"

Slowly, reluctantly, she nodded. She'd been determined not to tell him, but he was too intelligent to be fooled.

His hands relaxed. "You'll be safe. Go home to California. I'll come. I promise."

Tears scalded her face. "Jack, I can't leave you. I know that if I do . . ."

His fingers touched her lips. "Don't say it, Catharine. You've got to believe in me."

"I do. God, I do."

But she didn't believe in life. Not since Charles.

"Then promise me you'll go. If you love me, promise me."

"I love you."

The next morning, as soon as she'd finished breakfast—rice and a cup of weak coffee—Catharine walked purposefully down the hospital lateral. Spencer was at his desk, hunched over a lined legal pad, checking entries against a typed list.

"Spencer, I must talk to you."

He looked up vaguely. "Oh, Catharine. How are you this morning?" But he didn't wait for her to answer. His face twitched a little as another explosion shook the concrete walls. "Those bastards never stop, do they?"

Her voice sharpened. "I must talk to you."

He focused on her. "Is anything wrong?"

She felt a desire to laugh hysterically. The enormous shells exploded above with hideous regularity, the curved cement walls shook, and the acrid dust swirled through the tunnels, coating people, floors, beds, food, and medicine with the fine, dry dirt.

"Yes, something's wrong. I must speak to you in private."

"Easier said than done," he said drily.

People swarmed up and down the tunnel: soldiers, officers, patients, nurses, orderlies.

"Let's go to the vault."

He looked surprised, but nodded. "I have some last-minute..." He broke off and looked sharply around. Catharine understood. The arrival of the submarine was top secret, of course. Only a few would know it was coming; only a select few of the trapped thousands would escape in it. She should feel joy. Instead, she felt an aching coldness.

They waited at the east entrance for a lull in the shelling, then took the five-minute drive to the vault. Catharine didn't speak until they were alone, with the heavy door closed behind them.

She faced him and felt, with surprise, a pang of sorrow. Spencer had always been so immaculate, so very much in command of himself and his surroundings. It was heartbreaking to see him ill shaven, in crumpled, dirty clothes, his eyes red-rimmed with fatigue and worry. And he, too, lived with the expectation of coming horror, especially if he loved Peggy.

He rubbed his face tiredly, then said impatiently, "What is it, Catharine?"

"I should have talked to you a long time ago. In London. I'm sorry I didn't."

He managed a smile. "It can't be too earthshaking. The important thing is that the sub gets in tonight. We leave just before dawn and . . ."

"No. I'm not leaving," she said quietly.

He looked at her as if she'd lost her senses.

She had his attention. "Don't be absurd, Catharine. Don't you understand? We're getting out of this hellhole."

"No." She repeated it loudly. "No. I'm not leaving. I'm in love with another man."

He stared at her in disbelief. His brows drew together, and he flushed angrily.

"I can't believe it."

She realized, ironically, that Spencer had sensed nothing of her feelings this past year. Oh, hadn't they fooled each other. And what great fools they'd both been.

"It's true. I met him in London. Jack Maguire, the INS correspondent."

"A newspaperman?" His voice rose in distaste.

Her own anger flared. She clenched her hands, felt the hard metal of her engagement and wedding rings. She looked down and stripped them off without hesitation. They slid easily from her thin finger. She held the rings out to Spencer.

His eyes fastened on the shining silver and gleaming diamonds in hurt wonder. He didn't take them. "That isn't necessary, Catharine, and it's a bit melodramatic."

She stepped back a pace. "It is necessary. I want you to understand that we're finished."

Spencer's face looked thin, gray, and cold. "A man like that isn't your sort."

He was furious.

"I'm better qualified to determine that than you," she retorted. As she heard her own words, she hated their tone. She and Spencer had cared for each other once, long ago. There had never been great passion, but there had been liking and respect. Now that mutual regard was destroyed, shattered by their mutual betrayal. Yet, even so, how could they speak to each other in these corrosive bursts?

Then the question spurted out of her, the question she hadn't intended to ask.

"Why didn't you tell me about Peggy? For God's sake, why didn't you tell me in London?"

"Peggy?" He looked at once defeated, weary, heartsick. He didn't even attempt a denial. "How did you know?" he asked dully.

She told him of her foray to the vault and the embrace she had seen.

For the first time since Charles's death, she saw a sheen of tears in his eyes. "I'm sorry, Catharine. I should have told you, but I was afraid— if we divorced—that I'd lose my posting. And the work is so important to the war. I had to keep on. Then, when the posting to Manila came up, the ambassador said you had to come, too." Anger flashed in his eyes again. "But if I'd known you were involved with that fellow, everything would have been different."

Who should have spoken first? Who was at fault? Each had remained quiet for what seemed to be good reason. Now they looked at each other across an abyss of disappointment and unhappiness, both of them hurt for what might have been. For Jack and Catharine, it was forever too late because only the diplomats and their wives and a few nurses would escape to Australia aboard the submarine.

Spencer shook his head wearily. "Catharine, whatever is or isn't between us, you have to come on the submarine. You can't stay here. If you stay, you'll be captured or killed. The Rock is going to fall. It's only a matter of time, and not much of that."

"I will not leave without Jack."

He stared at her implacably. "You will come, Catharine."

20

Amea tugged on Catharine's hand. Catharine was awake with anticipation, but she moved slowly. It was ghostly in the dimly lit lateral. Catharine eased to her feet and edged her way to the narrow aisle between the cots that were jammed end to end. None of the sleeping women stirred, but Catharine wondered how many lay awake, knowing that they were being left behind to be captured when Corregidor fell. Amea went first. Catharine, Peggy, and the high commissioner's wife, Elizabeth, followed.

The high commissioner, Spencer, Woody, several diplomats, and two nurses were waiting silently at the intersection of the hospital lateral with the main tunnel. When the group was complete, the high commissioner led the way out through the east entrance. A bus waited. An MP stood guard while the diplomats boarded.

Catharine looked to her right and left, then decided this wasn't the moment. She would make her move at the last possible instant, when there would be no time left to search for her.

The bus lumbered slowly down the bomb-rutted road, skirting the larger craters. Catharine went over it in her mind. She'd considered every alternative, including making an appeal to Commissioner Sayre. She'd been on good terms with him, but she felt that beneath his genial exterior he was a tough professional. He would consider it very unprofessional for a State Department wife to refuse to escape from danger with her husband. Unprofessional and not permissible.

Only General Wainwright could overrule the high commissioner's orders as to who would leave on the submarine. Catharine had seen Wainwright several times in the main lateral. He was tall and thin to the point of emaciation. He seemed kindly, but he would scarcely be sympathetic, and he certainly wanted to be rid of as many civilians as possible.

That left her one recourse.

The group filed off the bus and walked silently down the gritty concrete pier. Heavy clouds scudded overhead. Only an occasional streak of moonlight washed over the pier, but it was light enough to see the double line of marines loading boxes on the docked PT. The PT, of course, would ferry the gold and the passengers out to the waiting submarine.

Catharine edged away from the group. Everyone was intent upon his own task. Now would be a good time . . .

"Ma'am."

She looked up.

A marine sergeant nodded toward the edge of the pier. "Please stay with the group, ma'am."

He was polite but insistent.

For the first time, Catharine began to be afraid, but she was determined. She wasn't going to leave. No matter what she had to do, she wasn't going to leave on that PT.

The marine stood between her and a chance to slip away in the darkness.

Catharine waited on the edge of the pier. The PT was moored alongside. On the other side of the boat, there was the open water of the harbor. When they boarded, no one would remark if she walked to the far side of the PT.

If she were quiet enough, unobtrusive enough, she could be overboard, and no one would notice.

The water held wreckage, of course. Worse—it held sharks. No one had swum since the bombings shattered the shark nets. Shark fins sliced through the water every day, grayish-blue masses of jellyfish bobbed in the choppy water, and stingrays slithered along the bottom.

Catharine could see the dark mass of the water moving heavily in the harbor. It would take a brave shark to be close to shore tonight with all the activity. As for the rest—she was a Californian born and bred and she wasn't afraid to swim in any water.

Her decision made, she relaxed. She wouldn't worry now or second-guess herself. It seemed such a dramatic act for Catharine MacLeish Cavanaugh. She could never have imagined a year ago that she would do anything this bold. Jack admired boldness and independence, but she feared not this time. He would be very angry because he thought she'd promised to leave if she could. He wouldn't understand, but she knew she had to stay. She had no choice. If she left him, she might never see him again. She had to stay.

Suddenly, the passing of the crates from marine to marine stopped.

Amea leaned close. "Something's wrong. The loading is way behind schedule."

Then Catharine heard Spencer shout, "But we aren't even half done."

A low, heavy voice rasped, "My orders are to rendezvous at 0600 hours. We are leaving now. Board the passengers."

"Wait a minute," Spencer ordered. "We have to get the gold out."

"This ship leaves in five minutes." It was the submarine commander.

The passengers began to move toward the gangplank. The high commissioner, his wife, some nurses, Peggy. Catharine stood still.

Spencer and Woody argued, but the commander shook his head. "I've got to make that rendezvous at 0600."

Woody turned to Spencer. "You and Catharine go ahead. I'll stay and . . ."

"No, it's my job. You and Amea go with the shipment. I'll stay. I know we can arrange for another sub."

"But Catharine will come with us," Amea said urgently.

Catharine backed up. "No. No, I won't go."

Spencer didn't answer for a long moment. Then he said woodenly, "Catharine will stay with me."

Amea gave a soft cry and hugged Catharine; then they were gone. Catharine and Spencer watched as the dark hulk of the PT moved out into the harbor.

Spencer ordered a sergeant to oversee the return of the remaining gold to the vault; then he turned to Catharine. She couldn't see his face in the darkness.

"Amea and Woody think you are staying because you love me.

"I'm sorry, Spencer."

He turned and walked away; she heard the echo of his footsteps on the concrete pier.

Peggy rested in the narrow bunk aboard the *Sunfish*. Nausea welled in her throat. She wished she could cry, but all her tears were gone. She stared with dry, aching eyes at the dim gray curving walls of the submarine. It had never occurred to her that Spencer would be left behind, so she hadn't told him. He was so busy with the gold, she'd decided to wait and tell him when they reached Australia. Another wave of nausea clawed at her throat. She bent up on one elbow and retched into the container that Amea held for her.

"My dear, I know it's awful," Amea said gently. "The heat and the motion. Do you think it would help if you got up and tried to walk for a bit?"

Peggy shook her head and sank back weakly onto the pillow. Mrs. Willoughby thought she was seasick, of course, but Peggy knew better.

Oh, dear God, what was she going to do?

Jack loomed above Catharine, his face hard, angry—and hurt.

"For God's sake, you could have gone without Spencer, couldn't you?"

She wasn't going to lie. Not to Jack.

"I could have gone."

He grabbed her arms, gripped her so tightly it hurt. "You bloody fool. Don't you know there's no hope? Bataan's going to fall any day. You know what it's like here."

She knew. Corregidor was running out of food, ammunition, and medicine. It might hold out for three more weeks. Maybe four. That was all.

"You could have been safe."

"I couldn't leave you, Jack. Can't you understand that?"

It took him a long moment to answer. Finally, he said gruffly, "All right, I understand it."

"I'm sorry."

His hands fell away from her. He looked at her somberly; then his face softened. "I love you, Catharine." He shook his head. "Yeah, I understand." He said wearily, "I've got to get you out of here. Somehow."

"Spencer's requested another sub. They'll take you, too," she said eagerly. "You're a correspondent."

"Spencer's not going to get another sub. I've got some friends in HQ. The escape hatch's closed. We're here. We're stuck here."

Catharine frowned. "Spencer will be very angry."

"Poor Spencer," Jack said drily.

"I mean, he'll be upset about not getting the gold out, but I guess they can throw it away, too."

"Throw it away?"

"Like the silver. He can't get the silver out, so he's having it dumped in the middle of the South Channel."

"He is? You mean he's throwing silver into the ocean?"

Catharine nodded.

"When?"

"They started last night. They're going to dump some more tonight, and the rest of it tomorrow night."

The damn moonlight. Jack wished for clouds. Just one cloud would help, but the luminous, shining tropical sky glistened above him. Jack inched forward and watched the marines, their backs bent with effort, as they lugged the containers from the low stone building to the half-ton truck. One MP stood guard by the door to the building. A second held a rifle loosely and slouched by the back of the truck.

Jack watched patiently until he was sure of the drill. No one was

checking the containers out of the building or into the truck. The
marines came and went in erratic bursts.

Jack moved closer and closer to the building until he crouched in
the shadow of a blast-twisted tree. The marines moved back and forth
between the truck. The MP on guard stood tiredly, feet spread apart.
He didn't pay any attention to the marines as they went in and out of
the building.

Occasionally, there would be a gap in the procession of workers.
When the next opportunity came, Jack took it. Jack appeared on the
trail between the truck and the door. The guard didn't notice as he
ducked through the door. In the dim light, Jack was just another man
in uniform.

Light shone dimly from a second doorway. Jack passed through.
Another guard looked at him incuriously. Jack walked to the corner,
bent, and lifted a wooden crate. For an instant, he staggered under its
weight, but he managed to turn and carry it without stumbling. He
hadn't realized how weakened he was from months of too little food. It
took all his strength to keep on walking. He trudged along the rough,
uneven ground toward the truck.

Halfway between the building and the truck he stopped. There
was a shattered palm to the left of the rail and a sharp drop past it into
a ravine. No one was coming toward him. He had to move before a
marine reached the truck and made the return journey. His throat dry,
his heart pounding, he plunged off the trail to his left. At the same time,
he shoved the crate away from him. Vines whipped against him; dry,
crackly underbrush jabbed and scratched at him. The crate thudded
down the steep slope. Jack reached out and grabbed hard at a bush
clinging to the side of the ravine. He hung there panting, waiting for
the shout of discovery, for the rattle of rifle fire.

Moments passed; his heart rate began to slow. His hands stung
from the nettly bush and his shoulder ached from the strain of carrying, then shoving away, the heavy crate, but he didn't care.

The most public act of his plan had succeeded. Now all he had to
do was find the crate in the tangled depths of the ravine, maneuver it

across the island to the point where he'd hidden his motorboat, cross seven miles of dangerous current to Cavite, evade the occupying Japanese, and find someone who would sell him a seaworthy boat for the silver.

Catharine didn't know the enlisted man who handed her the note just after breakfast, and he was gone before she could thank him. She recognized Jack's handwriting on the envelope and ripped it open.

The message was brief:

> Dear Catharine—Gone to Cavite in search of transport. I'll be back. Love—Jack.

Cavite.

The Japanese controlled the province. Much of the artillery fire that blasted Corregidor came from Cavite. Cavite crawled with Japanese.

Catharine's head jerked up, and she stared across the inky blue channel toward Cavite.

21

Three quinquis—wicks dipped in coconut oil, then set afire—
blazed in the nipa hut. The lights wavered and jerked as the sharp
ocean breeze slatted through the bamboo walls. They cast light and
shadow intermittently across the dark, impassive face of the village
headman.

"It would be very dangerous," he said in sibilant Spanish.

Jack's face didn't change, but he felt elated because he knew the
headman knew of a boat. It had taken Jack a week of cautious approach,
of moving from one native barrio to another, before he'd made contact
with a Filipino willing to bring him along an obscure jungle trail to this
meeting. But now Jack knew; a boat existed. Then his elation subsided.
Knowing and getting were poles apart.

"There will be no danger to you or any of your villagers," Jack said
in slow, emphatic Spanish. "All I require is the boat, with enough fuel
to cross the South Channel to Corregidor."

For an instant, the impassive face showed a trace of surprise. Jack
knew the headman wondered why any fool would go to Corregidor.

The Filipino said quietly, "A boat is worth very much. What can
you offer?"

"Ten thousand dollars."

The headman's dark eyes were uninterested. "American dollars are
worthless now."

"Ten thousand dollars in silver."

It was suddenly still in the smoky, ill-lit hut.

"Silver." The headman's face creased into a frown. "Where is this silver?"

"When I see the boat, I will take you to it."

"Do you take me for a fool?" the headman demanded derisively.

Jack picked up his pack from the floor. He opened it, aware that the Filipino watched with a catlike intensity, his hand resting on the knife in his belt. Jack plunged his hand into the pack and pulled out a small leather bag. He jerked open the drawstrings and poured out a stream of silver coins. The coins clattered into a pile, then glistened in the soft light of the quinquis.

The headman picked up several of the coins and studied them. He looked up at Jack. "It would be very dangerous. The boat must be brought here by night and camouflaged by day from the Japanese planes. If the crew were captured, it would mean their lives."

"Twelve thousand."

They bargained, Jack estimating how much silver his crate held, the headman estimating the food and medicines he could buy for his people.

They shook hands at eighteen thousand.

They stood shoulder to shoulder on the dusty patch of ground outside the outlet: nurses, doctors, soldiers, marines, ambulatory patients, civilians, off-duty support personnel. The crowd was silent except for an occasional shocked murmur when the night sky over Bataan exploded anew, each burst angrier, louder, more violent. Light moved in the sky, red, gold, orange, and pink; the noise was constant, the far-off roar of exploding ammunition like the thunder of an avalanche. The spectators watched somberly because they knew this was the deathwatch; this was the dying agony of an army that had fought beyond reason since December. Now it was April, and the bloody, convulsive end had come.

A woman sobbed somewhere in the darkness to Catharine's left, but Catharine's eyes were dry. She wished she could cry. Her throat ached with unshed tears—this was pain too deep for tears. Jack had told her so much about the young soldiers who had fought these dreadful months. Even if they survived, what would happen to them when they were captured by the Japanese?

And what would happen to those now standing here watching the fall of Bataan? Because if Bataan fell, Corregidor would soon fall. Capture now was certain. Some nights in the tunnel, men talked of what happened to those captured by the Japanese.

Everyone standing here would either die or be captured.

A curtain of fire shimmered across the night sky. Catharine lit a cigarette with trembling fingers. She drew deeply on it. She'd thought it couldn't get any worse, the terrible bombardments by day and by night, the endless shrill whining shrieks of the incoming shells, the mind-numbing detonations every few seconds, the lack of food, the heat, the dust, the flies, the quivering concrete walls.

But it was going to get worse.

Spencer frowned at the sheet of paper in front of him. He'd have Peggy . . . Then he remembered again; each time it was a twist of pain. Peggy was on her way to Australia. From there, she'd go by ship to San Francisco. The pain of her going ached deep inside him, but she was on her way home to safety. She was going to be all right.

Peggy would get over him. That would be best for all of them.

He wanted Peggy. He needed her, but he knew that it would never work out. A divorce would be a disaster for him. Divorce . . . A hot flicker of anger moved inside him. How could Catharine have become entangled with a newspaperman? The kind of man who didn't have a dollar in the bank and never knew how long he'd hold a job. Spencer knew about that kind of man: worthless, restless, undependable. Catharine would come to her senses. He should have put her aboard that submarine. Now, who knew what was going to happen. He'd requested Washington to send another sub. He felt suddenly empty, sick. The gold was too important for Washington not to rescue it. They had to take care of the gold. When the sub came, he and Catharine would get out. He'd work everything out with Catharine. After all, they were so well suited. They'd worked together as a team for so long.

His eyes moved restlessly, then stopped and focused on the chair where Peggy used to sit.

Shells whined overhead and exploded every five seconds, gouging out huge craters, rocking the main tunnel and the laterals, filling the air with the fine, sandy dust. Men crouched motionless along the tunnel walls, staring dully at nothing. Patients coughed and choked. The wan, thin nurses worked to keep men alive and wondered what for.

Catharine forced herself to get up every morning, to comb her hair, and to use a tiny bit of their precious water ration to clean her face and hands. She maintained a schedule, mornings in the wards helping write letters home or rolling bandages, afternoons sorting through the effects of the dead, packaging up the sad belongings that would be sent home along with the letters—should there ever be transport.

The men in the wards, those well enough to talk, were hungry for visitors. They wanted to talk about home.

Dennis talked about Cindy.

"Her hair, it's kind of like, did you ever see a field of buttercups, Mrs. Cavanaugh?"

Catharine nodded.

"That's like Cindy's hair, a soft yellow but a real yellow, you know."

Catharine smiled.

The shells exploded with monotonous, relentless regularity. Abruptly, there was a catastrophic explosion. The concrete walls shuddered. Pieces of concrete crackled and fell. The lights wavered, went out.

"Oh, my God," Catharine cried. Panic suffused her. She remembered the trembling darkness, the pressure, and the weight when she was buried in London.

"Mrs. Cavanaugh, don't be frightened." Dennis's voice was young, clear, and firm. "It's just the lights. It's happened before. They'll get them fixed. The tunnel won't fall."

Catharine's heart thudded so hard it hurt.

"It's all right," Dennis said encouragingly.

Tears pricked her eyes. He was comforting her, this boy who

couldn't move. This boy with no arms and no legs and no hope left in his life was comforting her.

She forced herself to speak calmly. "I'm all right, Dennis." And she was better. She could see the wink of flashlights held by the nurses.

"See, it's quiet now for a minute. You go up and get some fresh air, Mrs. Cavanaugh."

She wanted desperately to be up and out of the tunnel, away from the stygian darkness and the smell of blood, dirt, disinfectant, and urine.

"You won't mind if I go?" she asked.

"Oh, no. I'm okay."

She reached out through the darkness, found his thin cheek with its bristle of boyish beard, and touched him.

"I'll come back later."

She was halfway to the outlet when the bluish overhead lights came back on. Someone had switched to an alternate generator. She let out a deep breath and knew she'd come close to collapse. The darkness and the dirt reminded her terribly of being trapped.

When she reached the outlet and stepped outside, she blinked against the hot April sunlight. The thick haze of dust in the air didn't diminish the biting heat. Others streamed out of the tunnel mouth and stopped uncertainly to shade their eyes.

"Catharine."

She turned reluctantly to face Spencer.

"I've been looking for you."

"I work in the hospital in the mornings," she said dully. It was an effort to talk.

Spencer stepped closer, then bent forward. "We've sent for another submarine," he said softly.

Jack had said another submarine wouldn't come. What if he were wrong? What if a sub did make it in before Corregidor fell? Dear God, when would Jack return from Cavite?

She looked at Spencer eagerly. She was past pretense, past caring how her words might affect Spencer.

"Jack can go, too. He's a correspondent. They'll make room . . ."

Spencer's gaunt face hardened. "Not for him. Not if I can help it."

"Oh, no," she cried. "You can't do that. Not because of me. I'll go to the general. I'll tell everyone that . . ."

Spencer grabbed her arms, his fingers tight and hard. "He's all you can think about, isn't he? Well, where the hell is he?" Spencer looked around the clearing. "Is he hiding down there with the rest of the tunnel rats? Where the hell is he?"

"Let go of me." Her voice was icy, contemptuous.

Before the fury in her eyes, Spencer released her.

"He's gone to find a boat to get us off this island."

Spencer's face twisted in an ugly smile. "Is that what he told you? He's gotten the hell out, hasn't he? He got out while the going was good—and you gave up your place on the sub to stay with him. You're a fool, Catharine."

"He's gone to find a boat."

She almost taunted Spencer, saying it was more than Spencer had thought to do, would ever think to do, but even in her anger she knew that wasn't fair. Spencer was doing his duty as best he could. Did it hurt him so much that she had given herself to another man? She wished she could be clearly, coldly, and completely angry and excise Spencer from her thoughts. But she couldn't.

"Don't," she said abruptly. "Don't quarrel with me."

His thin shoulders slumped; his voice softened. "Catharine, when we get home, we could go to Carmel. Remember when we went there?"

Oh, she remembered so well—the dark cypress trees, bent and twisted by the Pacific wind, the thunderous, booming surf, and the clear, cold air so fresh it made the world seem new. She almost smiled; then her face closed.

She shook her head. "No." Her voice was weary now and full of sadness. "No, Spencer, it's all gone, all over. We can't go back. When we get home—if we get home—I want a divorce."

Spencer stepped back a pace. Once again, anger burned in his eyes. "He isn't coming back. You'll see. He's a worthless bum."

Catharine stared at him in shock. How could Spencer, always gentlemanly, genial Spencer be shouting at her? And her own voice was shrill, rising with anger. They'd never quarreled like this. Never. But so much had happened. They were hungry and frightened, in emotional turmoil. They had crossed a line when betrayal became clear, and now there was no buffer, no restraint, no kindness left between them.

She hated the harsh sound of her voice, but she was too shaken to stop. "Get away from me. Get away. Don't you understand? I love him—and I don't ever want to see you again."

"The Channel's mined." Billy Miller said it quietly, unemphatically.

Jack drew deeply on his cigarette and nodded. "I know. I sent word to the underground in Manila. They'll alert Corregidor, tell them we're coming."

Miller smiled, but the smile held no amusement. "What're the odds that message will ever arrive?"

Jack studied the boyish face of the navy lieutenant. "You don't have to come."

Miller smiled again. This time it was real. "I know. By invitation only." The smile slipped away. He looked through the dusk at an ungainly straggle of bushes that seemed to fill the mouth of the creek where it emptied into the sea. When he looked back at Jack, Miller's face wasn't boyish anymore. "That's government property. I don't care who you bought it from."

Jack took a last drag on his cigarette, then tossed it into the brackish water. He looked, too, at the odd heap of bushes. It was artful camouflage; palm trees and even a couple of firs lashed to the deck of the PT boat.

"You've heard of salvage," Jack said mildly.

Miller waited.

"Your guys holed the boat when it went aground near Masbate. The natives got it up and patched it. I'd say the transaction's according to Hoyle."

"Maybe," Miller said grudgingly. "But if we take that boat to Corregidor, you remember one thing: I'm still in the navy, and I follow orders."

Jack grinned. "You get us to Corregidor, and I'll worry about the orders."

"Just so long as we understand each other."

"We understand each other."

It wasn't quite an hour later, after the swift fall of tropical night, that Miller eased the PT out of the mouth of the creek.

It seemed to Jack that the roar of the motors was loud enough to rouse every Jap in the province, but it was too late to worry about that now. Jack stood next to Miller by the wheel. As the PT bucketed across the short waves, jouncing them, Jack peered through the night, trying to discern the hump that would be Corregidor. What were the odds that the underground would get the message? If they did, what were the odds they would relay it by short-wave radio to Corregidor? Moreover, what were the odds Corregidor would ignore the message, suspecting a Jap trick?

As he strained to see through the dark, Jack willed away thoughts of failure. He had to make it; he had to. If he didn't, Catharine would be killed or captured.

The breath shortened in Jack's throat. The boat must be close to the electronic minefield. He could imagine the mines swaying sluggishly beneath the dark water.

"Flash the lamp now," Miller said calmly.

Jack gripped the Aldis lamp and, as Miller had shown him, slowly and carefully flashed the message. He hoped he was getting it right. He hoped to God he was getting it right.

The sky above thundered with the express roar of airplanes coming in to unload their bombs. Light flashed on the island from the exploding bombs and shells. Jack didn't pay any attention. He kept on flashing the lamp, trying not to imagine the huge, powerful mines so close to the top of the water. If Corregidor ignored the message and didn't turn off the minefield, death would spring in this moment or the next. There would be an instant of incredible noise, force, and pressure. It would all be over.

He flashed the message, tried to breathe, and thought of Catharine. The boat slipped on.

22

Wainwright's headquarters were in lateral 3 which was about one hundred and fifty yards from the east entrance to Malinta Tunnel. Jack looked longingly at the water fountain at the lateral entrance. His mouth was still cotton-dry from the heart-stopping journey through the minefield. They passed two desks crammed sideways against the walls. Aides stood by maps, talked on telephones, filled out papers. About twenty-five feet into the lateral, an unshaded bulb dangled above Wainwright's desk. The bright, harsh light wasn't kind to the general.

Jack was shocked at the change in Wainwright since he'd last seen him. God, he'd aged. He'd never had an ounce of weight to spare, but now he was all bones. He'd lost his sunburn from Bataan; his craggy face looked pale and drawn.

The marine saluted briskly. "General, a civilian and a navy lieutenant just arrived from Cavite on a patched-up PT. The civilian says it's important that he talk to you."

Wainwright looked up from his papers. His glance swung from Jack to Miller, then back to Jack. He knew a civilian when he saw one.

Jack didn't waste his time.

"General, you know Corregidor can't hold out much longer. I salvaged a PT boat and found a navy lieutenant to sail it over here. I'm offering to take anybody off the Rock you want to send—as long as that number includes Catharine Cavanaugh, a State Department wife."

Wainwright stared at Jack unblinkingly. Jack felt a moment of panic. Wainwright had the final say. If he wouldn't let Catharine go . . .

"You're asking for enough food and fuel to make Australia?"

"Yes, sir."

Wainwright's light blue eyes narrowed. "Why the hell should I do that, son? I don't have an extra ounce of food—or fuel."

"If there's anyone or anything you want to get away before Corregidor falls, this is your last chance, sir."

"It's a damn long way to Australia."

"Nobody here has a better ticket, General."

A faint smile touched Wainwright's mouth. "I'd say that's right, son." He studied Jack. "Cavanaugh. That's the State Department johnny in charge of the gold."

"Yes, sir."

"Washington wants the gold," Wainwright said slowly. He paused for a long moment, then said gruffly, "That PT—you salvaged it? Well, I'm afraid I'm going to have to requisition it."

Jack found Catharine at the outlet.

When she saw him, she ran to him. He took her in his arms, and they clung to each other. Catharine didn't care who saw them. She was past caring about the judgment of others.

"I knew you'd come," she said over and over again.

Wainwright was impatient. "It's the only possible chance, and I don't have time to jabber about it. I'm going to send the gold out. You can go or not, as you wish. "

Spencer stood stiffly in front of Wainwright's desk. His voice shook with anger. "This is absurd. Maguire's just a newspaper reporter. He's a nobody; he's just trying to save himself."

"He crossed a minefield to get here," Wainwright rejoined. "That took guts." And something more, the general thought. He remembered Catharine Cavanaugh. He'd met her one morning when he'd visited the hospital. Any man alive on Corregidor took notice when he saw a woman, especially a woman like Catharine Cavanaugh. But his concern was to get the damned gold off the island before it fell. Wainwright rattled some papers on his desk. "The gold's going out."

Spencer stepped closer to the desk. "The gold is my responsibility. "

"You may accompany the gold," Wainwright said distinctly, "but the man in charge will be Lieutenant Miller."

It was a small party that boarded the PT. Spencer. Catharine. Jack. And two army nurses. Catharine had glimpsed both of them at work in the hospital lateral. Sally Brainard was a diminutive blond who always worked at top speed but had a cheery smile for every sick soldier. Frances Kelly was older, a tall, once heavy woman shrunken now by the months of privation. Frances's hair was streaked with gray and she looked perpetually worried, her brows drawn down in a constant frown.

Billy Miller didn't spare any of them a glance when they were underway. He and his crew were sucking the last horsepower from the blunt craft, and it bucketed across the water, slapping hard on the waves like a high-stepping trotter.

As dawn streaked the eastern sky, the PT nosed into a cove on one of the thousands of islands that make up the Philippines. Cautiously, the passengers and crew swam in the pale, clear water and spent the day resting in the shade of palms, always wary of Japanese patrol planes.

Each night, the PT charged across the water. The second night passed and the third, and the passengers survived. Jack spent his time with Catharine. Spencer moved restlessly from cabin to deck, checking and rechecking the canvas sheeted over the crates of gold. Every time he passed Catharine and Jack, his eyes darkened with anger.

Billy Miller knew he had an explosive situation on his boat that had nothing to do with the war. Miller knew he'd be damn glad when this trip was over. Each day they survived they bettered their chances of ultimate survival. The trickiest part of the flight was coming up on this, their fifth night. They were running hard toward Mindanao, the enormous southerly island in the Philippine chain. They had to make landfall where the navy had secreted tins of gasoline in the early days of the war. They had to find the fuel and take it aboard to have enough fuel to reach Australia.

Miller strained to see through the darkness. He'd checked his navigation, and he was almost sure they were getting close to their goal, but he didn't like the glitter of the whitecaps breaking in front of him, and he didn't like the smell of the wind. The back of his neck prickled because he knew what storms could do in this stretch of water.

The rain struck without warning as it can in the tropics, but he wasn't surprised. He had a single thought: they'd almost made it.

The hard, straight wind threw up huge phosphorescent waves that struck against them. Sharp, hard pellets of rain. The PT struggled up from a trough, then teetered on the lip of an enormous wave and careened down, down, down before it wallowed sluggishly in the trough and began its next labored ascent.

Miller struggled with the wheel. He had no time or thought for anything but the next moment, the next wave.

Jack held Catharine's arm with one hand and held to a stanchion with the other. Water rushed over the side of the PT, a gray-green wall that sucked greedily at them, tried to tear them loose and fling them overboard. Jack fought against the pull, holding to Catharine and to the stanchion with all his strength. When the wave was gone and they still stood, he shouted against the wind and the rain, "We have to get below!"

They bent low against the wind and rain, clinging to the boat when the waves washed over them, plunging forward in the lull between waves, finally lurching down the companionway to the cabin. As they burst through the door, every face turned toward them.

One of the nurses cried out, "We thought you'd been swept over!" Her eyes widened, and she looked past them. "Isn't Spencer with you?"

"Is Cavanaugh on deck?" Jack shouted.

He knew the answer when he looked at the strained faces of those clinging to any solid piece of wood for support as the cabin shook and moved.

Jack turned back toward the door.

"Oh, no," Catharine cried. "You can't go back up there."

She tried to follow Jack, but a seaman reached out and stopped her.

When Jack's head came even with the upper deck, the wind struck him full force; a torrent threatened to pull him headlong to the railing and overboard. He couldn't see. Rain streamed in a solid mass, hurled by the wind like water pounding from a fire hose. The PT moved like a wounded animal; each plunge went lower; each recovery was slower.

Jack clung to the railing and turned aft. He knew Spencer would be by the gold. The bloody, stupid, asinine fool. How could he still care what happened to that shipment when they fled for their lives, when the sky and the sea held enemies everywhere, when life and death hung in the balance?

Jack pulled himself aft, clinging to the railing with every ounce of strength and will. The waves crashed across the deck, tearing away anything not secured, pulling at Jack with deadly force. His eyes burned from the salt water; his body ached from the pummeling of the water. He lost count of time in the whirling maelstrom of wind and water.

The PT tilted forward. Jack lurched and fell to the deck. He looked up and an instant of pure terror transfixed him. A mountainous wave, thirty feet tall, loomed above him.

Then he saw Spencer.

Spencer's body hung limply alongside the railing, secured by a rope. Jack understood. Spencer knew his peril when the storm struck. He'd tied himself to a stanchion, but the rope was giving way. Spencer dangled limply next to the crates of gold, unconscious from a bloody gash on the back of his head.

Jack's eyes moved again, to the top of the mountain of green foam that hung over the ship, ready to break. When it did, Spencer would be swept overboard.

Jack looked again at Spencer, unconscious, helpless, unknowing. When the wave broke, it would be the final strain on the rope. Spencer would be washed away, pulled down into the churning water to his death.

The wave arched, curled.

Jack's chest ached as his heart beat in a frightened, erratic thudding. It was unlikely he could hold on for himself alone against the force of tons of water. If he moved now there might be time, just time enough, to fling himself forward, to find a safer place. If he stayed here and tried to help Spencer his own life would be threatened.

The wave that hung over the side of the PT was breaking now.

Frantically, Jack moved. One arm wrapped itself desperately around a metal stanchion, the other grappled for a hold on Spencer, pulling the heavy, inert body close.

He didn't have time to look up again, to see the gigantic wall of water as it curled over and thundered down upon them.

23

C louds scudded across the face of the moon. The storm had moved on as quickly as it had struck, but the PT boat slanted sharply to port and didn't move. The gargantuan wave had lifted the boat, then slammed it down onto a ridge of coral. When the wave receded, Jack knew that he and Spencer had survived, but nobody now had a ticket to Australia.

They were all congregated, looking at Miller in the fitful moonlight.

"We've got to get the women to shore," Jack said.

Miller didn't answer.

Spencer was propped against the bulwark. His voice was groggy but determined. "We have to wait until the tide comes in. We might float free."

"We'd have to check the screw for damage," Miller replied.

"Dawn comes in two hours," Jack said tensely. "We're three hundred yards off Mindanao, and Mindanao is crawling with Japs. Some Photo Joe will fly by in the morning, spot us, and it will be goodnight. We've got to get the women to shore."

"We don't know what's onshore," Spencer responded with equal anger.

"There's no hiding place out here, Cavanaugh. We'll be pop-up targets in a shooting gallery."

"So what do you suggest, Maguire?" Cavanaugh said sarcastically.

"Get the hell off this boat. Now."

"I'll give the orders," Miller said brusquely.

Jack clenched his hands in tight, hard fists. He looked across the moonlight-dappled water. He'd said three hundred yards. It might be five hundred.

There were two dinghies.

Jack turned to Miller. "Catharine and I are leaving now."

Cavanaugh pulled himself unsteadily to his feet. "Oh, I say, Maguire, you're forgetting whose wife she is."

Jack took a deep breath. "Your wife. Not your chattel. She'll come with me."

The anger and antagonism between the two men pulsed in the darkness.

Miller moved between them. "I'll say who leaves when."

"Then say, for God's sake," Jack demanded. "If we wait until dawn, we're dead."

Miller nodded slowly. "I understand that, but first, we'll try to get free one more time."

The motors roared to life, violent and harsh in the predawn quiet. Miller put the PT into reverse. The motors strained until the boat rocked back and forth.

Jack waited tensely. The noise was a dead giveaway if any Japs were near. His head swiveled around; he stared through the shiny darkness. He could see the women standing near the port gun, a gun that had no shells and was as useless as a chalkboard mock-up. Jack felt a sudden explosion of weariness. His body ached. How he had managed to hang on, to save himself and Spencer, he would never know, but he was paying for it. He wanted desperately to lie down and let exhaustion engulf him. Instead, he walked stiffly toward Billy Miller.

It was enough—even though the future held nothing but terror— to know Jack was there, only a few feet from her. Catharine watched him turn to walk toward Miller. She could feel the pain in his body. Very dear and brave heart. He was brave and gallant as few ever can be. She knew it because she had seen that wall of water. She'd broken away from the seaman, rushed up the companionway to the deck, and seen that mountainous wall of water break with a demon's thunder. The water had knocked her down the steps of the companionway. She'd feared they were lost, Jack and Spencer. When she found them there, Jack still clinging to the unconscious man, she'd known that she would never be more proud of a human being in her life than she was of Jack at that moment.

Now, once again, he was setting out to do battle, and he was exhausted. She knew it. Catharine took a step away from the nurses.

"Where are you going?" Sally asked, her bright eyes curious.

"I'm going to see what's been decided," and she moved toward the bow.

The first dinghy to shore carried Catharine, the two nurses, and fifty pounds of gold. A sailor paddled expertly through the clear patches picked out in the moonlight. The reefs protected the cove from the force of the thunderous surf. No one spoke when the dinghy slid up on shore. Catharine and the nurses splashed out of the raft to the sandy beach, then looked tensely around.

Catharine felt a hot lick of fear. Was the beach patrolled? They had no idea where they'd wrecked. This cove could be a stone's throw from the road into Davao, which was occupied by the Japanese. It could be a deserted cove far from any habitation. Mindanao was huge and very sparsely populated.

The choppy breeze rustled the dark vegetation that stretched beyond the beach.

The sailor moved past them and dumped the crate on the sand. The second dinghy slid onto the shore. Spencer and another sailor began to unload boxes of gold.

By the time the last transfer was made, sunrise flooded the water with a sheet of bright orange. The three women rested and watched in the shade of a coconut palm.

"I used to daydream about being shipwrecked on a desert island," Sally Brainard said ruefully. She offered a cigarette to Catharine and the other nurse, Frances Kelly.

Frances looked nervously at the gray mass of the jungle. "Do you think we should smoke? I mean, what if there are any Japs around?"

"Nobody's shot at us yet," Catharine said. She lit the cigarette and welcomed the sharply dry flow of smoke. She smiled her thanks at Sally. "Have you lost your taste for desert islands?"

"Yeah," Sally replied.

The three of them scanned the cove. In the early, misty light, it looked primeval. Only the unmoving bulk of the PT on the coral was a link to the world they knew.

Catharine managed a cheerful smile. "Oh, well, we've lived to fight another day. Who knows? Maybe we'll strike out from here and find Shangri-La."

"I'd trade Shangri-La for one day in Louisville," Frances said wistfully.

"What would you do if you could go home to Louisville?" Catharine asked, because anything was more cheerful than staring at the wild, unbridled jungle growth that surrounded the cove.

Frances drew slowly on her cigarette. A smile touched her eyes. "I'd go to Pop Boynton's Drug Store and order a chocolate malted."

"That sounds good," Sally said.

The harsh, explosive sound of breaking wood echoed across the water. The women jerked around and looked out toward the stricken PT. A sailor rhythmically swung an axe, smashing in the side of the boat. Two sailors swung fifty-gallon cans of fuel high into the air to fling them overboard. The dinghies plied steadily to and from shore, transporting the food supplies.

Catharine and the nurses didn't look at one another. The boat was their only link with the life they'd known and their only hope of reaching Australia. Every rending blow of the axe hurt.

"What would you do if you could go home, Sally?" Catharine asked, her voice unnaturally high.

Sally took a deep breath and talked about St. Louis, trying hard to mask the sound of the rhythmic pounding.

The boat sank an hour after sunrise. The small band of refugees sat on the beached dinghies and ate a cold breakfast of salmon and rice.

"The first thing to do," Spencer said when they'd finished, "is to find natives who can carry the gold for us."

"The first thing to do is find out where we are and get the women as far from the Japs as we can," Jack said determinedly.

Billy Miller ignored both of them. "We've got enough food for five days, maybe a little more. Everybody has a canteen of water." He looked at Spencer, then at Jack. "My orders were to transport the gold—and the passengers—to Australia. I can't do that now, but I'm still in command until I get this party—and the gold—to a senior officer."

"Billy, that gold weighs at least fifty pounds a box. We've got ten boxes. We can't carry it through the jungle. Why don't we bury it," Jack suggested.

"We aren't leaving the gold behind," Spencer said quickly.

"We might as well tie weights to our ankles as try to move that much stuff through the jungle. It won't help to have the damned gold if the Japs catch us. We've got to move as fast as we can to have any chance," Jack urged.

"We can't leave the gold behind," Miller said shortly, "but we can't carry the gold ourselves. We've got to get help."

Catharine scraped the last bit of salmon from her tin plate and ate it slowly. She shut out the sound of the men wrangling. It was odd to think that their lives were going to be tied to the fate of the heavy, dark lumps of metal that had lain in that vault on Corregidor. But she knew that the linkage went farther back than that, back to Spencer's hunger for success at whatever price. If she'd never met Jack in London, he would be safe. Her heart cried out at the thought. But she knew it was true. It was her fault that Jack was in danger now. Yet, he'd argued with her over that, told her he made his own decision to follow her—and never regretted it.

She looked up and saw his eyes watching her. She smiled. He smiled in return.

Perhaps those smiles made all the fear and danger worth the price. But the price would be higher yet. She knew that. There could be no safety for them on Mindanao. They were lost on a Japanese-occupied island. They had no arms. They had food for only a few days.

But Jack smiled at her and she smiled in return.

Love has moments of glory that only those who love can understand. Eyes that meet honestly and smiles that are as profoundly touching as any caress belong to a time and space that nothing can destroy.

Then Jack spoke. "I'll go with them, Catharine, to find native carriers," and fear closed again around her heart.

24

Night fell with the suddenness of the tropics, swathing them in impenetrable darkness. Catharine rested in the smoothed-out shell she'd prepared in the sand. After the blistering heat of the day, the gentle breeze off the ocean was cool and refreshing.

Why hadn't Jack and the other men returned? They might be hopelessly lost in the snake- and boar-infested jungle. They might already be prisoners of the Japanese.

They might be dead.

"Catharine." Sally's voice was thin on the night air.

Catharine's mind came back from its nightmare haunts. "Yes?"

"What will we do if they don't come back?"

Catharine didn't answer for a long moment. She thought of the lost colony of Roanoke. What had happened to those who waited? When no one came, did one party strike out, then another? Eventually, when the ship came in, no one was there. It took every ounce of Catharine's will to answer calmly.

"We can't expect them to come back immediately. Don't worry, Sally, they'll return."

When Sally spoke again, her voice was low and gruff. "Catharine, I'm frightened. I'm terribly frightened."

Catharine raised herself up on her elbow and reached out for the younger woman. She slipped an arm around Sally's shoulders and felt them shake with tears. Catharine pulled Sally closer, cradled her head against her shoulder. She felt the hot wetness of tears through her blouse.

"They'll come back," she said again, and she tried to believe it.

It was late afternoon on the third day when the curly-haired sailor from Michigan stopped his incessant pacing on the far end of the beach. He looked at the two nurses and Catharine sitting in the shade of the palms, at two other sailors swimming in the shallows, and at Wally Harris, the officer whom Miller had left in command. His mouth set determinedly, he crossed to the pile of sailors' belongings and picked up a bedroll.

"Jenkins." Harris's voice was sharp.

The sailor ignored him and continued strapping his bedroll.

"What are you doing?"

Jenkins looked at Harris defiantly. "I'm getting out of here. I'm not going to stay here and starve."

"We're under orders, Chris." Harris's voice was gentle now. "We have to stay here."

"Stay here?" The young sailor's voice rose and cracked. "Look around. This is nowhere. We'll stay here and starve. I'm getting out." He turned toward the jungle.

"Jenkins."

The sailor paused for an instant; then he ducked his head and broke into a lope. Within seconds, he was swallowed up in the thick jungle growth. For a few minutes more, they could hear the frantic sounds of his thrashing, uneven progress; then that, too, was gone.

No one spoke, but each of them knew the young man had gone to his death, Catharine thought.

It wasn't quite an hour later that movement sounded again in the jungle. They all scrambled to their feet and waited tensely.

Jack was the first to step out onto the beach. He looked quickly until his eyes found Catharine.

Everyone moved toward the returned men, and Catharine felt a surge of thankfulness. They all were back safely, Jack and Spencer and Billy. Behind them came a group of well-built Filipinos.

Jack came up to Catharine.

"Was it difficult?" she asked.

He nodded. "We wandered for a couple of days; then we found a track and followed it to a barrio. It was deserted, but we had been observed because some natives came up to us. They led us to another barrio and found some men who agreed to carry our stuff and lead us to some Americans hiding in the interior."

"Hiding?" She knew what it meant, but she asked anyway.

Reluctantly, Jack nodded. "Corregidor fell on May sixth. Wainwright surrendered all the troops in the Philippines to keep the Japs from killing everybody on Corregidor, but a lot of Americans on Mindanao fled to the interior; miners, missionaries, and soldiers who didn't surrender."

Catharine raised a hand to press against her lips. Corregidor had fallen and with it all the brave, wonderful people she'd known: the nurses, the doctors, the marines, the wounded. And Dennis. Oh, God, what had happened to Dennis?

Jack reached out and squeezed her shoulder. "Don't think about it, Catharine," he said gruffly. He took a deep breath. "Anyway, it means the Japs are in the saddle here, at least along the coast. They make sweeps into the interior, but there's plenty of room to hide. Unfortunately, we've landed not too far from Davao. There are Japs everywhere around here."

"How can we avoid them?"

"There's only one way." He reached down, picked up a broken palm frond, and began to trace in the sand. "Here we are." He made an X. "The main highway runs here." He sketched it in. "There are Jap patrols here and here." Then he made crosshatches on a large area west of them. "Our only hope is to move through here."

She looked at him, not understanding. "There aren't any Japs there?"

He looked down at the sand. "No, no Japs. If we can make it through, we can get to the mountains, and that country's so wild, we'll be safe."

"If we can make it through . . ."

"Manuel's the leader of the Filipinos. He swears he knows a way through." Jack shook his head. "We could see the swamp off to our left as we traveled, but we didn't dare enter. If you don't know your way in a swamp, you can travel in circles until you drop."

The swamp pulsed with life: the harsh caw of parrots, the whirr of insects, the splash of rats and snakes. The water was turgid and smelled dank and foul. But worst of all were the leeches. Once an hour the travelers stopped to remove the bloated worms. No matter how tightly they tied their pants' legs, the leeches squirmed past the constricting bands to fasten into their skin and draw blood until their bodies bulged.

After each pause, Manuel would once again signal a march, swinging his bolo knife to cut through a seven-foot wall of grass, each stalk an inch thick and wiry. He cut a narrow path, and the sharp-edged swamp grass sliced at their bodies, scratching and tearing any exposed skin.

Every step in the waist-deep water exhausted. It was an effort to move against the sluggish water, an effort to pull water-logged shoes from the mucky bottom. Hour followed hour, and their involuntary grunts of fatigue were a dull counterpoint to the squashing sound of their steps and the thock of Manuel's bolo knife.

Spencer wavered once or twice, and Catharine knew the ugly gash at the back of his head still throbbed. She and Sally and Frances stumbled forward, the humid heat draining their strength. Insects swarmed over them, biting all exposed flesh, raising huge welts on their faces and hands. But Jack stayed close to her, always ready to help her through particularly difficult patches.

They finally stopped in midafternoon for food, clambering up onto an enormous fallen tree trunk. Catharine stared down at the murky brown water. How long could they bear to move through it?

They drank from their canteens and shared three cans of Vienna sausages among the nine Americans. The cargadores, each of whom carried a crate of gold, rested, too, but none of them seemed weary. They laughed and talked quietly among themselves and shared a lunch of rice and camotes, a kind of sweet potato. The food, little as it was, gave them the energy to start again when Manuel signaled time to move on.

The afternoon was a burning misery of heat and fatigue. Catharine no longer thought in terms of how long. She bent every effort to lift one foot at a time, step after step after step. At sundown, when they stopped, she stood unmoving in the water, too tired even to look for a place to rest. Jack took her elbow and helped her up onto a fallen log to wait while the men built a platform of vines and saplings so they could sleep out of the water. When it was finished, the women climbed up and collapsed on the uncomfortable springy platform, too tired even to think of food. Jack brought them a mixture of rice and salmon served on plantain leaves.

Each day, they moved more slowly, the physical strain telling ever more deeply on their malnourished bodies. One foot after another, day after day.

Finally, the fourth day, the water fell to their thighs, to their knees, to their ankles. They looked at one another, their faces and hands inflamed with insect bites, their skin mealy from the water, their legs pocked with marks from the leeches, and hope flickered in their eyes. They'd come through the green hell. They'd reached the end of the swamp. One last time, they performed the familiar sickening ritual, the men turning away to provide the women some privacy as they made their leech search.

Catharine was last. She didn't want to look, but she could feel the bloated black bodies on her skin. Sally held a burning match to a leech embedded in Catharine's calf. She shuddered as the worm contracted and fell away, slipping down her leg.

Billy Miller was already waving them into a huddle. "Manuel says we need to move fast. A Jap patrol may be along here any time now. We've got to get past it and get up into the mountains. If the Japs catch us, they'll intern civilians, kill military personnel."

So one fear supplanted another. Now they no longer watched for snakes, stripped away leeches, and fought the insects and heat. Now they listened for the thud of approaching feet or the crackle of gunfire.

They skirted the villages, keeping to rough paths and trails. Once they hid, faces pressed into the dust, bodies hugging the ground, as a Japanese patrol rattled by. Then Manuel, prodding them to run, led them across the road and ever upward into harsher country—climbing, always climbing.

Catharine thought it would be better in the mountains, but their shoes, rotted by swamp water, fell away from their feet; the tender skin blistered in angry red and white patches as they stepped on nettles and rocks. Their muscles, abused by the muck of the swamp, throbbed as their legs, unaccustomed to climbing, struggled to keep pace. At first, the cooler air was invigorating after the stultifying heat. But it grew ever cooler as they climbed higher. They began to shiver in their worn cotton clothes and wore any extra pieces of clothing they still possessed. The terrain worsened: steep-sided canyons; sharper, tougher gradients; overhangs; and impassable slopes.

Manuel led the cargadores at a tireless pace. Spencer and Billy Miller followed close behind, the sailors and nurses came next, and Catharine and Jack brought up the rear.

One afternoon they came to a shallow stream, icy water swirling over a pebbled bottom. Catharine dropped down, eased off her shoes, and plunged her blistered feet into the sharply cold water.

"I wish I could stay here."

Jack looked up at the enormous hardwood trees towering into the sky, their limbs so thickly leaved the afternoon sun couldn't pierce the canopy. It was dim, cool, and very quiet. He grinned. "Actually, I'd be happy to trade for Chicago—and a beer at Delancey's Saloon."

Catharine didn't smile. She shook her head. "This is all crazy."

He studied her for a long moment, then nodded. "I know. Destination to nowhere. But what else can we do?"

"Stop."

"And let the Japs catch us?"

She didn't reply.

He reached down and pulled her up. "Come on, Catharine, we're going to make it, you and I."

Tears burned in her eyes. "Make it where, Jack?"

His hand tightened on her arm. "I don't know. Nobody knows, but we're going to finish the course, Catharine, you and I, together."

Was it the word together or was it the warmth of his hand? Catharine wasn't sure, but somewhere she found the strength to bend down, slip her blistered feet into the ragged canvas shoes, and follow him.

They came around a curve and found the others. Below the path, the sheer side of the mountain fell away for hundreds of feet. They could look down, down, down the tree-shrouded mountainside to the glitter of a stream far below.

She looked at the ribbon-like path. Was it even four inches wide? It edged along the rock face; part was crumbled away. There was a space, perhaps two feet across, where the path disappeared. Between the one edge of the path and its beginning past the break, there was no barrier from a drop down the mountainside.

The Americans watched silently as the cargadores moved along the gritty path, then disappeared around the bulging rock. No sound broke the intent silence above the gorge. Finally, all the cargadores were gone. Miller looked at his group.

"I'll go first." He nodded at Jack. "Bring up the rear, Maguire."

Miller didn't look down. He spread-eagled himself against the rock face and began to inch outward on the path, one foot at a time. It took him several minutes to pass the broken spot; then he was gone around the edge of the rock.

A ruddy sailor took Sally's hand. "I'll go first and you follow."

Catharine didn't watch them. She didn't watch Frances go with the second sailor. Catharine watched Spencer. His face looked like a death mask, colorless and drawn. He stood stiffly by the trail, but he didn't look out over the dark gorge that slashed between mountains or at the path.

Only Catharine, Jack, and Spencer remained.

Catharine reached out and touched Spencer's rigid arm. When she spoke, her voice was carefully casual. "I'll go first. You can come behind me. Here." She took his hand and was terribly aware of Jack watching.

Spencer didn't move.

Catharine tugged gently on his arm.

He licked his lips. "I don't think . . ."

"We can do it. Don't look down." Again, she gently pulled on his arm. Catharine could sense his fear.

Slowly, she stepped toward the path—and Spencer followed. Catharine moved out on the exposed path; Spencer came, too. They moved slowly, so slowly, an inch at a time, their bodies pressed against the rock face. He stopped once. His ragged breathing rasped loudly in the terrible silence.

"We're almost around the curve." Her voice was soft and gentle. It was a lie. They were at the point of dreadful emptiness where the path fell away. They must step over nothing to reach the narrow ledge that continued around the side of the cliff.

Catharine looked down to gauge the distance she must step; vertigo swept her. She fought the sickening dizziness.

"I can't do it. I can't." Spencer's voice was a thin whisper.

"One foot at a time." She said it again, then again. She lifted her foot. Two feet of sheer emptiness to the other side. She mustn't stop. She knew that. If she stopped, it would be impossible to start again. Her foot moved out over nothing. Then, blessed relief, she found the beginnings of the other side and stepped firmly; but her forward momentum checked because Spencer stopped.

Straddling the emptiness, Catharine turned her face and saw him pressed against the rock face, his body trembling.

"Spencer, I need your help. Step this way, just a little."

He stayed against the rock face for a long moment; then his face turned toward her. "I can't."

"Spencer, remember the summer we met and how we used to go canoeing? Do you remember how still the pond was? It smelled like moss and cedars. It was so quiet, almost as if we were the only people in the world. Do you remember that? It was so peaceful. Think about the pond, Spencer, and how it looked; then you can come closer to me. That's right. Move a little closer. Now we're on our way. I'll step over here, and you can follow." She was over the break now; Spencer must step, too. "Remember the green and the stillness, and put your foot over here, yes, a little farther, and now you're on your way. Let's make one more big step . . ."

Step by step, word by word, she drew him across the gap and around the cliff face until the path widened and eager hands reached out to pull them to safety.

Jack was coming around the curve when Spencer reached out, pulled Catharine into his arms, and held her tightly. She looked over Spencer's shoulder and saw Jack's face.

Jack lowered his head, brushed past them, and didn't look back.

25

Catharine curled into a tight ball, trying to get warm. They were jammed, head to toe, into the one-room living area of the nipa hut. The hard ridges of the bamboo floor cut into her shoulder and side. No matter how she moved, she couldn't get comfortable, although the hut was unimaginable luxury after the harrowing journey through the swamp and up into the rugged mountains. Finding the hidden camp of refugee mining engineers had been the most marvelous piece of luck, though actually it wasn't luck at all. An Ata tribesman had come down the trail to meet them with information that refugee Americans were hidden deep in a gully three days' travel ahead. The three days were a nightmare of perilous crossings, exhaustion, and, once, a near brush with a Japanese patrol searching for fleeing American soldiers.

They reached the hidden camp shortly before dusk. They were made so welcome that once Catharine had to turn away to brush tears from her eyes. They ate roast chicken and hot rice for dinner, described their adventures, and heard equally exciting stories from the three married couples and two bachelors who had evaded Japanese capture. The miners' camp had all the luxuries of a rustic mountain hideaway in the Ozarks: water piped through a bamboo trough from a nearby rushing stream, an outdoor privy tastefully hidden in a clump of bamboo, and three nipa huts built on bamboo stilts like the native Bukidnon dwellings.

A nurse slept on either side of Catharine. She doubted that anyone slept well. It was too crowded, too cramped and uncomfortable. She was terribly aware that Jack was on the other side of the sala. It might as well be a million miles away. Ever since she and Spencer crossed the narrow trail and Spencer held her in his arms, she hadn't spoken to Jack alone.

She knew it wasn't jealousy on his part. She knew Jack too well for that. It went deeper than that. It struck to the very core of their feeling for each other.

Catharine moved restlessly, then forced herself to lie still. She mustn't disturb the others. Their journey had been so long, so difficult, that everyone needed rest. She wished she could rest, but every fiber of her being cried out for Jack. He was so near. If only she could reach out and touch him . . .

Spencer stared sightlessly into the deep well of darkness. Not even a spear of moonlight pierced the damp wall of vegetation that masked the gully. He didn't mind the hard ridges of bamboo. He felt exultant, triumphant. Against all odds, they'd saved the gold, ferried it out of Corregidor, plucked it from the sinking PT, and carried it through swampland and over mountain trails to safety.

Relative safety.

There wasn't any reason to expect the Japanese to find this camp. The natives liked Americans, and most of them simply slipped away into the jungles and highlands when the Japanese soldiers appeared. All he had to do was keep the gold safe until the American ships came. They would come, of course. Spencer smiled in the darkness. There was no doubt about it—he'd certainly be due a commendation for his work. Actually, it should cap his career. In gratitude, the Department would surely approve his request to return to England—and with a promotion, of course.

His smile slipped away. Catharine and this absurd infatuation— of course, it would come to nothing. The fellow was just a newspaper chap. Catharine must have been out of her mind. But she'd not had much to do with the fellow the last few days. The muscles ridged in his jaws. He didn't like to think about it, didn't like to imagine Catharine and the fellow together. He pushed away the hurtful images. Catharine had never turned passionately to him. That rankled more than the thought of losing her. But if he could have Peggy, he would be the gainer—except that it would be hard without Catharine to manage the kind of life that was necessary. Suddenly, he could smell the coal dust and the damp, heavy fog of London; but he didn't picture Catharine. Instead, he saw Peggy looking up at him with her sunny smile, drops of fog glinting in her thick reddish blond hair. Peggy turned toward him, her blue eyes full of love. He could feel the taste of her mouth and the softness of her body.

Peggy sat motionless, her face turned toward the dusty window, but she wasn't looking out at the dun-colored troop train as it thundered by on the main line. Her train had been sidetracked for three hours now while troop and equipment trains flashed by. They would be very late arriving in Chattanooga, but she didn't care. She dreaded her arrival. Her mother would be at the station. And Rowley. And she would have to begin her lie.

Peggy moved restlessly in her seat; the familiar bubble of nausea rose in her throat. She swallowed once, twice.

"It's the heat, dearie." The big woman sitting beside her smiled sympathetically. "Here, I've got a fresh lemon. Nothing like lemon to help when you don't feel so good. I've just been to see my son in Norfolk." The smile fell away. Abruptly, tears glistened in her dark brown eyes. "He didn't say, but I know they'll be leaving soon." The big woman's hands crumpled the newspaper she held. "Bobby's seventeen."

Seventeen. Peggy thought of all the young men she'd known on Corregidor. So young and now, who knew what had happened to them. Or what would happen to this woman's Bobby. Peggy reached out and clasped the woman's hands.

The woman gave herself a shake, like a big dog coming out of water.

"Here, now, I didn't mean to burden you with my troubles. I 'spect you have troubles of your own." She looked down at Peggy's hands. "Are you on your way to see someone?"

Peggy paused for just a moment, but she'd made up her mind. She looked down at the plain golden band on her left hand, then turned toward the woman. "No. My husband's somewhere in the Philippines . . ."

The quarrel erupted shortly after breakfast.

In honor of their arrival, the miners and their wives broke out a precious tin of coffee and served a steaming cup to everyone. Jack stood a little apart from the main group. Catharine watched him. She wanted to approach him, but there was something forbidding in the hard set of his face. When he finished his coffee, he walked slowly toward the group and stopped in front of Billy Miller.

Miller looked up warily.

Jack jerked his head toward the miners and their wives. "They've been hospitable. We owe it to them not to abuse that hospitality."

Miller looked at him steadily. "What do you mean, Maguire?"

"We need to get that gold the hell out of here."

Spencer raised his head. "Wait a minute, Maguire. That gold's none of your concern. You're—"

Jack cut in. "It's everybody's concern, Cavanaugh. The word will get out about the gold one way or another, and then the Japs will start looking for it, and they won't give up."

"And just what do you suggest? So far as I know, the local bank's closed," Spencer said sarcastically.

Jack ignored him and turned to Billy Miller. "You're the man in charge. Do you want to endanger these civilians?"

One of the miners stepped forward. He was a huge man, well over six feet, with a leonine head and powerful arms and shoulders. "What's all this about gold?"

Miller hesitated, then said reluctantly, "We're in charge of a shipment of gold out of Corregidor."

The miner looked toward the group of cargadores. "Is that what they're carrying?"

Reluctantly, Miller nodded.

Spencer stepped forward and spoke to the miner. "We're carrying out a special mission for General Wainwright. It's critical that we protect the gold."

The miner studied Spencer for a moment, then said brusquely, "Look, we're civilians—and we have our wives with us. We've kept ahead of the Japs so far, but we don't need any extra problems. You and the rest of your party are welcome to stay with us as long as you want to—but not the gold."

Spencer flushed and turned on Jack. "You're really a brave man, aren't you, Maguire?"

It was abruptly quiet. Monkeys swung in vines near the tops of tall trees, occasionally pausing to chatter back and forth. Brilliantly colored parrots cawed loudly.

Jack Maguire tensed. A dull red flush suffused his face and neck. He lowered his head a little as a large animal will as it prepares to attack.

Catharine called out sharply. "Jack. Jack, don't."

It hung in the balance. The big miner took another step to stand between Jack and Spencer. Slowly, the color drained out of Jack's face. Then he turned his back on Spencer and again addressed Billy Miller.

"You're the man in charge. You know what I'm talking about. We've got to get the damned gold to a military camp."

The miner nodded. "We've heard of a group of guerrillas deep in the interior. There's a U.S. Army colonel in charge."

Now it was Spencer's face that turned red with anger. "Miller, it's idiotic to head out God knows where. These people are Americans. It's their duty to protect important government property."

Miller ignored Spencer. "The general would prefer that a ranking officer be in charge of the gold. We'll take it to the guerrilla camp." He looked at the miner. "Where is it?"

The miner shook his head. "A long way. A very long way."

"Do you have any maps?"

A second miner, a small, wiry man, nodded. "I do. As a matter of fact, I'll come with you. I'd like to join up with the guerrillas. And I speak enough Visayan to help us get fresh cargadores when we need them."

Miller looked at him gratefully. "We'd be glad to have you."

"We'll leave the women here," Jack said, speaking to the larger miner.

"That will be fine. We'll take good care of them."

Spencer frowned. "Of course not. We'll all stay together." He looked at Catharine. "You'll come, Catharine, won't you?"

Catharine felt the full force of Jack's gaze. His dark eyes ordered her, implored her.

She understood what he was doing. He wanted to protect her and the two nurses. He wanted to separate them from the gold and the danger it could bring. She loved him for it, but she wasn't going to be separated from him in this wild, frightening country. She was going where Jack went so long as she could lift one foot after the other. If he left her here, what kind of danger would he meet trying to retrace his steps and find her again? And these miners—they were kind and generous and willing to take them in, but if Japanese patrols came too near, they would have to uproot and flee. She could end up following these strangers deep into the interior with no way to get word to Jack.

"You will come, Catharine." Spencer spoke harshly.

"Yes." The look in Jack's eyes hurt her. "We must all stay together," she said quickly.

Jack looked at her for a long moment, shrugged then turned to Billy Miller. "We'd better get started."

Catharine felt his anger inside; it hurt more than a physical wound. She needed him, needed his support. She was frightened deep inside, frightened of the jungle, frightened of the Japanese, frightened that she couldn't stay up with all of them, do her share. She needed him now, needed him more than she ever had before. Oh, God, Jack, please don't be angry. Please understand.

She would talk to him as soon as she possibly could.

Once again, they climbed steep hills, skirted the edges of preci-pices, followed rushing mountain streams, walked until each muscle cried out for rest. Their thin cotton slacks and blouses offered little pro-tection from the cool mountain air. At night, they stopped at native huts. One room would hold all of the Bukidnon family, perhaps twelve or more, the party of Americans, their cargadores, and the gold.

Each evening, the women walked down to a stream, pulled off their muddy clothes, bathed quickly in the icy rushing water, rinsed out their clothes, and put on something clean from their packs. None of them had much to wear: a couple of pairs of slacks, blouses and underwear, and one pair of shoes, which were wearing thin. Sally had tied a cotton bandana around one foot to keep the sole attached to her shoe. Catharine cut a scarf into squares and used the soft cloth to line her shoes.

Sally squealed when she stepped into the cold water. She crouched down, splashed water on herself, and began to shiver. "I swear to God, if I ever get home to St. Louis, I'm going to sit in a hot bath for three months."

No one answered. Frances, the second nurse, was older. She'd managed to keep up, but it was with a tremendous effort.

Sally moved quickly. Hopping out, she dried off with the small, square towel that she'd tucked into her pack at the last minute before they left Corregidor, dressed quickly, then gently reached out to help Frances. "Come on, pal. Time to join the polar bear club."

Catharine stripped too, and stepped into the stream. It was so painfully cold that it took her breath away, but it felt wonderful to wash away the dirt and mud. There was always mud because the rain fell almost every day. She shared a bit of her precious soap, then helped Sally dry off Frances.

As they started back up the faint trail toward the hut where they would stay the night, Catharine said quietly to Sally, "I'll talk to Jack. We're traveling too fast for Frances."

It was almost dusk, so Catharine couldn't see Sally's face very distinctly. But she heard Sally's soft words clearly. "It's about time you talked to him, isn't it?"

The light from the quinqui wavered from the night breeze that rippled through the ill-fitting bamboo walls. Jack sat on the far side of the room, talking in slow Visayan to the village chief, the teniente. Catharine sat with her back against the ridged wall. She'd never felt more alone in her life. Every available inch of space in the one-room hut was absorbed by the party of Americans, their cargadores, and the teniente's family. Frances's elbow crowded Catharine on her right. Billy Miller's bony shoulder pushed at her from the left. The room throbbed with warmth, the smell of dirty bodies, and a pungent odor of partially cooked pork. Despite their hunger for meat, the Americans had declined the pork. They'd seen it butchered, seen the writhing mass of worms in it, and watched it sizzle for too short a time above a smoky fire. Instead, they'd eaten the hot rice and shared hard green bananas.

Catharine watched the light from the quinqui flare briefly and illuminate Jack's dark, strong face. She wondered how it could be that two people could love as they had loved, with a passion that rivaled the heat and power of an exploding volcano, and sit in a small, confined space and be as distant as the poles.

He didn't glance at her once.

She would have known. She couldn't have missed it.

Where had their love gone? Why didn't he know with an absolute, unwavering instinct that he was her heart, her soul, the only link to reality that would ever matter to her?

His face looked heavy, somber, in the uncertain light. He seemed totally intent upon his labored conversation with the flattered teniente.

Catharine couldn't see the color of his eyes in the dim light, but she didn't need to see them to remember their brilliance, the vivid aquamarine brighter and clearer than any sea. She could see the strong fullness of his shoulders, powerful arms that had once held her so gently, so lovingly.

She wanted him. She wanted to love him, to feel his lips on hers and the wonderful warmth and strength of his body. Desire pulsed within her. She tightened her hands into fists, into tight, hard balls. Couldn't he feel this current between them?

Then, just for an instant, so quickly it might never have happened, his head turned. His eyes looked across the wavering darkness at her, and Catharine knew that he wanted her, too.

Jack waited impatiently at the edge of the clearing. The Americans arranged at each night's stop for a new team of cargo carriers because the natives didn't want to go too far from their home area. The fresh cargadores leisurely began to arrange their burdens. Jack lit a second precious cigarette and knew he was squandering his small hoard. Why didn't Miller push them harder?

He drew the smoke down into his lungs, and some of his irritation dissipated. Frances was having a hard time keeping up. And what difference did it make when they reached the guerrillas? Once, it would have mattered. It might have meant he was that much nearer to being with Catharine—if she'd stayed in the miners' camp as he had intended. But Catharine hadn't stayed. None of them had stayed, so his objectives to get the damned gold away from the women, to protect them from the Japanese, wasn't being realized. What difference would it make when they reached the guerrilla camp? Not a damn bit.

Catharine had made it clear, very clear, that Spencer came first.

The cargadores had their loads arranged now and were listening to the teniente, who spoke first to Miller, then to the men.

Jack looked across the clearing. The women were climbing down the notched log ladder from the hut, Frances first, then Catharine and Sally.

It shouldn't hurt so much.

Catharine was beautiful in the soft, misty early morning light. But she was always beautiful, even when Spencer pulled her into his arms and held her as a husband may hold his wife.

Jack wanted to look away, but he couldn't. He'd managed to avoid her ever since the day they'd left the miners' camp. There wasn't anything left to say, but now, as he watched her climb down the ladder, the old excitement churned inside him. It was hell to be so near her and not be able to touch her. It would be better, far better, to be away from her. As soon as they reached the guerrilla camp, he'd break free from this group. The miners had told them the latest word. The Japanese had ordered all Americans to come into Davao. Those who didn't would be killed when they were found.

Jack finished his cigarette and walked toward the cargadores. He'd stayed close to the leader the last few days, avoiding any contact with the other Americans. Especially Catharine. He walked swiftly, then paused and felt his face grow rigid.

Catharine was walking toward him. Her face was pale, almost luminous, in the dim morning light. Her incredibly violet eyes looked enormous. Despite fatigue and hunger, her face was strikingly beautiful: the soft curve of her mouth, the high cheekbones, and deep-set eyes. He wanted to turn away. But she stood squarely in front of him, barring his way. The others moved sluggishly behind them.

There was no artifice in her face. There was only pain.

"Jack, please, don't be angry with me."

He felt unutterably tired. Wearily, he shook his head. "I'm not angry."

Tears glistened in her eyes.

He felt a hot ache in his throat.

"You've avoided me—ever since the day we crossed that broken path."

Jack looked away from her face and stared down at the uneven ground strewn with leaves, broken fronds, and pieces of bamboo. "I wanted you to stay with the miners. I wanted you to be safe," he said harshly.

"I would rather be dead than be separated from you."

His head jerked up. When Spencer was in trouble, he turned to her—and she helped him. When Spencer ordered her to come with him, she came.

His mouth would have quivered, but he held his face rigid. He swallowed once, then said shortly, violently, "Sure." Turning, he walked swiftly away, shouldering past the cargadores to start up the trail.

26

The moment came with shocking suddenness.

Jack finished his breakfast of rice with a little bit of coconut milk and looked at their missionary host, Dr. Michaels. He spoke to him directly, and there was an abrupt and complete silence among the group that had struggled together since leaving Corregidor.

"Is there any chance, sir, of finding a boat along the coast?"

Dr. Michaels was oblivious to the effect of Jack's words among his fellow refugees. The missionary considered the question, then smiled gently. "Perhaps an outrigger canoe. Everything else has been taken over or destroyed by the Japanese."

Foreboding swept Catharine. She leaned forward, her tin plate forgotten in her lap, and watched Jack's face.

There was so much power and passion in his face. He looked more alive than any man there in the dim half-light of early morning. There was a fierceness about him, the same sense of unfettered drive suggested by a hawk poised to soar.

Jack frowned. "If we could find any kind of halfway decent boat, maybe . . ."

Billy Miller interrupted, his drawl puzzled. "Man, what do we need with a boat? We're only a day's hike from the guerrilla camp."

Jack lit a cigarette, drew deeply on it, then answered mildly enough. "I'm striking out on my own from here on, Miller."

Miller frowned. "You can't do that."

Jack smiled. "Miller, I'm not in your navy. And I don't give a damn about the gold. Take it to the guerrillas. Dump it in the ocean. Do whatever you please, but count me out."

Catharine stared across the crowded sala. The missionaries and their wives listened curiously, excited by the arrival of these strangers. But the two nurses glanced at Catharine, then pretended to study their food. Spencer looked pleased.

Catharine stared at Spencer. How could he have so little understanding of her and her life? How could he not sense the enormous struggle within her?

The moment of decision had finally come. She realized that this moment would determine the course of her life. It was to be a public moment in a peculiarly private place.

Last night when it was time to plunge down into the dank, wet gully, she had been reluctant even though their new guide nodded reassuringly. The cargadores led the way as always, using their bolos to whip back the clinging tendrils that hung from the trees and shrubs. Catharine had been certain they were going into a dead end. The vegetation looked impenetrable. Catharine followed and tried to repulse a shudder at the gloom and darkness. The trail had wound down and down. They'd arrived just as night fell at the well-hidden camp of the missionaries, a cluster of five nipa huts on stilts near a rushing stream. The missionaries themselves, several families and two nurses, had greeted them cheerily. Catharine's sense of imprisonment subsided, although she slept with a feeling of dread and uneasiness.

But she hadn't imagined this moment. Nothing in her past had prepared her for this moment. She'd always avoided confrontations, though she'd come to understand since meeting Jack that her heart and mind were capable of great and sustained passion.

Jack didn't look her way when he stood and smiled down at the missionary.

"If you can loan me a guide to the coast, I'll be on my way."

"Of course, young man. We will be delighted to help out."

Spencer watched with a half-smile. He looked satisfied. It was, Catharine realized, a look she disliked intensely. Billy Miller frowned but said no more.

Slowly, Catharine stood.

Someone near her gasped. It must have been one of the nurses, Frances or Sally. Catharine heard the sound, followed by a sudden, taut silence. She was terribly aware of the hush and the startled faces turned toward her. She could feel the blood draining from her face.

Jack, too, looked across the crowded sala at her. For an instant, he seemed a distant stranger, his eyes questioning, his face somber.

They all waited.

She was a very private person, but now, in this very public moment, she must make her choice. She could not delay because she knew Jack too well. He had made his decision. He would leave the group, and he would never return.

She faced the most profound crisis of her life. Everything that she had ever known and experienced came together, with the clear understanding that her life came to nothing if she didn't follow where her heart led.

Catharine closed them all out of her consciousness. She looked at Jack across the crowded sala and spoke to him alone. "I am coming with you."

Again, as if from a far distance, she heard the sharp intake of breath and heard, too, Spencer's harsh call of her name, but she closed out the sound as she had closed out the presence of the others. She looked at Jack, waited for his answer, and knew that there need not be an answer. She saw his face, the face of a man who no longer believed in miracles and was watching a miracle happen.

There was for that moment in the nipa hut, so far from safety and from the reality of life as they'd known it, a clarity and greatness that could never be surpassed.

She was moving across the congested space when Spencer grabbed her arm and jerked her around to face him. An angry red flush stained his face; his mouth twisted in fury. "You can't do this, Catharine. You can't make a fool of me, do you hear?"

Catharine knew Jack was lunging forward. She held up a hand to stop him as she pulled free of Spencer's grip. She looked at her husband and felt a surge of anger. So this was Spencer's feeling—concern for his status, for his standing. It was as it had always been. He didn't love her. She had been an accomplished, useful, decorative wife and once a mother—nothing more. She felt free—no matter what society might think or say. She owed Spencer nothing more.

"You are making a fool of yourself," she rejoined quietly. "What I do or where I go is no concern of yours, Spencer, not anymore."

"You are still my wife." He rasped the words.

"We have not been husband and wife for many years," she said wearily, hating this public exchange but determined to be honest for Jack's sake.

"The fellow's a boor, a second-rate, seedy newspaperman."

"He's the finest, bravest man I've ever known. I love him—and I'm going with him." Her words hung clearly in the stillness of the sala. Catharine struggled across the crowded room and realized that some of the missionaries frowned darkly and drew away as she passed. She lifted her chin, looked at Jack, and reached out to take his hand.

They climbed down the ladder of the hut. When they stood on the ground, he pulled her into his arms, and his smile exploded.

"You're wonderful. I always knew you were wonderful, but that was magnificent, Catharine."

He gave her a quick, hard hug, then took her hand and turned toward the faint path that plunged into the heavy growth.

"Where are we going?" she called out.

Jack was still grinning. "Hell, I don't know, but it doesn't matter, not so long as you're with me."

Catharine didn't hesitate, and she didn't look back at the nipa huts.

She didn't pause either at the sound of Spencer's angry voice shouting her name. She was only a few feet up the jungle path when the sound was gone, lost and muted in the tropical growth.

The barrio was deserted. Not even a single pig wallowed in the heavy mud at the edge of the clearing.

Jack paused where the trail flared into the clearing, one hand up to keep Catharine behind, the other raised with his bolo held high.

It was eerily quiet, the light filtering through the tall trees, shining down in slanted bars of silver, falling across the nipa huts that had the unmistakable air of abandonment.

Catharine watched tensely as Jack moved soft-footed through the clearing and cautiously checked each hut. Their cargadores waited with her at the edge of the clearing. When Jack returned, he made no effort to be quiet. He stopped beside one hut and knelt. Catharine joined him and looked down, too.

He was staring at a print in the soft ground, the small, mitten-shaped print of a tennis shoe.

He looked up at her. "Japs," he said briefly.

Catharine said nothing, but she wondered how long the print had been there. Had the Japanese been here since the brief shower that morning?

Catharine looked around the ominously quiet clearing. She'd learned to know barrios as they trudged up to mountain heights and down again to the coast in search of escape. The tribesmen always welcomed them, shared what they had, and looked shyly but with great interest at Catharine. She'd learned to expect the solemn gazes of the children when she took quick plunges into mountain streams to bathe. She'd become accustomed to the giggles of the younger wives and the shy friendliness of the older women, but this was the first time they'd entered a barrio to find no one, only the sharp call of the macaws and the occasional chatter of treetop monkeys.

Their head cargadore, Vincente, frowned. "We can't stay here."

"It's all right now," Jack replied.

"I don't like it either," Catharine said uneasily. "Jack, what are we going to do?"

The cargadores were busy making a fire. It would be their usual lunch: boiled rice and boiled coffee with a fresh banana for dessert.

"I think I'd better take a look ahead."

Catharine pushed away from the bole of the coconut tree. "I'll go with you."

"No." At her quick frown, he explained. "This is just a reconnaissance, Catharine. I can move more quietly by myself with Vincente. You'll be safer here. I'll post a look-out."

She understood the logic, but she didn't like it. She hated this ghostly, deserted barrio. There was nothing but silence and the imprint of a Japanese sneaker on the damp earth.

Catharine felt a wave of despair when Jack and Vincente left, but she smiled and raised a hand in farewell. She was being foolish, a combination of fatigue and fear. It was certainly good to have an afternoon to rest, and Jack and Vincente could move faster without all of them. They would find a boat, and she and Jack would be on their way. She pushed aside her memory of the Pacific and its endless empty space. What kind of boat could Jack find that would be seaworthy enough to get them to Australia? How would they sail it? He would have to find, too, a navy man willing to risk the journey. That, perhaps, would be the easiest task of all. The island, with all its incredible wilderness, was a refuge for growing numbers of Americans, including the army and navy men who had ignored Wainwright's order to surrender.

Perhaps they were only hours away from escaping the Philippines. Catharine wandered aimlessly around the barrio. Perhaps it had been a prosperous small community. There were almost a dozen huts on stilts. She wondered where all of its citizens had fled. Her walk reinforced her sense of oppression. The cargadores had doused the fire and were stretched out asleep in the shade of a hut, except for Pilo serving as a sentry. Catharine hesitated, then climbed up the ladder of one of the huts, where there was a broad bamboo sleeping platform against the back wall. She crossed to it and sank gratefully down. She smiled a little as she drifted into sleep.

It was a sound that woke her, brought her upright, one hand tight against her throat: a mélange of noises, the thudding of feet, a frantic thrashing through thick undergrowth, shouts, a high, broken-off scream.

Catharine knew even before she flattened herself to one side of the opening to look down into the clearing. From her height, she could see perfectly. She could see the blood welling from the throat of Pilo, her favorite among the cargadores, a slender, laughing young man who liked to whistle American songs. Now he wavered on his feet; his hands came slowly up to try and staunch the flow of blood. The Japanese soldier raised his sword, swung again, and Pilo's head rocketed backwards to bounce against the hard-packed dirt.

The sun-drenched, blood-splotched clearing wavered in her sight. Catharine pressed hard against the side of the nipa wall, knowing what must come, knowing with a growing horror that they would find her. She would be a woman and an enemy for them to do with as they chose; she had no means of protection, no way of resisting.

A noise close at hand, a sound of movement very near, a small crackle obtruded over the shouts in the clearing below.

Her head turned. She froze, an animal's instinct; the horror in the clearing was transcended by the horror so close at hand.

The cobra, patterned a brilliant black and yellow, moved slowly across the outside wall of the hut, then paused at the doorway. Its hooded head swayed gently in the rectangular opening.

"You must go back up into the mountains." The teniente looked nervously over his shoulder. "The Japanese are everywhere, all up and down the coast. They are driving the people from their barrios, capturing Americans, and putting them into camps. I would not be here myself, but I had to come back to get some medicine for my old mother. You must go back up into the mountains." The teniente spoke with finality.

Jack wiped the back of his hand across his cheek. It was sweltering in the seacoast barrio. Beyond the barrier reef lay the surging Pacific and, thirteen hundred miles away, Australia and safety.

"A boat," Jack began.

The teniente didn't even bother to answer. He just shook his head. "No boats," he said again with that tired finality. "They sank them all. You must go back up into the mountains."

Jack and Vincente took time to get some supplies—a sack of rice and some peanuts. They didn't talk as they toiled back up the trail toward the barrio where they had left the others.

It was Vincente who was in the lead and saw first. He gave a cry, a deep, tearing cry, at the sight of his younger brother, Pilo. Vincente ran, flung himself down, and, rocking back and forth on his haunches, stared at the severed head, covered now with clusters of flies and maggots.

Jack burst past him, thundered into the clearing, and saw the splotches of blood, drying pools now, and the bodies.

"Catharine, oh, God, Catharine!"

He plunged from the nearer bodies to the second and knew she wasn't there. His mind filled with ghastly pictures of Catharine with the Japanese and what they would have done to her.

"Jack," whispered a strangely taut and careful voice.

He stood very still. Was his mind gone now, too burdened by horror to accept the truth? Then it came again, the restricted and fearful call of his name.

"Jack. The middle hut. Look." The words were even, toneless.

He looked up then, saw the hut, and didn't see Catharine; but hanging in the doorway, the enormous black and yellow cobra swayed nervously.

Jack slowly started forward, pulling free his rifle as he walked.

The cobra saw him; the hood expanded to its full extent.

Jack walked slowly, so slowly, but he was determined to be close enough that his shot couldn't miss. The cobra swayed back and forth, excited, angry, sensing a threat.

The words, higher now, louder, spilled from the open doorway.

"Be careful. They can spit venom."

The cobra's head began to turn, seeking the source of noise behind it.

Jack brought the rifle up in one smooth movement, sighted, and pulled the trigger. The explosive sound reverberated in the clearing, and the cobra's hood blew apart.

When Catharine was in his arms, neither of them spoke. They

clung to each other, held to each other. Slowly, strength began to flow between them.

"I'm sorry," he said finally. "I should never have left you."

"If you'd been here, you'd be . . ." She didn't say it, didn't want to face it, put the horror into words. Tonelessly, she told him what had happened, how the Japanese soldiers had laughed as they killed the last of the men in the clearing, then started to search the huts.

"The cobra stopped them. They left when they saw the cobra."

"How long was it before we came?" Jack asked.

"An hour."

An hour of terror, waiting for the cobra to crawl into the hut, drawn by the heat of her skin, an hour when all that saved her from death was absolute will.

Jack took her hand in his.

"What are we going to do?" she asked.

He looked at Catharine, her face pale and strained, and he managed a grin. "Well, kid, it looks like we missed the last boat, so we're going to take a trip to the mountains."

A trip to the mountains—it meant days more of slogging along trails, hoping to avoid Japanese patrols, negotiating narrow paths, skirting crevasses, hiding, hunting for food, always one step away from disaster, not knowing where they were going or what lay ahead.

Or what would happen when they got there.

27

Jenny held up the worn cotton blouse, once white, now a kind of bluish gray. "If I scrub it one more time, it's going to disintegrate." Then she grinned. "What the well-dressed refugee wears—any damn thing she can lay her hands on."

Catharine smiled and used a tiny swipe of soap on her own blouse. The icy mountain stream swirled past; her hands tingled from the cold, but it was pleasant to joke with Jenny as they did their morning wash. She and Jack were fortunate to have found this group of mining engineers and their wives. They'd been with them for almost a week now, sleeping in the sala of the hut that belonged to Jenny and her husband, Calvin Mackey, and their young son, Roger. The Mackeys, in their early thirties, were friendly, cheerful, and unshakably optimistic. Jenny was a languid redhead who managed to accomplish a great deal of work in their primitive camp without looking as though she was exerting herself. Her husband spent his free time studying a dog-eared map of the province, trying to determine where would be the best spot for an American landing, which Catharine considered the acme of positive thinking.

It was communal living. Catharine hated imposing on the Mackeys, taking away the privacy which she knew must mean so much to them. Jack had hired workers from a nearby tribe who were putting up a hut for them.

When they moved in, they would be alone for the first time since they left Corregidor. She remembered those snatched hours, hours gouged out of time in an exploding hell, but hours that would always be precious in her memory. As she scrubbed away on the blouse, forgetting she had only that tiny piece of soap, she wished she could be beautiful for Jack. Her slacks were ragged; her blouse was paper thin. Catharine didn't even have a mirror anymore. She'd lost so much in these months on the trail. She knew she was far too thin. Her hair hung in a thick, unruly braid down her back because her hair had gone so long without being cut. She squeezed the blouse and spread it to dry beside Jenny's wash on the sun-warm rocks. As she began to wash a shirt of Jack's, she asked abruptly, "Jenny, do you have any lipstick?"

Jenny looked up in surprise, then with sudden understanding said, "Sure. I'm saving it to celebrate liberation, but I'd be glad to share."

Catharine already regretted her impulsive question. None of them had extra of anything. It wasn't right to expect this newfound friend to share. "No, no. I just wondered. I wouldn't want..."

Jenny was already digging into the pocket of her shorts. "Look. Here are my prizes." She pulled out a half-dozen bobby pins; a tiny vial of perfume; a compact with an unbroken mirror, which she proudly displayed; and a lipstick, which she uncapped. The smooth, dark red gloss shone like a ruby.

"I can cut it in half..."

Catharine refused that largesse and finally accepted a sliver of the lipstick when Jenny agreed to take four cigarettes.

They laughed as they made their trade. Jenny confirmed Catharine's estimate of her generosity when she promptly offered Catharine a cigarette.

Catharine shook her head. "That's not fair. You keep it for Calvin."

"Oh, he doesn't smoke, which is marvelous because I get all he finds. Come on, take one, and let's have a smoke."

They dried their hands and stretched out comfortably on the bank of the stream in a patch of sunlight.

Jenny blew a light stream of smoke into the sunlight, watched it dissipate, then said teasingly, "Are you planning a second honeymoon?"

It was a good-natured question, a light relief from the underlying fear that marked their days. Catharine's hand paused in midair, and her cigarette burned for a long moment. The silence expanded, and Jenny suddenly flushed.

"Sorry," she said in confusion. "I didn't mean to offend you."

Impulsively, Catharine reached out and touched Jenny's arm. "You didn't offend me. It's just . . . I don't know exactly what to say." She took a deep breath, then said quickly, "Jack and I aren't married."

"But I thought he said . . ." Then Jenny's face matched her flaming hair. She sputtered and tried again. "I mean, golly, that's all right." She heard herself say that, found it wanting, and started over. "For heaven's sake, I don't care."

There was no censure in Jenny's voice, only warmth and an eagerness to be supportive. For the first time in a long time, Catharine began to relax. Sitting on the warm rocks, she told Jenny about Jack. When she was finished, when she had told all of it, including the hard truth that Spencer, her husband, was in a camp only a few miles from here with the nurses and the missionary group, she looked reluctantly at Jenny.

"Don't be defensive," Jenny said abruptly, her voice clear and certain. "You've done your best, Catharine. It isn't as though Spencer loved you. I know you feel guilty, but if we were home, you would get a divorce and marry Jack. We aren't home." Some of the life seeped from her face. "We may never be home again, so don't regret this chance to love Jack. When it comes down to it, there isn't anything in life that matters but love."

It was just before sunset when Catharine and Jack moved the last of their goods into their new hut, which sat almost a hundred yards from that of the Mackeys. They ate dinner with the Mackeys, then walked slowly up the dusty path to their own hut.

Catharine felt unaccountably shy. It had been so long, so very long since she and Jack had been alone. For so many weeks now, there had always been someone else present: their traveling companions, the cargadores, Americans with whom they stayed as they plunged deeper into the interior. As she climbed up the ladder and stepped into the hut, she turned to watch Jack duck through the low doorway.

He was too thin. She must insist that he eat more, but he was always so careful to see that she and any others had full plates. She sometimes felt as if she were being buried in a mountain of rice and fruit, but they must be grateful for the fruit. Someone had heard through the jungle grapevine of the hideous condition of the prisoners at the Davao Penal Colony, where hundreds of American and British prisoners of war were being held. The men were suffering from scurvy, rickets, and beriberi— all symptoms of an inadequate diet.

"You're too thin," she blurted out, then felt like a fool. Was that the best she could do the first moment they were alone together?

His prominent bones jutted beneath his skin; his shirt hung loosely on his large, now spare, frame.

"You can fatten me up, Catharine. I've arranged for a native to bring us chickens when he can. Can you do something with chickens?"

She glanced at the native stove at the far end of the room and nodded.

They stood only a few feet apart in the fresh-smelling hut and stared at each other; neither knew what to say.

Jack reached out his hand. "I love you. I promise I'll make you a real home someday."

She moved then, stepped into his arms, and smiled up at him. "Oh, Jack, you Chicago fool, I don't care about that. All I care about is you."

He stared down at her, a quizzical look in his eyes. "You know, that's funny, but I know you really mean it. You've lived in finer houses than I could ever have and you don't care, do you?"

"And I never will."

She looked up at him, at his dear face, his dear, thin face, the strong nose accentuated now, his jaws protruding, his dark eyes sunken, but she didn't see the deprivation or fatigue. She saw a love tough enough to last a lifetime, however long or short that might be.

She reached up and gently stroked his cheek. His hand caught hers and brought it to his mouth. He kissed the palm of her hand, and sudden tears stung her eyes.

"Love me, Jack," she said softly.

"Did I ever tell you I was the luckiest man in the world?" he asked.

She shook her head.

"I am. I fell in love with the loveliest woman in the world, and she loves me back. No man can be luckier than that."

Lucky. That was how he felt and, she realized, how she felt. Here they were, refugees in a strange land, subject to death if captured, yet both of them rejoiced in each other, knowing that these moments, this kind of love, were the essence of life. Together they could meet the uncertain future, no matter what happened.

As the last shafts of sunlight speared through the doorway, Jack picked her up and carried her to the bamboo sleeping platform against the far wall. When he stood beside it, he held her and looked down rue-fully. "This won't be the most comfortable bed we've shared."

"It will be wonderful," she said softly. Her hands reached up to bring his face down, her mouth sought his, and she gloried in the touch of his lips and the taste of his mouth. She felt a sweep of sheer happiness, the kind of happiness that only rarely touches human lives.

When they lay together, their clothes tossed aside, and she felt the long length of his body, she laughed softly. He paused from touching her shoulder with the tip of his tongue and looked at her in surprise.

"I'm so happy," she said simply. "Oh, Jack, I was afraid today. It had been so long, and I feel that I'm ugly. My hair is wild, and I'm too thin."

"Ugly!"

She laughed again at the outrage in his voice.

"Ugly. Why, Catharine, you will always be lovely, always—now, tomorrow, years from now."

There was an Irish lilt in his voice. Again, she felt the heat of tears in her eyes.

He caressed her, murmuring her name, and she stroked his back and tasted of his cheek. Then his hands were not so gentle but triumphant and urgent. She felt the heat of his passion and welcomed him in a wild and joyous union.

Spencer leaned forward, his light blue eyes intent, accusing. "There isn't sufficient security."

Frank MacPherson's teammates on a Georgia rural football team in 1928 described him as built like a cement outhouse with a personality to match. He hadn't changed much since then. They would have recognized the way he hunched his blunt, square head on his bull-like shoulders. "You got a key to some safety deposit box?" he rasped.

Spencer's narrow patrician face stiffened. He lifted his head. "This shipment is important, very important. It is of the highest priority."

MacPherson shook his head like a bull irritated by gnats. "Mister, I got men with malaria. I got Japanese patrols busting their guts to find us. I got women and children to protect. You tell me gold is important. Important to who?"

"The Department of State," Spencer replied.

MacPherson lit one cigarette from the stub of another. He had to find quinine, somewhere, somehow, and this ass wanted to talk about gold. Well, he knew what Spencer could do with the gold.

"You don't like the security here?" MacPherson demanded. He didn't wait for an answer. "I'll tell you what, sonny, you take your gold and put it wherever you want. Okay?"

Miller, standing to the side of the log-built table in the guerrilla's clearing, moved restively, but MacPherson ignored him. Then Miller shrugged. What difference did it make? He'd done his job as commanded by Wainwright. He'd brought the gold as far as he could and delivered it to the care of the ranking officer, Colonel Frank MacPherson. That was as far as Miller's writ ran, and, frankly, he felt the same way about the gold. Let Spencer have it.

Spencer's entire demeanor changed. He smiled at the colonel. "That's good news, sir. Don't worry—I'll take very good care of the shipment. " He turned and gestured toward the lead cargadore. He'd get the stuff hidden better than it was here.

That night, stopping along the trail and staying with a Bukidnon family, he was too elated to feel his usual sense of disgust at the dirt and poverty of his hosts. He ignored the betel-stained lips of the adults, smiled graciously, and accepted rice for dinner. His mind still whirled with feelings of triumph. He would write Peggy and tell her all about it. She would see how well he'd handled the situation.

Peggy . . . As darkness fell and he rolled up against the side of the sala wall to sleep, he felt a wash of longing. It been so long since he'd seen her. That last night on Corregidor when she left by sub was in April. Now it was sometime in October. How long would it be before he saw her again?

With gas rationing, private cars were few and far between on the roads. They had to stop for a long troop train just outside of town. Peggy looked occasionally at Rowley's profile as he drove up the narrow, winding road on Lookout Mountain. She felt a rush of tenderness. Rowley was so patient and kind and generous. He was using his gas to take her for an outing, saying she needed some fresh air. She couldn't spend all her time at the Red Cross rolling bandages, especially now. That was as near as he came to making any comment about her pregnancy. He didn't ask her about her "husband." She wondered if he would turn away from her if he knew the truth. Peggy sighed, leaned back against the car seat, and closed her eyes. Sometimes she didn't think she could keep on going, but there was the baby growing inside of her. She clung to the thought of that new life.

When Rowley parked the car and got the basket out of the back, they found a picnic area that looked out over the lemon yellow and fiery orange of the Smoky Mountains in their October glory. It was a peaceful hour. They didn't talk of much, but it was as healing to Peggy's spirit as balm. She had a wonderful feeling that everything someday would be all right. She didn't know how or where or when, but the feeling was there, and she smiled at Rowley.

Catharine had known for several weeks, but she didn't tell Jack. She wasn't altogether certain why she didn't tell him. She knew it was a mixture of reasons: love, fear, and an almost superstitious reluctance

to put it into words. Then she made a pact with herself; she would tell
him after Thanksgiving.

They had fled their hut along with the other residents of their
refugee camp twice in the last two months, each time because the
jungle grapevine warned of a Japanese probe. Twice, the rumors had
been false, and they'd returned and celebrated their homecoming with
the Mackeys and the Contis, another mining family that had a hut a
hundred yards away on the other side of the clearing.

Each time, they'd crossed paths with the missionary group,
Spencer, and the two nurses. Each time, Catharine and Jack had moved
on farther to avoid them, although Jack objected. "What the hell,
Catharine, let them stick up their noses. We don't care."

She wouldn't discuss it because she knew Jack didn't understand.
Perhaps it was growing up in Pasadena, perhaps it was still a niggling
sense of failure and betrayal, but she didn't want to face the disap-
proving glances. Still . . .

A Filipino in a barrio down the mountain had promised them a big
turkey for Thanksgiving and Jack had gone to get it. Catharine tried to push
away the internal dialogue that absorbed her these days. She had to tell Jack.

It was a year ago at Thanksgiving that she sat with no appetite at
the heaped table at the U.S. Residence and tried to smile cheerfully,
but her every thought was with Jack. The next day, they'd taken turkey
sandwiches, gone to the beach, and made love in the sun-spangled
afternoon. She could never have imagined at that time what lay before
them: the horror of Corregidor, their escape, this nomadic existence
on Mindanao, hoping to evade capture by the Japanese, praying that
someday the American forces would return.

She would never have imagined either that she could have found
the courage to leave her husband publicly—but it wasn't a matter of
courage, she knew that. It was a matter of her own survival. No matter
what the cost, she had to be with Jack.

The hut quivered, and she knew he was back and climbing the
ladder. He poked his head in the opening. "Come on down and see
the bird."

When Catharine climbed down, she saw Paco, the Mackey's cook, holding an enormous turkey carcass.

The Mackeys looked out of their hut, grinning, the Contis were coming up the trail from their hut.

Jack pointed at the turkey. "Okay, ladies, here he is. The finest turkey available. I'm confident that when you ladies have finished with him, our dinner will rival dinner at the Waldorf."

"Do you sell stock in gold mines, too?" Jenny Mackey drawled.

Jack looked at her reproachfully. "Ye of little faith. This is going to be our most unforgettable Thanksgiving." He pulled his pack around from his back and propped it on his knee to open. "For example..." One by one, he pulled out, with appropriate pauses for exclamations of admiration, a small bottle of pickled olives, two cans of green beans, one can of condensed milk, and, miracle of miracles, a tin of coffee.

Catharine, too, was caught up in the laughter as well as the preparations. She and the other women started the turkey baking at dawn in their green-wood oven. They boiled camotes and baked a cake, which they frosted with the whipped condensed milk.

When the two families, Catharine, and Jack sat down to their Thanksgiving dinner in the Mackeys' sala, just before midafternoon, Calvin Mackey said grace: "Dear God, thank you on this very wonderful day for our safety. Help us to go forward and do all such good works as you have in store for us. Bless this food for our sustenance and us to thy service. In Jesus Christ's name, amen."

It was, Catharine thought, an unforgettable day. After weeks of rice and more rice, with an occasional chicken and eggs, it was a celebration indeed to eat the baked turkey and to share the small servings of canned green beans and the heaping mounds of fluffy camotes. They finished with the cake and dark, thick coffee that, to their deprived senses, could certainly match any served at the Waldorf.

Dishwashing was brief. They carried their tin plates to the nearby stream and dipped them down to wash away the few leftover crumbs. Then the three couples lounged comfortably in the Mackeys' sala and talked politics—was Roosevelt really the best man for the job?—and plotted the Pacific campaign while the Mackeys' son tirelessly chased the Contis' daughter around the clearing.

It was almost dusk when Jack and Catharine walked hand in hand up the path toward their hut. Catharine walked slowly. Her footsteps lagged.

Jack paused. "What's wrong, honey? Are you tired?"

She looked up, but the brilliant setting sun was in her eyes. She couldn't see his face clearly. No, she wasn't tired. She was gathering her courage because now she had to tell Jack.

28

As she spoke, everything happened in dreamlike, slow motion.

Jack stared at her.

Catharine felt a kind of shriveling inside, a sense of empty despair and utter aloneness. Was he shocked or, even worse, repelled? Why in God's name did he look at her like that, his face almost waxen in the smooth yellow light. When he moved, it seemed to Catharine that he moved so slowly. He rose and walked toward her. Oh, God, he was holding out his arms. In the paleness of his face, she could see eyes shining with tears—and tenderness.

Jack wanted to shout, to rampage through the wilderness to seek safety for Catharine. He knew there was no safety, and now there was worse danger for her. Yet, it was danger that spelled the miracle of creation, danger that could bring forth a human life, his son or daughter, the child he had never expected to have.

"Oh, God," he said softly, breathing into the soft darkness of her hair, so aware of her body and its vulnerability. "Oh, dear God, Catharine." He cradled her face in his hands and looked down at her. He couldn't talk; he could only stand there and wonder how he could protect her, realizing that he couldn't. For once in his life, in his brash, irreverent life, he could struggle and fight to no avail because the days would pass and the ultimate reality of life and death would be Catharine's to face.

"It's all right. Jack, it's all right." Her voice was high and tremulous; he realized she was comforting him.

He put his face down against hers, felt the softness and warmth of her cheek. "I love you," he said huskily. "I love you so much." That was all he could offer, all he could give in return for the miracle of creation, but through a haze of tears he could see the joy in her smile. He knew that as paltry as he felt his offering to be, it was enough for Catharine.

Jack was so careful of her. He helped carry the clothes to the mountain stream and insisted upon doing the washing himself. He foraged down the mountain for food, more food. He went as far as the coast, seeking medicines and canned milk and cotton to use for baby clothes.

She was so thin that even as she reached the sixth month of pregnancy, there was little to show. Jack redoubled his efforts to find food, and he wouldn't listen to her pleas to stay close.

"You've got to have more food, Catharine. The baby needs it."

When the baby first kicked, she held his hand to her swollen abdomen and he grinned in delight. "He's going to be a punter."

By the eighth month, she was heavy and slow-moving. But she seemed almost to blossom as the time grew nearer. And, no matter how awkwardly she moved, Jack watched and smiled, his eyes filled with love and pride—and fear.

The days passed, and Catharine knew the time was almost upon her.

Catharine lifted her head to look through the doorway. God, if it would only stop raining. Torrential rains had slammed against the peaked roof of the hut for almost a week now. Jack had been gone since the day before the rains began. She always smiled as he left, assured him she would be fine. As soon as he was gone, as soon as there was no rustle of movement on the trail, she would lie down on the sleeping platform, close her eyes, and try to will away the terror that weakened her bones and made ugly pictures in her mind. She could be brave when Jack was there, when she could reach out and touch his hand, when she could see him turning to look at her. But when he was gone, the fear prowled in her mind like a starved animal, ravenous to destroy.

She was terribly afraid.

Her labor with Charles had been difficult. She'd been in labor twenty hours; she'd heard, through the grinding pain, one doctor call to another, "I can't get this baby!" Charles was born with angry bruises on his cheeks, and the doctor told her later, "Well, you're a lucky girl. If you'd lived a hundred years ago, we'd have lost you—and the baby, too."

There would be neither doctors nor forceps this time.

Catharine pushed herself awkwardly up from the camp chair. It had been one of Jack's prize acquisitions. He'd found it at an abandoned plantation and carried it miles through the jungle to her because she had such difficulty trying to sit on the sleeping platform. She moved heavily toward the kitchen. It was time to fix her dinner. She no longer had nausea, but she had very little appetite. She must eat, so she did. Sometimes, she felt if she ever saw rice again she would be actively ill, but that was all she had. She put on the water to boil and measured out the brown rice, then turned to look toward the doorway. Thank God, the rain was easing. She would go down the ladder in a little while and walk to the stream—perhaps do the washing. It helped to keep busy and disregard the fact that the baby would be coming in just a month now, if her calculations were correct. Sally had come twice to check her and to give advice. She'd promised to come and help when Catharine went into labor, but Jack wasn't satisfied. This last trip was to see if he couldn't find a doctor. Also, they'd heard a rumor that there was a store of baby formula at another refugee camp, and Catharine begged him to try and obtain some. She was afraid she couldn't nurse, and there was no milk available. In reality, her fears were darker than that. If she didn't survive the labor, then Jack must have something to feed the baby.

Catharine put a lid on the rice pot and reached out to hold onto a roof pole. She was tired now, always tired, and it was difficult to move. They had fled three times ahead of Japanese search parties. The last escape from the probing Japanese patrols had been a nightmare, a fighting struggle along sticky clay trails while the rains battered against them, but Jack had been determined to get as far away from known Japanese search areas as possible. The Mackeys and Contis had moved, too, but not as far as she and Jack. Catharine missed the women. It would be nice to see them again and play bridge and talk about silk stockings and movies and shopping in grocery stores. She was smiling as she lifted the lid to check the rice; then she sighed. She was lonely, and the fear that haunted her was much worse when she was alone. Surely Jack would get back tonight.

The ladder which led up to the doorway always gave a little under the pressure of a climber. There had been no call such as Jack usually gave, but Catharine recognized the sudden jolting quiver of the hut and turned, a smile beginning to grow.

The light from the quinqui wavered fitfully in the currents of air that moved through the nipa leaves of the walls. The quinqui didn't give much light, but it gave enough to illuminate the sala and the doorway, which had been a frame for the misty grayness of the rain. Now it framed the head and upper torso of the Japanese soldier staring nearsightedly into the room. The gold rims of his glasses glittered in the soft light of the quinqui. He had a rounded face and a broad, flattened nose, but it was the eyes, magnified behind the thick lenses, that mesmerized Catharine. The eyes burned with lust and cruelty.

He walked slowly toward her, his lips spread in a loose smile. His uniform was wet. Little spatters of dampness sprayed out as he began to unbutton his pants. His rifle hung over his shoulder. He reached up and dropped it behind him with an impatient shrug.

Catharine pressed back against the far wall of the kitchen area. She licked her lips. Oh, God, the gun, the .45 that Jack had taught her to use, was across the room on the floor beside the sleeping platform. The soldier was between her and the gun and coming inexorably nearer.

He would kill her baby.

If he threw her down, if he raped her, he would kill her baby. The baby was nearly due. She often felt the baby's movements now, abrupt, thumping kicks that made her gasp.

He gave a little laugh. Saliva oozed from the corners of his loose lips. He was so near she could smell weeks of sweat and dirt. His pudgy hands came towards her.

The fear moved in her with a vitality and life of its own—the fear for her baby. She moved awkwardly. The heat of the cooking pot seared her hands, but she gripped it, raised it, and flung the boiling water and rice at the soldier's face.

He screamed and raised his hands to his face. Catharine plunged past him but careened into a box of stones and lost her balance. As she fell, she tried to protect her swollen abdomen. She landed heavily on her hip, wrenching her back but she was moving, sobbing and struggling for breath.

She was almost to the sleeping platform when he was beside her. He bellowed and kicked. Unendurable pain exploded in the side of her leg. Even as she screamed, her hand found the little pile of clothing that covered the gun. She clawed for the gun despite the agony of using her hands. She loosened the safety catch, aimed, and pulled the trigger.

The explosion jolted her arm. There was an eddy of cordite, a burning stench, and the smell of blood. The blood spurted in a high arc. Her shot had blown through his throat. His stocky body slumped tiredly to the floor, his eyes glazing into emptiness.

Catharine stared in horror. She leaned to one side and vomited, gagging and retching until she could vomit no longer. Tears furrowed down her face; the pain in her hands and leg throbbed.

Finally, sick and filled with pain, she struggled to her feet and stared down at him. She still cried, but she stared down at him, unrelenting, because he would have killed her baby. Her chest heaving, she walked unsteadily toward the doorway. Was he alone? Were there others with him? No one had come at the racketing sound of the shot. He must have been alone or ahead of his company, perhaps a forward scout.

The horror shifted now in the back of her mind. Had they found Jack? Was Jack dead?

Catharine held onto the rough-edged frame of the doorway and stared out into the misty clearing. The rain was almost over now.

The heavy fronds of a fern rustled to the right. Catharine whirled around and raised the .45, then sighed and sagged against the doorframe when a slender boy ran into the clearing. He had brought them chickens, an occasional bag of rice, and, sometimes, news of the Japanese patrols.

He paused at the foot of the ladder. "Miss, you must hurry and go away. The Japs are burning and killing. They're coming this way."

"Where are they coming from?"

He pointed to the south.

From the south. That was where Spencer, the American nurses, and some of the missionary families were hidden.

"There are other Americans. That way." She pointed. "Will you warn them?"

He shook his head. "No time," he called. "No time. I must go tell my family." He turned and ran to the west.

Catharine called after him, but he was already gone.

The Japs were coming, and Spencer and his companions didn't know.

It was hard to turn back into the bloodied room where they had been happy, but she limped around the grotesque figure of the dead soldier. She worked swiftly even though her burned hands stung. First, she wrote a note to Jack and pinned it to the nipa wall beside the opening for the door. He couldn't miss it. If he came . . . But she had no time now to think of that. She stuffed essentials into a basket: the little vial of painkiller and the single hypodermic that Sally had given her, some twine and scissors. All the while, her mind refused to think of going into childbirth, alone on the trail. But the fear throbbed inside. She stared at the basket. *What else, what else, think, dammit, Catharine, think!* Matches, a blue enamel basin, the little pile of diapers and two little blankets made from a tablecloth for which Jack had traded his pocketknife, the precious box of boric acid powder to use to clean the baby's eyes, the Mercurochrome, a change of clothing for herself and Jack, cold rice—and the.45.

It was awkward maneuvering down the ladder, its rungs still slick from the rain, while carrying the basket, but Catharine twisted sideways and took her time.

She paused at the edge of the clearing. A faint trail led to the west, the way Jack had gone, the way to safety—but she turned south, plunging into the thick foliage. Pushing vines and ferns out of her way, she found the trail and plunged ahead.

It was dark now, and she estimated she must be very near Spencer's camp.

Then pain burst within her without warning. She reached out helplessly and clung to a twisted rope of thick vines.

29

"God, please." Catharine said aloud, her voice harsh and deep. "Don't let me lose my baby—please."

She knew that pain, that deep, wrenching, pulsing pain. The pain eased, fell away. Panting, Catharine tried to walk. God, she had to walk. Tears burned down her face. She didn't try to wipe them away; she just kept on walking, one heavy, limping footfall after another. The trail widened, and she was in the clearing. A faint, luminous glow of light was hanging above her from a quinqui in a hut.

"Spencer." Her hoarse, desperate call pierced the quiet of the night.

A pale beam from a flashlight cut through the darkness.

Catharine shielded her eyes and stared up. "The Japs. They're coming."

Pain jolted her again; she bent over, clutching the basket.

The match flame wavered in the breeze. Jack shielded it with his hand.

The words were scrawled hugely on the piece of cloth: "Japs. Gone to warn Spencer and girls. Then to west."

No salutation. No signature.

He looked inside the hut, at the disarray and signs of hurried flight, and at the stiffening body of the soldier.

He'd come from the west. He knew he wouldn't have missed her. When had she left? He'd met a Filipino an hour from their hut who told him of the Japanese search party.

Catharine had gone the way they were coming.

Jack clattered down the ladder and set off in the direction of

Spencer's camp, running, thrashing through the night, his heavy pack banging against his back.

Flames crackled against the night sky. Jack crawled on his belly, slowly, and felt the heat. He strained to see through the swirl of smoke. When he did see, he felt such a rush of rage that for a moment he thought his head would explode.

The bodies were piled in a heap close to the nearest burning hut. Jack recognized one of them: Billy Tremartin, the three-year-old son of a missionary couple. Then Jack saw the bodies of Paul and Polly Tremartin. When the soldier had finished with Polly, he had taken his bayonet and rammed it into her.

Jack buried his face in his hands, but he couldn't blot out the images of horror: elderly Mrs. Farris, her skirt bunched around her ample waist, her legs sprawled wide; her husband, his chest pulpy from the bayonet thrusts.

It took Jack an agonizing fifteen minutes to be certain that Catharine wasn't a part of the carnage—not Catharine, Spencer, or the nurses. Catharine must have reached them and warned them. Why the missionaries hadn't fled, he didn't know. But he had one hope of finding Catharine and the others. One word—west.

Sally Brainard clutched the .45 pistol. She lay on a tilted slab of rock overlooking the trail. She didn't know how to shoot a gun or reload it, but she was going to kill anyone who came near them. When she heard a machete flailing through the vines, she stiffened, aimed the gun, and waited.

The misty, half-seen light of dawn filtered grayly through the canopy of immense trees. Sally narrowed her eyes. Then she drew her breath in sharply because she heard Catharine's scream. It rose with a sob, then cut off to nothing. The baby must almost be here, but Sally mustn't think about that now; she had to kill the Japs, every last one of them.

Sally's finger tightened. The trigger was stiff and hard to move. The foliage jerked and fell away. The man came around the curve.

Sally braced herself to fire; then she screamed. "Jack, oh, Jack, thank God."

"Push, Catharine, push," Frances commanded.

The pain blotted out everything. Frances's voice came from a long distance. Catharine tried to respond, but the pain was too strong. She felt a scream deep in her throat, but she stopped it. Her hands scrabbled against the gritty, uneven floor of the cave.

She was dimly aware of Spencer, his face haggard in the occasional light from the flashlight which Frances used so sparingly. It was Spencer who had known about the cave and had insisted they make the difficult journey down the steep slope to its safety.

The pains were coming frequently now. It was almost time. It hurt too much to think. There was no time now. Perhaps this was the way her life would end—with a deep, riveting pain that would never stop. She would push—God, she would—but if the baby was like Charles, then there was nothing she could do.

"Push, Catharine, now."

It wasn't Frances's voice.

Catharine was panting and moving with the pain, but she lifted her head. Even in the dim, fitful light, she knew.

Jack gripped her hand, gripped it so hard, and talked to her. His voice was the rope over an abyss. There was a final crescendo of agony, and they were all calling and crying. She heard Jack's voice over them all.

"The baby's here. The baby's here!"

Jack found Spencer sitting wearily by the edge of the stream, his back against an enormous banyan root. The gurgle of the water swirling over the chunks of rough rock made a dull, steady roar and had covered the sound of Jack's footsteps. Jack paused for a moment. Spencer looked years older than he had in Manila. His khaki shirt and pants were creased and dirty. In Manila, he had often worn immaculate white linen. Now his hair was thinning and hung lankly down onto his forehead. He needed a shave.

Spencer looked up, slowly pulled himself to his feet, and waited, his face furrowed with exhaustion. Jack picked his way across the jumble of boulders and stopped in front of him.

"Frances says you carried Catharine the last half mile."

For a moment, Jack didn't think Spencer was going to answer; then Spencer lifted a hand to rub wearily against his eyes and said, "Half mile? It seemed like a hundred."

"You saved her life. Hers and Amelia's."

Something flickered in Spencer's light eyes. "Did you think I'd leave them to die? For Christ's sake, what do you think I am?"

"A very brave man," Jack said quietly.

Slowly, Spencer shook his head. "No. My guts were shaking like jelly. I kept thinking about the Japs and how they were going to find us."

"You stayed with her."

For a long time, Spencer didn't say anything. He took a cigarette from his pocket, lit it, and drew the smoke in deeply. "Catharine was my wife for eight years—and the mother of my son." Then he shook himself briskly. "Well, I'm going to be on my way. You don't need me anymore." He frowned. "You've got food for the baby?"

"Pounds of it. Dried formula. I got it this last trip."

"Good." Spencer picked up his pack; then he paused again. "Look, I'll tell you. No need to talk to Catharine now, but when we get back to the States, I won't cause any problem about a divorce." He shoved his hair back. "Catharine can file against me. I made up my mind this last month. I won't contest. I've written Peggy a letter. I'm going to marry her when I get home. I plan to send the letter out with the next batch of stuff that a sub picks up."

"Catharine told me about her. She says she's a special person."

Spencer paused in tightening his pack. "Did Catharine say that?" At Jack's nod, Spencer grinned. "Do you know something? Catharine's right."

When Spencer started up the trail, Jack stared after him fondly for the very first time since they had met.

Spencer paused at the top of the gully and raised his hand in farewell.

When he was out of sight, Jack turned to walk back toward the cave. He heard his daughter faintly cry and broke into a run. The sun was coming up in a sweep of gold and mauve and pink. Jack's heart felt full and light. He felt lucky now that everything was going to work out. They were going to make it, he and Catharine and Amelia—and Frances and Sally—and Spencer, too.

Then malaria struck.

30

The specter of malaria was constant. It had been only a matter of time after they ran out of their last supply of quinine, which everyone took as a preventative.

Frances came down sick first. Then Amelia.

Amelia cried fretfully; her skin felt hot. Catharine held her close and tried to get her to nurse, but her tiny mouth wouldn't fasten on a nipple.

She had to eat. And the fever. Catharine remembered the way Charles's face had felt—the dreadful, hideous dry heat. Panic and horror bubbled inside her. She began to shake; long, deep shudders racked her body.

"Amelia, Amelia," and there was a sob in her voice.

Footsteps slapped across the bamboo flooring. "Here now," Sally said briskly, "that won't do our little girl any good." The nurse reached down and scooped up the baby, then paused to pat Catharine's shoulder. "You lie back now, dear. You're still weak from labor. Don't you worry—we'll get Amelia eating again. I'm going to give her some water right now."

"Fever." Catharine's voice was high and rising. "She's got a fever. She's going to . . ." Catharine clapped her hand over her mouth and rocked back and forth on the bamboo sleeping platform.

Sally looked at her worriedly. Putting Amelia in her makeshift bassinet, the nurse eased Catharine down. "You rest now. I've got a little something here for you." She held a drink to Catharine's mouth and waited patiently until it was gone. When Catharine lay quietly, the nurse turned to the baby. She, too, felt the flaming skin and bit her lip.

If only she had some medicine. She looked across the hut at Frances huddled on a pallet.

The rains pounded against the hut. Water splashed through leaks every foot or so apart, sounding eerie and mournful.

It was past dinnertime when Jack returned. The minute he clambered up the ladder, Sally was on her feet. Her fear was evident as she moved toward him, demanding, "Did you get some medicine?"

Jack was already opening his backpack and lifting out the small vial to hand to her. She hurried to the bassinet and lifted Amelia. The baby lay limply in the nurse's arms.

Catharine raised up on the sleeping platform, her hair streaming down behind her, her face pale and frightened.

"Jack."

He came to her and reached out to take her hand, but his face turned toward the nurses and his tiny daughter. "Is she ... I hurried as fast as I could."

"She's worse," Catharine said painfully, "and today she couldn't nurse. Oh, Jack, she couldn't nurse."

"Sweet girl, sweet girl," Sally said softly as she held a spoon to the tiny, slack mouth. "Oh, good girl." She looked up and smiled. "She's taken it. I got it all down her, and earlier, Catharine, while you slept, I mixed an aspirin with water."

She nodded reassuringly at Amelia's frightened parents. "She's a tough girl. And she took her medicine. She's going to be all right." Sally spoke as strongly and brightly as she could. She wished in her heart that she could believe what she'd said. And Frances was in very bad shape.

Jack looked at Sally. "When will they be strong enough to travel?"

Sally didn't answer. She thought of the sweeping sheets of rain that drenched anyone stepping outside for even a minute and stared at Jack.

"There's a sub coming."

Once his words would have electrified them all with joy. They knew, of course, as the word swept around the country from pockets of guerrillas to hidden refugees, that occasional U.S. subs touched in at out-of-the-way spots to bring messages and medicine and pick up escaping servicemen. They'd talked about the subs and how, one day soon, it would be their turn to leave.

The rain splatted, hissed and gurgled against the nipa hut.

"I don't know," Sally said uncertainly. "I just don't know, Jack."

Frances died three days later. As Jack and Sally wrapped her in the faded quilt that would cover her in her last resting place, tears slipped down Catharine's face. Frances dead. And Amelia so terribly ill.

It was later that night that Sally woke Jack and beckoned for him to come past the partition into the kitchen area. She whispered so that Catharine wouldn't hear.

It was gray and ghostly in the hut. Catharine looked blankly around when she woke; then consciousness and fear returned together. She struggled to get up, realizing that odd, unaccustomed sounds had awakened her. She stared at Jack, who stood by the bassinet—his full pack was on his back. Sally stood beside him, and she, too, was dressed for travel.

"You just got back," Catharine said slowly, wondering if she were caught up in an odd and fretful dream.

Jack came and sat down on the platform. He bent over and kissed her cheek.

"You just got back." She said it louder and knew this was no dream.

"Catharine, the sub will be here in five weeks. It takes twenty days to cross to the rendezvous point."

"What are you telling me? Jack, where are you going?"

"You have to rest and get your strength back. I want you to eat a lot and try to walk, even here in the sala, because you must gain strength to walk to the coast—I've arranged for a guide to bring you in a couple of weeks, when you are stronger."

"Jack, you'll be with us."

His face was drawn and white, his nose almost pointed, his jawline a ridge of bone. "Sally and I talked it over."

Catharine clawed to get up and to see past him, to look into the bassinet. "Amelia, where is Amelia, where is my baby?"

Jack gripped her shoulders, then pulled her roughly into his arms.

"Sally and I are going to take her ahead, Catharine. We've got to find a doctor for Amelia."

He had the baby formula in his backpack, matches, and dry wood to make a fire to heat water, and the one bottle and worn nipple that a guerrilla had gotten for them from a storekeeper in Davao.

They'd rigged a carryall for Amelia, a sling that hung around Jack's neck. She nestled in the crook of his arm. They'd taken a single piece of oil cloth and fashioned a shield from the rain.

Jack and Sally were ready to leave at dawn.

Catharine took her baby from Jack and held her in her arms. She kissed the tiny dry, hot face, smoothed the silky fringe of reddish hair, and willed Amelia's eyes to open, but she lay slackly in Catharine's arms—hot, limp, quiet. Then Catharine put Amelia in her sling and held one tiny hand.

Catharine and Jack didn't speak. They stood close together for a moment. She pressed her cheek to his; then he turned and was gone. The rain shunted down, a dusky gray curtain, and all the world was rain.

Catharine stood in the opening; the chilled rain splashed and hissed.

Catharine stared out into the opaque world. "The rain . . . Charles got all wet . . . he was wet and chilled and then . . ." She lifted her hand, pressed it against her mouth. The wetness of the rain mixed with the hot wetness of her tears.

Catharine fixed her meal and dutifully picked up her spoon and took another bite of rice and another; then she set down the spoon. But she had to eat. She lifted the spoon again. Jack had arranged for a guide to lead her down to the coast—she had to keep her strength.

"Hello, hello there, Catharine."

Catharine jumped up from her dinner, rushed to the doorway, and looked down at Spencer, waving from the ground. The rain had stopped three days before. Catharine was scheduled to leave in the morning to begin the arduous journey to the rendezvous point.

"I saw Jack and Amelia and Sally . . ." Spencer began.

Catharine moved quickly. She was down the ladder and clinging to Spencer's arm. "You saw them? Where? When? How was Amelia?"

"They were only a few days from Masamis and scheduled to take a banca the next day. She's better, Catharine. Not all well yet, but the medicine was helping. Jack said she was eating."

Tears spilled down Catharine's face. She tried to speak and couldn't.

"Anyway, I wanted to check on you while I was this way."

"What are you doing back here? I thought you were already across the island."

"I've come back for the gold."

"The gold," she said sharply. "But, Spencer, isn't it hidden in an area under Japanese control?" Spencer had put the gold in a cave not far from the one where Amelia was born. That was the area where the Japanese had rampaged, killing scores of missionaries and refugees. They still controlled that territory.

"I'll be careful."

She wanted to warn him not to do it, to leave the gold where it lay until the war was over. For God's sake, there was a submarine coming for them. But she had no right now to tell Spencer what to do.

She said only, "Come with me tomorrow, Spencer. I'll be glad of your company."

But Spencer shook his head; his light eyes glistened in a way Catharine knew.

"I was assigned to bring the gold home. I'm going to do it."

Twenty days of struggle, days of slogging through the lowland jungle and pausing every few hours to burn off the leeches, bloated a disgusting bluish black with their blood; days of climbing, skirting thousand-foot drops and roaring falls that plummeted down mountain gorges; days of fording streams while crocodiles sunned on the banks, their eyes watchful. Every day Catharine remembered how

Spencer had said Amelia was better, but still she wondered if her baby was alive.

Catharine pressed forward, never admitting fatigue.

They skirted Japanese-held towns and slipped alongside Japanese-patrolled roads. Twice patrols spotted them, but they escaped into thickets of jungle. They were a day's march from the beach where the Americans were gathering when Catharine awoke with fever and chills and couldn't rise.

The guide knelt by her side. "We're almost there." He tried to lift Catharine.

Catharine peered through eyes glazed by fever. She licked her lips. "Can't." It wasn't surrender; it was the recognition of truth. Catharine burned with the hot onset of malaria; the fever alternated with racking chills. Through clenched teeth, she ordered the guide to go ahead. "Go on. Find Jack, and tell him."

The guide, Eduardo, found a deserted schoolhouse and fixed a pallet for Catharine. He placed water near her in a newly scoured milk can and promised to return with help.

Catharine heard him dimly. The words were insubstantial and meaningless. She huddled against the schoolhouse wall and shook with chills or ached with fever. Pictures and places rolled in her mind. She slept and waked and slept again. The images moved in her mind: her father's face, heavy with sorrow; Charles laughing, his blue eyes dancing with delight; Spencer and Peggy clinging to each other that bomb-splintered night on Corregidor; and Jack turning toward her, the love in his eyes bright and clear as the shining arch of the sky at a sun-flooded dawn.

Spencer gestured impatiently for the cargadores to keep pace. He moved at a half trot at the head of their column. It wasn't far now—another half mile at most. They hadn't seen a sign of the Japs. He began to smile. By God, this would show them all. No one in Washington could say Spencer Cavanaugh didn't complete an assignment. He would receive a commendation; there would be a promotion. He might even be given his choice of assignments. He would take London, of course. That would please Peggy. She loved London, even during the dark days of the Blitz. Or was it really that she loved him? He felt a swell of happiness. Peggy was safe in the States. He would go for her. This was going to turn out all right. It was going to be a triumph. And he'd manage in the Service without Catharine's money. He could make it known, subtly, of course, that it had been a mismatch with Catharine, that she'd left him for another fellow, and he'd turned to an old friend. It wouldn't be good that Peggy had been his secretary. Perhaps he should ask for an assignment in Washington until after the war, then request a posting where he'd never been.

Light-arms fire rattled in the little valley as the Japanese patrol began shooting.

The bullets stitched a bloody line across Spencer's chest. As he fell, his mind formed one last thought—Peggy.

God, it was so hot. That was fever; fever killed Charles. Amelia. That last time—she was hot, tiny and hot. Catharine tried to say her name. She heard the scratchy sound. "Amelia...please, God, please let Amelia live."

She shook with the terrible, racking chills of malaria, and at the same time sweat beaded her face, poured down her chest and back, bathed her legs. Catharine struggled to reach the water. She must drink water or she was going to die.

Going to die ... was she dead now ... she and Charles ... Amelia ... please, God, let Amelia live ...

In the wavering mistiness, she saw Jack.

She struggled to pull herself up and felt the strong grip of his hands—and she was in his arms ... in his arms ... where was Amelia?

Jack, Jack. The dream was so real. No, this was no dream; Jack was here, his touch warm and loving. The feel of him told her the best truth, the most wonderful truth, even before he spoke.

"Catharine, love, you're all right—and Amelia's all right. She's fine. She's wonderful. I'm going to take you to her."

"Amelia. My baby?"

"Catharine, she's all right," he told her loud and clear. "Amelia's with Sally and she's eating and we have milk for her. Catharine, she has the brightest, bluest eyes, and she's fine. They're waiting for us, and I've got bearers and quinine and the sub will come tomorrow. Catharine, it's all right. We're going home. You and Amelia and I are going home."

31

The cold, damp air whipped across the slate-gray deck. Far above, the flag snapped against the gray sky. Catharine looked up and felt again the surge of thankfulness. An American flag. An American ship. They were lucky beyond measure, she and Jack and Amelia.

A sharp, aching stab of sorrow twisted inside her. If only Spencer could be here, too, on his way home to Peggy. If only . . . Tears ached at the back of her throat. She had his last letter home, one written to Peggy. A bearer had brought his blood-stained pack to the Americans waiting for the submarine. That was all that was left of Spencer. But no, that wasn't so. She had so many good memories of him, and she would always remember his bravery the night Amelia was born.

Amelia stirred in her sleep. Catharine pulled Amelia's blanket tighter to shield her from the sharp air. The baby sighed and made a contented, sucking sound.

The fog parted and Catharine leaned forward.

"There! I see it. Do you?"

Jack's arm tightened around her shoulders.

The fog shifted ahead of them. Shafts of sunlight sparkled down on deep blue water. There, directly ahead, shining in the soft light, glistened the Golden Gate Bridge.

Tears stung Catharine's eyes. The Golden Gate. America. And the dawn of a new day for the three of them together—she and Jack and Amelia.

ABOUT THE AUTHOR

CAROLYN HART (Oklahoma City, OK) is the winner of multiple Agatha, Anthony, and Macavity Awards. She is a founding member of Sisters in Crime. Her prolific career has included the enduring Death on Demand series as well as the Henrie O and Bailey Ruth books. In 2007, she received the Lifetime Achievement Award at Malice Domestic.